Wings Over The Watcher

Wings Over The Watcher

PRISCILLA MASTERS

First published in Great Britain in 2005 by
Allison & Busby Limited
Bon Marché Centre
241-251 Ferndale Road
London SW9 8BJ

http://www.allisonandbusby.com

Copyright © 2005 by PRISCILLA MASTERS

The moral right of the author has been asserted.

A catalogue record for this book is available from
the British Library.

10 9 8 7 6 5 4 3 2 1

ISBN 0 7490 8212 7

Printed and bound in Wales by
Creative Print and Design, Ebbw Vale

Priscilla Masters was born in Halifax and is one of seven adopted children. The family moved to South Wales where she lived until she was sixteen when she went to Birmingham to work and then to train as a nurse. She is married to a GP and now lives in Shropshire. She works part-time as a nurse.

Other titles by Priscilla Masters:

Prologue

In different locations in Leek, a Moorlands town in Staffordshire, three separate tableaux are being performed. Joanna Piercy is writing to Matthew to try and explain recent events; Korpanski is filling in his insurance form after his wife has had a minor prang with the car and an unknown person is penning love-letters to a local doctor.

It seems that no one could lead a more mundane life than Beatrice Pennington, a woman who joins Joanna's cycling club, anxious to regain her figure by dieting and keeping fit. Unexciting, middle-forties, married, a part-time librarian, grown-up kids left home. Her life appears unremarkable. But weeks later a drama unfolds around her. A month after Beatrice begins her quest for health and glamour her distraught husband arrives at the police station to report her missing.

At first Joanna assumes Beatrice has decamped with another man. Evidence certainly seems to point this way. But as Joanna begins to peel back the layers of Beatrice Pennington's seemingly uneventful life she begins to realise: Beatrice was no ordinary woman at all.

Her complex story begins to absorb and intrigue Joanna. Until she receives word. Matthew is returning home.

This is a story which explores same-sex stalking, its reasons, the effect it has on both the stalker and the victim and the consequences of such obsessive behaviour.

Chapter One

Although a letter is a good way to break significant news it has its drawbacks.

As Joanna Piercy was finding out.

She was sitting at the table in the dining room, haunting Dido music playing softly in the background, supposedly to help her concentrate but her mind kept tracking away. On the table in front of her, neatly set out, was a pad of white notepaper, an envelope and a retractable ballpoint pen. The bin at her feet was full of scrunched up paper balls of the same notepaper. She had made her preparations. But she could not find the right words. They would not come to her aid to help her to explain this difficult thing.

Dear Matthew, she began again.

She cupped her chin in the palm of her hand, staring into the distance. She could go no further. Matthew had a penetrating instinct for the truth. He would quickly sense any evasion or lack of sincerity. And he could sniff out a lie – even from the other side of the Atlantic.

She took a sip of the sharp, dry wine from her glass, let it sit on her tongue for a second, then swallowed it. She bent over the sheet of paper again, arms curled around it protectively, though there was no one in the room to peer over her shoulder. She was alone. Quite alone. Seconds later she scrunched the paper up again having added only five more words, *I'm so very, very sorry.*

She lifted her head to stare into space, knowing the problem. Writing a letter was the coward's way out.

Not hers. She should have boarded an aeroplane to Washington DC and spoken to him, face to face.

For a moment she was transfixed by the image of Capitol Hill and the White House. Washington seemed such a long,

long way away. As did Matthew.

She stared out through the window at the square spire of Waterfall church. She could hear some holidaymakers from the barn-conversions joking. They were standing in front of the stocks, laughing at something. (Probably something about bondage – it usually was). Distracted now she watched them push open the gate and wander through the churchyard. She felt a certain envy for this cluster of happily-marrieds in t-shirts, jeans and comfortable trainers. It looked cosy and a million miles away from her current situation. Which needed resolving. She bent her head again to stare at yet another blank sheet of notepaper. *She must write this letter. She must find the right words.* From somewhere. She had put it off for long enough and watched the problem expand – as troubles do when they are not confronted. It made it worse that she recognised the problem for what it was – an evasion. She was by nature a fighter, someone who put her fists up and prided herself on not running away from battles.

So what was she doing now?

Retreating.

Hiding. Being a coward. Ducking the issue. There were plenty of phrases for it. And they all meant the same thing. She was not facing her situation or dealing with it but running away, trying to pretend it did not exist.

Dear Matthew, she wrote for the sixteenth time before being distracted again, this time by a couple of youths in a red Ford Escort revving their car up and skidding onto the gravelled car park of the Red Lion.

Again she stared through the window. The intractable problem was that there simply weren't the words in the English language to tell a man nicely that he was not going to become a father.

She gulped in air.

He wouldn't believe her.

She could picture his face as clearly as though he was

sitting opposite her, in his customary chair, legs stretched out in front of him, his eyes studying hers, as he sometimes did, usually with that odd question. But this time full of doubt and suspicion. In spite of everything she smiled. Matthew's chin lengthened when he was dubious about something. It became pointed and sharp, altering the shape of his face subtly so he looked sceptical and suspicious. Her heart suddenly skipped a beat. She missed him. And she did not know whether he would ever return.

He'd been gone for three months now. Three eventful months during which they'd hardly spoken. Typical Matthew, he'd immersed himself in his new project – studying gunshot wounds in Washington DC – and left her to make her decision alone. Except in the end it had not been she who had decided. The choice had been torn from her while she had hardly been aware. And so the problem had, in the end, slipped away into nothing.

And now she must tell him.

Dear Matthew, she began again.

The distraction this time was a photograph hanging on the opposite wall, of him holding a tiny baby. Eloise. And there was a puzzle. Who had sent her flowers when Matthew had left?

Eloise. Matthew's daughter who had always returned her cold dislike with her own brand of pure, undisguised hatred.

Who had rung her twice and asked, in that odd, childish voice of hers whether she was "OK"?

Again, Eloise.

Of all the strange relationships that existed in this world this one was the strangest. An initial hatred between them which had softened, blossomed even, as Eloise had grown from a difficult, intelligent child to a strong-willed young woman.

Joanna smiled again at the photograph, remembering. Eloise used to swear blind that she could remember it being taken. Even though she had patently only been a few months old at the time. She must be making it up. So when would the fable subside? If ever?

Who knows. Like the infant who had died, nature herself would decide.

Joanna bent over the sheet of paper again. This was a task that must be done.

Three miles away, on the outskirts of Leek, in a square, modern house on the Westwood estate, someone else was writing a letter. But whereas Joanna had struggled to find the right words, this pen was swiftly smothering sheets, finding phrases easily.

"*I knew the very first time I met you that this was no ordinary encounter. I knew you wanted me as much as I wanted you. But the confines of our lives are so cruel. Sometimes my passion absolutely engulfs me. Overwhelms me. Threatens to drown me. I love you. I don't know how many times I have to say it. I love you. We will be together, one day soon. Maybe we should move away from this gossiping little town where people feel they have the right to comment on us, on our love, on our relationship.*"

The writer bit the pen and smiled.

At the other end of the town, in another neat, detached, estate house, Sergeant Mike Korpanski was scowling and chewing his lip. No easy words for him.

"*Dear Sir*", he tapped out, two-fingered, on the computer. "*With reference to my letter of the fourteenth of June.*" Blast," he exclaimed, deleted the type and retyped, *June. The car was locked and parked in a side street while my wife was getting the dry-cleaning from the shop. When she returned the vehicle had rolled backwards by itself and smashed into the vehicle behind it, causing some damage. It subsequently turned out that she had omitted to apply the handbrake properly.*"

He swore under his breath. "Bloody woman."

Eight hundred quid's worth of damage. And all because she'd forgotten to pull the handbrake up – hard. How many times had he told her, "The handbrake's loose so leave the car in gear if there's even the hint of a slope."

Out of the window went his No Claims Bonus.

He swore again, swigged at a can of lager and looked through the patio doors at his son, kicking a football around on the lawn. "Come on, Dad," he shouted at him. "Let's do shots at goal."

"One minute, Rick." He held his finger up to emphasise the point.

Before suddenly, unpredictably, his anger burst through again.

"Bloody hell, Fran," he shouted in the vague direction of the kitchen. "Why didn't you leave the car in gear?"

She stood in the doorway, slim and dark, one hand on her hip, a dishcloth in the other hand. "If you'd adjusted the handbrake, Michael Korpanski," she said severely, "it wouldn't have rolled. I told you it wanted sorting."

He cursed again and bent back over the claim form, grumbling softly. Typical woman. To turn her own stupidity back on him and make *him* feel guilty. And he knew more than anyone that motoring offences hung around your neck for years. He'd have to fill in this trifling little incident every time he applied for fresh cover. He gave a long sigh then scanned down the lengthy document. And to add insult to injury there was a £250 excess. He looked at the garage quote for repairs on his own car. Rear bumper, lights. A new exhaust. And that was before he had any idea what the damage had been to the other car.

He cursed again.

Joanna had given up even trying to write the letter. The words were simply too elusive, the problem too subtle to explain in a letter and besides – the evening was too perfect to struggle with this over-dose of emotion and guilt. She stood up, opened the window and caught the scent of summer jasmine on a late spring breeze.

Guiltily she glanced back at the table, at the brimming waste-paper basket, the sheets of paper – and made her excuse.

She could think better on her bike. Work out precisely what to say and how to say it without sounding false.

Before she could argue or change her mind she pulled the window shut, ran upstairs, fished her cycling shorts out of the drawer, struggled into a short sleeved cycling-top and ran back downstairs.

Two at a time. Three minutes and she could be out there, the wind ruffling her hair, moving through the grassy moorlands, taking pleasure from the sight of fields of grazing cows and sheep. Feeling the pull of her muscles as she took the hills.

The paper and envelope seemed to reproach her.

She ignored them.

She could think better on her bike.

Korpanski had completed his insurance form, pinned his explanation to it and was venting his anger out on the football, booting it towards some goalposts he and his son had rigged up, at the opposite end of the garden to the house. Fran Korpanski watched him indulgently through the window.

Only one of the writers is still at the task.

"I remember the very first day I ever saw you. I noticed your eyes first. Your beautiful, brown eyes. Those and your quite flawless complexion. Amazing for a woman of your age. Your eyes seemed to alter when I walked into the room. They appeared to get bigger and grow more luminous and look at me with such a melting look of love. You are such a caring person, you know, one of the few I have met. Someone who really understands. So many people these days are too busy to listen to the rhythms of life and love. They ignore their own feelings and so miss out on these subtle messages which cross the air, such as the ones you send out to me every time we meet. I live for those occasions.

Adieu, my sweet, sweet love. I think I shall see you again very soon. One of the great advantages of living in a town as

small as this one is that it is quite easy to "bump" into some-
one – if you want to. You see I know your routine.
Thoroughly. I know where you live, where you work, what
time you leave your house in the morning. I often take the dog
for a walk at around that time purely so I can watch you fly
out through the door – such a busy person. I watch you unlock
your car door. Sometimes, sitting inside, you fiddle with the
radio as though the station is not to your taste and someone –
your husband? has altered it. Classic fm seems to be your pre-
ferred station. I like popular Classics myself. I have heard the
strains of familiar music as you pass me, unaware that I am
there. Invisible. That is how I like to be – sometimes. Only
sometimes. I watch you reverse down the drive. Quite fast.
Rather than be noticed by you I generally hide behind the rho-
dodendrons. The large, pinkish clump near the bottom. That is
a very long, overgrown drive you have leading to your house.
Victorian, I suppose. I sometimes watch you through the win-
dow on dark evenings so I know how you spend the times
when you think you are alone. My father once said to me that
when someone is thinking about you, you are not really alone.
    You never are.
    Do you find that a comforting thought? That you never are
really alone?
    I do.
    I am greatly comforted by the bond that exists between us
and the love we share. I often wonder how much of every day
you spend thinking about me.
    How little am I alone?

She heard his key in the lock first and hurriedly placed the
letter in an envelope, slipping it swiftly between the pages
of a novel she was reading. A wonderful, exciting book
about a man who sees a dead woman walking towards him
at a cocktail party. The first chapter gave her such a thrill of
excitement that she had read and re-read it many times
over. Such a clever writer. And she loved a good murder
story.
    He was rattling the doorknob.

"Darling. Are you in there?"
She opened the door and smiled.

She streamed down the hill, dipped into Caldon Low, before climbing up towards the hills, honking hard as she ascended until she finally reached the Winking Man, breathless and tired but seeing her life with a clarity she could never find in the cottage.

She had been pregnant. She had not wanted the baby and Matthew had known that – just as clearly as she had known he did.

This he had not been able to forgive – the fact that she had rejected *his* child so he had left her to work in the U.S., leaving her to make the choice – alone. It was an impossible choice.

Then nature had intervened and taken the decision from her with a miscarriage. But Matthew didn't know that – yet. She could not find the right words to explain what had happened and her unexpected response to events.

And now all she knew was that she wanted Matthew back. She wanted to see him, to say all that she had held back over the years. She wanted their relationship to stop pretending, hiding behind half-truths and euphemisms. It was time to move forward.

Into the future.

Chapter Two

Joanna returned from her bike ride in rebellious and positive mood, action her intent. She would not write the letter but apply for leave, tell Matthew she would spend a few days in Washington DC with him and obey her instinct – to speak face-to-face. She would ring him tonight.

Once she had made her decision she felt happy, buoyant, optimistic and sure that they would work their lives out. She fished a poetry book from the shelves. Nothing romantic now or morbid, but one of her very favourites. Practical. One that reflected her *ready-for-action feeling*.

'Stitch! stitch! stitch...
Sewing at once, with a double thread,
A Shroud as well as a Shirt.
Work! Work! Work!
While the cock is crowing aloof!
And work – work – work,
Till the stars shine through the roof!'

She read it through three times, loving the words and their incessant, pounding rhythm, pouring herself another glass of wine. She glanced at her watch. It would be morning in Washington DC. It was a Thursday. She had to take a chance that he was free and not working. She did not want to leave a message but speak to him and warn him of her intent. Once she knew his imminent plans she could easily apply for leave. She was due some anyway and there was no major investigation in progress.

It is astonishing how quickly one can be connected with a phone a few thousand miles away. And even more astonishing that glowing optimism can be so quickly dissolved in such a brief exchange.

She dialled his number, waited for a while, heard it ring twice before it was answered. A matter of less than a minute.

"Hi there." It was a singsong, female voice.

"I'm sorry. I was trying to connect with Matthew Levin."

A giggle. "I'm so-o sorry." More than singsong and female it was a seductive, suggestive voice. "Matthew is uumm – kind of – unavailable right this minute." Another giggle.

And she was cut off.

Joanna stared at the phone, speechless, furious. And jealous. How dare he. When they had so much to work out between them. She could read between the lines. It was obvious what was going on. She cursed and cursed and then felt suddenly giddy, as though her feet were no longer quite connecting with the floor.

Matthew?

She sat for a long while, wondering whether the unknown female would tell him someone had phoned, a woman with an English accent and that he would read her number, realise it was her and ring back. She waited, expecting the call but the phone was silent. She picked up the receiver, heard the dialling code and knew she had put it straight back on the cradle. Next she checked her mobile had a charged battery and a good signal.

But both telephones remained silent.

Maybe the unknown female had not told him about the call.

She sat in the growing dark, wondering. What position was the girl with the giggly voice in to be able to answer his mobile? What was she doing with his mobile? What was Matthew up to? And where did that leave her?

She preferred not to think.

Curled up in her chair, her third glass of wine in her hand, she allowed herself to work things out, step by step. Maybe the reason Matthew had remained so silent was that he had met someone else. Maybe she and her problems seemed far away and unimportant, insignificant.

It made sense. Their relationship always had been too complicated. Somewhere, written into the hardware of their tangled lives together had been doom. From the first.

So she may as well acknowledge it.

Friday May 28th 8 a.m.

Korpanski stomped into the office they shared, thunder making his face heavy. Joanna looked up from her computer screen. *Right then*, she thought, *make my day. I can match you for aggression.*

"Morning," she said warily.

He began at once. "Glad you didn't stick 'good' on the front of that."

"Still whingeing about your car?"

"Bloody woman," he began, "You'd be whingeing if it was *your* car. Hundreds of pounds' worth of damage. Insurance levels." Then he realised what she had said. Immediately he moved towards her desk. "Everything all right, Jo?"

And suddenly it was all too much. She could feel weakness and tears move in close.

"I rang Matt last night," she said.

Korpanski waited.

"A perky little voice answered."

"Doesn't mean anything," Mike responded gruffly. "She might be…"

"It was morning there, Korpanski," she said. "And she didn't exactly sound like a business acquaintance."

"I think you're jumping to conclusions a bit fast."

"I'm not jumping to conclusions, Mike," she snapped. "I'm putting two and two together."

"But he must know about…"

Slowly and deliberately she shook her head.

Korpanski looked shocked. "You're kidding."

She excused herself. "It all happened so quickly. And…I tried to write. Mike, it isn't easy."

All of a sudden Korpanski crossed sides, from female buddy to male to male. And closed ranks. "He's got a right to know. It was his kid too."

Korpanski the father. It was all she needed.

She knew now she needed to justify her actions – or lack of them. "I thought I'd go over and spend some time with him. I've still got a week's annual leave owing. But now – well – I don't know."

Korpanski merely stared at her, the only sign of a response a pulse thudding in his right temple.

Joanna caved in. Sniffed. "Let's get on with some work."

The detective sergeant grunted and settled down behind his desk.

It would be a long day.

11 a.m.

Doctor Corinne Angiotti had finished her morning surgery. A receptionist had brought her a cappuccino and an almond biscuit plus a huge pile of mail. Mainly pharmaceutical promotions, letters from consultants about patients, results of tests. And so on. A bubbly blonde with soft brown eyes, in her early thirties, wearing an unflattering brown skirt and loose cream blouse. She worked her way steadily through the pile of mail until she reached a hand-written missive in a square blue envelope.

She jerked backwards.

Not another one.

Why didn't she leave her alone? The woman was mad. Insane. Obsessed. She wanted to tear the envelope in half, quarters, eighths. Sixteenths. And then fling it on a fire somewhere. But we never do, do we. We always open them first.

Her eyes scanned the words and she felt ice-cold. Frightened. As she drank her coffee thoughtfully she wondered. What on earth could she do about it?

It was notoriously difficult to deal with problems like this. As a GP in a small market town, she knew if any of this leaked out the notoriety would finish her. Always to be pointed out as the focus of a middle-aged woman's affections. She would be the object of ridicule. Unless she could persuade her to stop.

Corinne sat motionless, her hands in front of her on the desk. What perturbed her was this. What had she done to spark off this response? Had she somehow, subliminally, given out all the wrong messages during the supposedly formal consultation? If so this situation might well arise again – and again.

She cast her mind back.

She had first met the patient during a routine appointment at the surgery not long after she had joined the practice, one short year ago. Beatrice Pennington had attended for a routine blood pressure check. Corinne had found it high and suggested her patient return for another check with the practice nurse. Nothing abnormal had happened then. She could swear it. The wretched woman had seen the nurse and had another check but the reading had again been high and the nurse had referred Mrs Pennington back to her.

That was when it had all started.

She had suggested her patient have a heart tracing and then return so they could discuss some simple medication.

Corinne had felt then that something was not quite right. But she had been unable to put her finger on it. The patient had held her hand. Not that unusual. Reassurance sometimes went with a touching of the hand. But it had been for slightly too long. Not enough to make a fuss about but she had moved her hand away, still feeling the hot pressure from her patient. That had been all. She could swear it.

So when – exactly?

It had been during the following conversation. She had mentioned the word 'stress'. This had led to marital confidences being leaked. Her husband was boring.

Corinne had answered flippantly. And now she knew that she had said the wrong thing. That many men were boring – in large doses – especially husbands. It had been an innocuous comment. Said with a smile. Nothing. Nothing at all. But all the same, Corinne's hand began to shake as she tried to drink her coffee so a little of the froth on the cappuccino blew onto the letter.

Beatrice Pennington had read so much into the casual state-ment. Dissatisfaction in her marriage mirroring her own bore-dom with the marital state and, creepily, an affinity with her doctor that Corinne herself really, truly, did not return.

But could she convince the woman that this was the case? Slowly she shook her head. No.

Recognising that something was not quite normal she had suggested her patient consult the practice nurse in future, returning to her only once a year for an annual check. Her patient had looked crestfallen, disappointed. Little lines had appeared either side of her nose. So fatally she had relented, agreed to see her every few months. And that had been the beginning of it all.

As a medical student Corinne had spent an extra year studying the psychology behind the doctor/patient rela-tionship so she understood about manipulation, about child, parent and adult interaction and she knew exactly the position she was being manoeuvred into. Yet she was pow-erless to prevent it.

So had started a pathological doctor/patient relationship which she had watched, as though from the sidelines, with a feeling of unreality, just as powerless to stop.

Six months ago, during a dull and otherwise uneventful November, the letters had started.

Always unsigned.

It had been the final straw, the last act in a sick joke.

In fact she had known from the start who they were from. People use their own pet phrases and somehow she could see the pale sweating face in front of her as she peeled the words off the page.

Likewise she could hear herself bleating in her own phrases to the General Medical Council, that Beatrice Pennington had a vulnerable, lonely personality, that she was a woman who suffered from low self esteem, that...

She was bored with it herself. But she had not been intim-

idated until recently. Here, in the surgery, she had felt safe
– protected. But... She shivered at the thought of the
woman hiding in the drive. The worst was, she knew the
very bush she hid behind. Large, straggly, thick and overgrown. She felt like hacking it down. Hacking them all
down so the drive was a long, clear, safe stretch. She would
never drive down it again without peering into every inch of
vegetation.

She had hoped they might even start a family within the
next couple of years. They had been getting so settled and
Leek had seemed the right sort of town to bring children up
with traditional values. They had been so relieved to move
out of London and all that London had come to mean. Oh.
It all seemed so ruinous. And as clearly as she could hear
herself explaining her actions as innocuous she could picture the traditionalists taking the return view – that she herself had provoked this. Invited it. Desired it for some per-
verted reason of her own. And Pete's history didn't help.

The awfulness was gradually engulfing her. She could not
stand this.

She glanced down again at the latest letter, read a line or
two. *Miss out on these subtle messages which cross the air...*

It is quite easy to "bump" into someone...

And quite suddenly she felt blind panic. They would have
to leave Leek and become fugitives again. Leave this town
she had grown to love so much. Drag Pete away from his
job as a teacher in the school where he had finally rebuilt his
confidence after the truly awful experiences in
Wandsworth.

And slowly anger crept in to replace the panic. This *stupid, wicked* woman who could wreck lives through her desperation to find affection. Whose imagination invented situations that were about as real as Billy Liar's. Whose
wicked and pervasive letters were about to ruin her own
life. Corinne Angiotti gave a soft, animal growl. Beatrice
Pennington would NOT get away with it.

As she sat, paralysed by her fury and hatred of the

woman who was slowly dismantling her future she knew something else too. She was not going to sit back and allow this to happen. Not this time around. This time they would not run. They would stay and fight.

She drank the still-warm coffee quickly. And by the time she had drained the mug reality had set in. And how did she think she could stop her?

Could she, Corinne Angiotti, Birmingham Graduate in Medicine, MB ChB, MRCOG, DCH and so on, really brazen it out, witnessed by all the friends, neighbours, patients who had grown to know her in the last year? Corinne gasped. Because she knew herself too well. She simply couldn't do it.

She crossed to the window which looked out on a busy, noisy crossroads. It forced her to face reality. So what was the solution? Continue like this? Waiting, hoping for her patient to gradually realise that her odd and irrational feelings were not reciprocated? How long would that take?

Really? If ever?

Corinne felt the beginnings of real despair. She didn't know whether she could stick it out.

"Bugger," she whispered and stood up wearily.

It wasn't even as if she could confide in Pete. He had his own devils to wrestle with. Or the senior partner who would always put the good of the practice first. In fact she had no one she could turn to.

She felt suddenly, terribly alone.

What could she really do to stop her?

Answer – the logical one. She would ask her to come in during surgery time, explain that she was deluded, that she, Corinne, was a happily-married woman, still in love with her husband, who felt no love for her patient, apart from the responsible feeling appropriate for a doctor towards her patient. She would encourage her to develop new interests outside the home and to adopt a more healthy attitude.

Finally she would suggest she consult another doctor in the future.

There. That was that.

She felt cleansed.

Until.

She dropped the letter in the bottom drawer of her desk and for some reason locked it, removing the key and threading it onto her own personal bunch of keys.

That was when she was aware of a cold feeling, ice-cold enough to paralyse her.

Because the letter had been dropped on a pile high enough to graze the roof of the drawer.

There was no room for any more.

Chapter Three

Thursday, 24th June, 8 a.m.

Sunshine poured in through the window of Waterfall Cottage and skimmed across the dark, oak table, nothing on it except a white notepad, closed, a plain white envelope and a retractable ballpoint pen, all sitting by a vase containing drooping, dead red roses. The room was empty. In fact the cottage was empty. At 8 a.m. Joanna was already pedalling across the road north towards Grindon Moor then turning into Onecote and down into Leek. On such a blue, bright morning, she felt depressed, confused and angry. Only the rhythmic pedalling healed her until by the time she arrived at the station her mind was calmed and her legs aching.

Korpanski was scowling over the letter he'd received in the morning post.

Dear Sir,

Thank you for your letter of May 27th. We note that your car was parked on an incline with the gears not engaged. We note also that it appears that the handbrake was not adequately applied. Could you let us have the following information.

When did a mechanic last check the handbrake? And to your knowledge was the handbrake in any way faulty or needing adjustment?

Korpanski swore, flung the letter down on the hall table and left for work.

It is a hawthorn hedge, newly christened with fresh, green leaves, still iced with the late, white flowers of May. But the scent is not so pretty – it is that of a decomposing carcase. Maybe a badger has died, a fox or a rabbit, a dog or cat run over by a car or caught by a predator. Or perhaps it is something else. Something larger. Whatever it is it is attracting flies.

It had been the last straw – that appeal, the familiar blue envelope at the top of the pile of her morning's mail, sticking out of her pigeonhole.

"Don't you think it is time to come out into the open? We have been discreet for long enough. However our families might be hurt – sooner is better than later and time is ticking by.

I cannot hide beneath the umbrella of concealment any longer. Corinne. I want the world to know."

Deluded she may be but Corinne's hand shook as she read through the words twice over.

In the bottom drawer of a desk the blue notepaper and envelopes lie silent. At last.

"Someone to see you, Joanna."

She looked enquiringly at the young PC. "I don't like mysteries, Cumberlidge," she said crisply. "Who is it?"

"I don't know, Ma'am." He'd caught the uncharacteristically sharp edge in her voice and adopted a more formal tone. "He asked for you by name."

"Description?" she asked lightly, ashamed that she had allowed her poor humour to leak into her dealings with a junior officer.

"Middle-aged man." He thought for a moment. "Balding."

No one sprang to mind. "Thank you. Then show him in." She stood up and watched as a tall, awkward man bumped into the door frame. He was slim and angular, with thinning, greying hair, a shining bald patch on his crown. He was around six foot tall, wearing a Harris tweed jacket – badly fitting over round shoulders and loose over the back. His trousers were creaseless and baggy-kneed and he wore brown brogues on his feet. Joanna made a swift assessment: old-fashioned, conventional, unimaginative, no criminal record.

She didn't recognise him.

But held out her hand anyway. "Mr…?"

"Pennington. Arthur Pennington. You know my wife,

Beatrice." He had a flat, expressionless voice with a local accent.

Old-fashioned names too. Arthur and Beatrice. She searched her memory for a Beatrice Pennington and failed to find her.

"I'm sorry," she said, smiling to take the sting out of her words. "I don't recall..."

"She's been coming to the cycling club for a couple of weeks. On a Sunday."

Then she *did* remember. Quite clearly. Because the woman had seemed so very ordinary. Another overweight, middle-aged woman with straight, brown hair, who had turned up to the cycling club on a brand new bike saying she needed to "get fit" and "lose some of the..." She'd slapped an ample midriff bulge with a giggle then introduced herself as Beatrice Pennington. Her self-deprecating humour had amused them all and they always welcomed newcomers. Besides – they'd instantly admired her both for her good humour and for her effort. So after a brief discussion they'd made a quick adjustment to their proposed route, turning it into a figure of eight in order to drop her after ten miles and then continue with the rest.

It was quickly obvious she wasn't going to cope with the usual thirty mile ride.

It is hard to look ungainly on a bike. Cycling is a sport in which you can look good on a flat or downhill even when it's your first time out. Provided you don't wobble too much. And you can always either go-slow or push up a hill. But Beatrice somehow managed to do the impossible, look clumsy on her machine. She wobbled constantly, braked too hard, losing her balance and panicking then putting her foot down. She sweated her way up the first incline and slowed them right down. Yet Joanna and all the others continued to admire her indomitable spirit and good-humour. It didn't seem to faze her that she was lagging far behind so they encouraged her every few minutes, dropping back to chat to her. It was obvious Beatrice had found the hills hard work and her legs were clearly not used to the exercise but she had gritted her teeth and persevered and to her credit had managed the ten miles, waving them off happily as they'd finished their ride.

She'd joined them for a few more weeks, her form gradually improving, then as suddenly as she had started, she had stopped coming. Last Sunday they'd waited for ten extra, precious minutes, finally setting off without her in a downpour. Joanna had assumed that, like many others before her, Beatrice had found the attempt at fitness simply too tough.

Now, four days later, Joanna was looking at her husband.

Unexciting was the word that came into mind as she recalled fragments of conversation and conjecture.

Pagan, one of her two cycling buddies, watching the bike and rump wobbling ahead. "Wonder what's started this off."

Pat, married teacher, whose husband spent all of Sundays fishing, "New man." Said with a twinkle.

"Doctor's orders," had been Joanna's explanation and the three had giggled like chummy schoolgirls and freewheeled down the hill, overtaking Beatrice's squeaking brakes.

"Need some oil," they'd thrown back as they rushed past.

Arthur Pennington adjusted his glasses.

"Sit down, Mr Pennington," she invited, feeling unaccountably sorry for the man. "I do remember your wife. Of course I do. Quite well, in fact. She's getting quite good on her bike, isn't she?"

Pennington practically tossed his head as though this was of no interest to him so she didn't pursue the subject. "What can I do for you?"

His pale, shining forehead was corrugated from brow to receding hairline with anxiety. "It's about her," he said, "my wife, Beatrice. She's gone."

Joanna felt a sudden quickening. So Pat had been right. Beatrice had had a lover and it *had* been that which had lain behind the fitness attempt.

And now?

Surely it was obvious. She had left to be with him.

Something in her crowed for all middle-aged women who

are married to unexciting men who take them for granted
and break out. It was the clichéd stuff of modern fiction.

But one look at her husband's face was enough to stub
that idea out. Arthur Pennington was suffering.

She made a feeble attempt at mediating. "When you say,
"gone", do you mean she's left you?"

"I don't know," he said. "I don't know what's happened.
I only know she's apparently disappeared. She isn't home. I
expected her back from work last night around six and they
said she hadn't been in all day. She didn't come home at all
last night. I lay awake, right through the night, waiting for
her, Inspector. So where is she? We hadn't had a row or a
fall out or anything. I just don't understand."

In cases like this the usual story is that the woman has
decided to leave her life – her husband – her children – her
home – everything – either temporarily or permanently.
And Joanna had secret knowledge from the mouth of
Beatrice herself, which put her in a position of cognisance.

*"Actually," she'd confided at the top of a very steep hill, her face
as red as a beetroot with the effort of the climb, "I am married.
I do have a husband. But I also have someone else."*

Joanna had been simultaneously startled, excited and
intrigued. Her first thought had been: You could not judge
by appearances. "Really?" had been all she'd managed.

"Yes." Beatrice's face had been solemn – and at the same
time almost ethereal with this hidden love. "Oh yes," she'd
confessed. "Someone quite special." And her face had
reminded Joanna of old, religious paintings, which portrayed
adoration.

So this news from Arthur Pennington was hardly unexpected.

Joanna came back to the present. Pennington was staring
at her, his head to one side, chicken-like, waiting for her
answers.

And party to this secret knowledge Joanna was uncomfortable. Did Arthur Pennington know about *the someone*

else? Did he have any suspicion that his wife had this secret life?

She was aware that she must approach this nutty little problem with great delicacy so she sat right back in her chair and adopted a friendly, informal approach. "Let me ask you a few questions, Mr Pennington."

He sat very upright. "Go ahead," he said with a tinge of bravado about him.

Korpanski chose that moment to barge into the room, spied Pennington and apologised. Joanna seized the opportunity to ask the aggrieved husband whether he would like a tea or coffee, knowing that he could probably do with something a little stronger.

Pennington elected for a tea, she for a coffee and Mike withdrew to act as tea-boy.

While she resumed the questioning. "Has your wife packed any clothes?"

"I don't know," he said vaguely. "Women have so many, don't they?"

So he didn't know the contents of his wife's wardrobe. What man did? Matthew? Mentally she shook her head. He no more or less than most men. Women's wardrobes were a testimony to their complicated psyches. All those hidden parcels for projected transformations they would never achieve. *"I've had it for ages, dear"*, mistaken never-worn purchases and old favourites women could never bear to part with – the size 10s they would never again wear – retained simply to remind them of the waist they once had, the size they once were, the person they would never again be. The clothes they had been persuaded to buy against their better judgement by well-meaning friends or overbearing shop assistants. *"You look lovely in fuchsia, madam."* When it was the last colour they should ever wear. There were the evening dresses they could not wear again because *"everyone's seen it before"*. And lastly there were the fashions, which would "come around again". The yachting trousers and jackets. The expensive suit bought for a wedding. And in Joanna's case two dresses of significance. The fancy, floaty frock she had bought for Daniel's christening when she had been his godmother and a red evening dress worn at the Legal ball on the last occasion when she had seen Matthew out for an evening with his wife.

Then, like most women (and Joanna assumed that she and Beatrice shared this other characteristic of the female sex), right at the bottom of the wardrobe were all the shoes which were either the wrong colour, or had suited only one outfit – ever – or were far too uncomfortable and made you feel like Hans Christian Anderson's mermaid – that you walked on razor blades or shards of glass. And maybe, right at the back, hidden even beneath the shoe-boxes, some women even concealed old love-letters or money – or gifts they never should have accepted. Burglars know this – that the back of women's wardrobes is invariably worth their attention.

But, looking at Arthur Pennington, Joanna guessed that all this was pure mystery.

"Are any suitcases missing?"

He thought for a minute, pondering this new question. Pennington did not hurry. Was incapable of sudden spurts of effort. "I don't think so. I haven't really looked in the loft. I just came straight down here. She's never gone missing before. It's completely out of character. Nothing like her at all. I'm worried, Inspector." His pale eyes looked as helpless as a baby's. "What if something's happened to her?"

She regarded him. *Something has but nothing you would recognise or understand.*

She was quick to reassure him. "Look – Mr Pennington. It's really unlikely that she's come to any harm. Hospitals are very quick to inform relatives if there's been an accident. There wasn't one in Leek yesterday anyway. It's much more likely that she's with a friend."

"I've checked her closest friends."

"I'll need a list of them. What about your children?"

"We've two. We've a son who works on the oil rigs and a daughter who works in London for an advertising company.

I haven't rung them. She won't be there."

"You should still ring and check."

"If you think it's necessary. But I tell you. She won't be with either of them. Our daughter lives in a tiny one-roomed flat with her boyfriend. There's *physically* no room there. And as for Graham – well – he's somewhere in the North Sea."

"What about your wife's passport? Is that missing?"

He looked at her incredulously. "I don't know. I haven't checked that. Beatrice wouldn't have gone abroad without telling me."

He just didn't understand, did he? This was not the Beatrice he knew – or thought he knew. This was the other woman. The different woman. The one he probably never had known.

Her sympathy was tinged with exasperation. "Look – Arthur – Mr Pennington. In most cases like this the wife turns up a bit later and no harm is done. I suggest you go home and check through the items I've mentioned. See what's missing. I'm sure she'll turn up somewhere."

Korpanski interrupted them with their drinks, taking a while to fuss over milk and sugar before sitting at his own desk in the far corner and silently witnessing the interview. Joanna was more than usually aware of him. She wished he wasn't there.

With the result that she was frowning as she continued with her questions. "Just for the record where does your wife work?"

"Leek library." Pennington was just beginning to run out of patience. "But as I said she didn't turn up at all yesterday, Wednesday. It's their busiest day – being market day and all that. They were very annoyed."

Joanna sensed that to Pennington the word *annoyed* meant something deeper. Anger, frustration, inconvenience.

"She didn't phone in sick?"

"No – she didn't. I don't recall Beatrice ever being sick. It's most odd," he mused. "She set out for work as normal. She wasn't unwell. *Where* did she go if she didn't go to work? *Why* did she set out on her bike as usual if she had no intention of spending the day at the library? She deceived me."

Joanna nodded and Pennington failed to notice.

But in every disappearance there is an exact point at which a person exits from one life to enter another. So – you pretend you are going to work, setting out as normal. You might even travel for a mile or two along that road. But at some point you veer to the right or left, depart from your normal route. And the farther you travel along this strange and unfamiliar road the farther you are away from your old life. Sometimes the void between the two becomes so wide, so vast, that it is a no-man's-land you can never ever cross again.

And the little Joanna knew about the missing woman seemed to underline a person who could take this route. There had been something very fervent about the way Beatrice had gritted her teeth and driven herself up the hills on her bike, pulse racing, sweating. Finding it physically tough – yet performing it without complaint or giving up. And at the top Joanna had seen more than simply the glow of exercise achieved. She had witnessed something else. The nearest she could get to it was a child presenting its mother with a school-made Mothers' Day card or a home-baked cake offered for tea.

Oh yes. There had been love lying behind Beatrice's effort and it was not for the bespectacled man sitting on the other side of Joanna's desk.

In the corner of her eye she could see Korpanski's chair turning into the room, knew his eyebrows were rising, that his dark eyes would be wide and innocent and that he would deny that he had been both listening and inventing a solution. But basically they both knew already that this was a "domestic". Something between husband and wife. Nothing to do with the law. This was the story of a woman who simply wanted to escape the humdrum nature of her mundane life.

It didn't interest her. And glancing across at Korpanski's face she knew it wouldn't interest him either. But she must feign concern.

"One last question," she said. "What about money?"

"What do you mean?"

"Do you have a joint bank account? Has any money been withdrawn?"

"I don't know. Yes – we do have a joint bank account but I haven't looked in it."

"Then I suggest you get a statement. What about her car?"

"She's been cycling to work lately. Getting fit," he said disparagingly.

It answered just one of the tiny little questions which the mind will inevitably ask. How was it that Beatrice's form had improved so dramatically during the few weeks since she had joined the cycling club? She had not admitted that she had been cycling into work every day. Joanna smiled. More evidence of feminine deceit.

"Her car's still in the garage," Pennington said disconsolately.

She stood up then, agitated with a silly vision of Beatrice Pennington being whisked off in an exotic sports car to a destination unknown, like the final scene of Grease. Into the sunset of fantasyland.

The idiotic picture made her anxious to dismiss the husband so she shook his hand, suggested he do the "homework" she had set him and watched him shuffle out with a feeling of despair. He had a shock waiting for him. He was about to turn over his wife's life and find something nasty crawling beneath the stones.

She was torn, as a woman and as a policeman, something between sympathy and admiration.

The woman won.

"Go for it, Beatrice", she muttered under her breath. "Go for it."

Chapter Four

Korpanski watched her close the door behind the sad man. "Anything interesting?"

"Nope. Just a woman who got bored with her husband and has legged it. Probably with some fancy man." She leaned back in her chair and smiled, picturing Beatrice Pennington – happy at last – just as she had been when she'd reached the top of the hill under her own steam and surveyed the panorama beneath her feet. The vision gave her a feeling of warmth. At least someone was happy.

Korpanski gave her a sharp look. "You're looking like the cat that got the cream. Heard from Levin, have you?"

"Nope." She turned back to her computer screen and pretended to read off last month's crime figures. Korpanski's eyes were too penetrating sometimes. He read her when she didn't want to be read. "No, I haven't."

"He's a..."

"Mike. Please," she appealed, "leave my private life alone." It was hard enough fighting her own devils without Korpanski acting as St George, brandishing his chivalrous sword at her side.

He was sitting on the corner of his desk, his leg swinging. "Sometimes it's difficult," he observed, slipping back into his chair and moodily staring at his own computer screen.

She hated the silence between them and jerked her head in the direction of the door, knowing they should move away from personal things and return to safer ground. They were colleagues after all but it was a tightrope they constantly teetered along. "It's simply a case of an errant wife," she said – calmer now. "An errant wife who has, coincidentally been coming out cycling with the ladies of Leek for a few weeks. Even more of a coincidence is that during a bike ride a couple of weeks ago she confessed to having a secret lover."

"Ooh." Korpanski was grinning. "I love a bit of scandal."

"She missed coming out with us on Sunday and, according to her husband, disappeared yesterday instead of going to work in the library. I wish all disappearances were as simple to resolve."

"What dangerous lives some people lead."

"Mmm." She leaned back in her chair and eyed him up slyly. She never could resist teasing him. "Talking about excitement, did you get your little insurance claim sorted?"

Without warning Korpanski's face went puce and the muscles in his neck stood out like ropes. "That little episode," he exploded, "is about to cost us a bloody fortune in lost No Claims and Excess. I could kill Fran for her carelessness. And typically she's shifted the blame onto me just because the handbrake was a bit loose. And now the insurance company have started asking awkward questions. I *told* her always to leave the car in gear. Women," he ended furiously.

He paced the room for a moment, stopping in front of her desk.

She braced herself for another onslaught but just as abruptly his face had softened with concern so she answered his question before he even asked it. "No, Mike," she said. "I haven't heard and I'm not ringing."

"I didn't think you were so proud," he said, "or so jealous."

The words stung like salt water sprayed across her face.

"He'll damn me one way or the other, blame me completely and probably disbelieve me. I'm dreading the inevitable fall out. If he's met someone else then maybe it's just as well. It'll be easier – less complicated."

"You don't mean it, Jo."

"Don't I?" She gave a long sigh. "Don't I? Ever since I first met Matthew he's come with a rucksack full of complications. First of all a wife – Jane. Then a daughter, Eloise. And now this. Quite honestly I wouldn't mind just for once a relationship *without* complications. Something nice and simple."

"You'd find it boring, Jo." He jerked his head towards the door. "Like them."

She didn't answer.

"But this wasn't your fault, Jo. You couldn't help it."

She leaned right back in her chair – so far she was brushing the wall behind her. "And you think he's going to believe that?"

"If Levin knows you at all he'll know you would never lie. You'd always face up to the truth – however hard. If he doesn't trust you, Jo, he doesn't *know* you."

She felt vulnerably grateful to Mike for his implicit faith, wisely said nothing but twiddled her biro between her fingers and wished very hard that Matthew Levin shared the same trust. His face, initially vivid, quite without warning, began to fade. It blurred as did his voice. She knew then he could become less important to her if he didn't come home. But would stay forever far away, tucked tidily in a small corner of her brain.

She looked up at Mike and he stared back at her then moved in closer and touched her shoulder. "Come on, Jo. It'll all…"

"Don't use any of your damned clichés on me, Korpanski," she warned. "I don't want it. It's *not going* to come out in the wash. At some point Matt and I are going to have to talk face to face and sort this out. If he even wants to any more." She stared into the distance, picturing Matthew's cold stare the night before he had left for Washington DC. "And I can tell you. I'm dreading it. He's going to say things to me which'll stick with me all my life. No one on earth can hurt you like a lover," she finished under her breath.

And yet the unwanted pregnancy might not have been such a bad thing. It had merely forced them to face the issue instead of running away from it. In some ways she was glad it had happened.

Korpanski's eyes flickered. He straightened up, chewed his lip and said nothing.

They worked solidly for an hour or so at their own desks before he squeaked his chair backwards. "Hey, Jo." He rustled through the sheaf of papers. "Nothing much here. How about a pub lunch?"

And because she knew this was an olive branch when it was she who had been unreasonable she grinned. "Nothing I'd like better."

Halfway up the High Street of Leek is an ancient pub called The Black Bull. It is all you can possibly want in an English pub. Atmospheric. Beams low enough to crack your head on, cheap, good food, nosey bar staff, cold beer and darts instead of one-armed-bandits and warm lager. Plus – the absolute bonus for a couple of inquisitive detectives – a nice little huddle of copper's narks in the corner who shifted uncomfortably as they entered. They must have nothing for them. Perfect. Mike and Joanna found a table in the corner, ordered their food and drinks at the bar and settled down, both facing inwards towards the door. Police always like to see what's going on around them.

Apart from the narks they recognised a few more familiar faces. Some who were uncomfortable to see them and swivelled around, presenting their backs, making the child's mistake – that if the detectives were not in their sights they, in turn, were invisible to the two detectives. Others came over and chatted more easily – and innocently. Joanna tucked into a Caesar salad, Korpanski to steak and kidney pie with plenty of chips. She pinched a couple and couldn't resist a dig. "You know, Mike," she said, "the moment you stop burning muscle at the gym you'll put on weight like a retired rugby player."

He stuffed the food in anyway. "Ah, but you see I won't give up going to the gym. Way o'life, Ma'am."

She enjoyed the teasing. It was essential to them now, this sparring.

"And anyway." He jabbed his fork at her Caesar salad. "That's no food for a lady cyclist."

She suddenly threw back her head and laughed. "Oh, Mike," she said, "the only time I can really forget about Matthew is when you're around."

Korpanski's eyes were very dark, different from Matthew's which were a warm – or cold – depending on his mood – green. Korpanski's eyes were so dark you could not always tell the iris from his pupil, particularly in this poorly lit corner of the pub. Joanna had always thought the eyes and his muscular build were probably a throwback to his Polish ancestry.

It was the eyes which met hers but instead of responding to her capricious remark he bent back over his food and continued chewing stolidly.

Work is a neutral subject.

"What are you going to do about your missing woman?"

"Not a lot," she said idly. "There isn't much cause for concern here. I suppose we should make a few enquiries, try and find out just who her Romeo is. Just as long as we know she's safe we don't need to intervene at all. It isn't police business."

Korpanski merely grunted. The case didn't really interest him either. He'd just been making conversation.

Once or twice during the meal he did look up and almost spoke but he had finished his first course before he broached the subject that always lay between them.

"So how is Levin getting on?"

"I don't know." She felt she needed to qualify the remark. "He emailed me to say he'd arrived safely and that the Pathology Department was really welcoming and very well set up. He was glad he'd gone and he felt he'd learn a lot."

"And?"

Joanna took a long swig of her J^{2}O and made a face. "That is it. Sum total of contact between the subject and yours truly. I knew he would leave me alone. It's his way. He never wants to influence people, you see. He's a great believer in free choice. And he wanted me to make up my own mind about... Well – you know."

"But in the end it wasn't your decision, Joanna. Doesn't he even know that?"

She shook her head, swizzled the ice cubes around in the tall glass. "Nope. The trouble is I know what I'd ultimately have done. So does he. So in a way it makes no difference. It's hardly the issue."

Korpanski didn't even need to ask.

"But you're right, Mike. It wasn't my decision in the end. It was taken away from me. Some might say by a wiser being." Her smile was asymmetrical, atypical, twisted and heavily cynical.

"And you're really saying he doesn't know?" Korpanski was incredulous.

"Yes. I'm really saying he doesn't."

"He doesn't know he isn't going to be a father?"

"Don't make such a big deal of it. I told you, Mike." Her tone was forbidding any more questions. "I thought I'd write."

"But you can't find the words." There was something positively scathing in his tone now.

She shook her head, waited for him to say something else, disliking this evidence of bonding between the two men – even if it was conducted at a distance of thousands of miles.

"You don't think a man has the right to know these things?"

"Of course – but…"

"I'd fucking kill you."

And Mike Korpanski, at last, having blurted out his truthful opinion, fell silent. And so did she, having shot him one long glare.

He finished his food, drained his beer and slapped the jug back down on the table. "Coffee?"

She shook her head. "No. Let's get back. I have a feeling Pennington might return. I sort of set him a number of tasks to carry out."

They walked back up the High Street, through throngs of

shoppers – even though it was a Thursday and traditionally the quietest shopping day. The old habit of half-day closing had practically disappeared from the Moorlands market town and most of the shops now stayed open through the afternoon.

The police station was at the top of the High Street, beyond the war memorial and the bus station. It was an ugly building, modern brick, squashed in behind an old mill. The old police station had been a Gothic, Victorian piece of architecture, designed to give the police status and instil fear into the criminal fraternity. But it had been impractical and, like many other *Ye Olde Police Stations,* had been sold off.

They were scarcely in through the door when Joanna knew her prediction had been correct.

In the small, square waiting area, Arthur Pennington was sitting solemnly on a bench, knees pressed together, back ramrod straight. He was obviously waiting for her. This tiresome little man. As soon as she entered he jumped to his feet and caught at her sleeve. "Detective Inspector. Joanna. Miss Piercy. Please."

And just as suddenly and unexpectedly she felt a wave of pity for him.It simply wasn't his fault that he had developed these habits designed to irritate. He wasn't to know that of all things she hated it was having her sleeve pulled or her arm pinched, purely to gain attention. Neither did he know that somehow his dumpling of a wife had battled to transform herself into something else. But not for him.

She jerked her elbow so his hand fell away. "Let's go into my office," she said. "It's more private."

She felt Korpanski's eyes following her through the door and knew they would joke about this later. But with a certain frostiness. She just wished he wouldn't venture his opinions on her private life.

She led the way along the corridor, two steps ahead of Pennington whom she could hear breathing behind her heavily. She didn't speak as they climbed the stairs and entered the small office she shared with Korpanski, grey-walled, maroon-floored, small and square, filing cabinets in the corner, a computer link on each desk. Characterless, business-like, efficient. She liked everything about her office except one aspect. Its window overlooked a brick wall. She had been offered vertical blinds to cover the view but she felt, somehow, that it was a stern reminder to her, that police cases frequently reflected just that – a brick wall. It is only when you study the structure that you realise there is no uniformity in old bricks. There are stains and marks, hollows where frost has penetrated and destroyed some of the baked clay, ridges where the mortar has worn more quickly because of wind and weathering. Irregularities of the grouting, thick, thin, pale, dark. Even sometimes clues of previous structures, that abutted the wall, nail-holes, screw-holes, marks where hinges or ropes have worn grooves. She had once felt that the wall lacked inspiration. These days she did not.

She sat down behind her desk, motioning the nervous, upset man to the low armchair in front of it. She was well known for ignoring all the PC rules about being approachable, not hiding behind a desk, being open and so on *ad nauseum*. She was a policewoman. A Detective Inspector. Not a social worker. She *liked* the desk between her and her interviewees. She was here because she was in a position of authority and that was how she liked it. People who knew her respected it. As, eventually, did people who did not initially know her.

She studied Arthur Pennington's face and read puzzlement in there. Nothing but puzzlement. No grief or guilt, no anger or jealousy. Only complete confusion. He simply didn't understand where his wife was. Once again she felt the unexpected wash of pity.

"You were kind enough to give me some suggestions this morning," he began. "I haven't been to work today, you know. I just couldn't. I wouldn't have been able to concentrate. I mean where *is* she?"

"I'm sure she's all right."

He turned on her. "How can you know that for certain?"

"I don't know it for certain," Joanna replied coldly, "but I know the statistics indicate that most women of this age who 'go missing' have," *(gone off with a lover, whispered her voice)* "not come to any harm. They are perfectly safe. The best thing you can do is to be patient and wait."

He opened his mouth, fish-like, to speak, shut it again without saying anything. But his eyes bulged with the effort.

"Mr Pennington, I feel I should remind you. Your wife is a grown woman. Old enough to make her own decisions. If she hasn't got in touch with you it might well be because she doesn't want you to know where she is. Give her some space."

He blinked. Looked still more upset, his face collapsing in on itself so he suddenly looked like a very old, wizened man. He was patently telling the truth when he claimed that he hadn't slept last night.

"I don't know where to start," he said, almost tearful now.

Another emotion washed over Joanna – just as unexpected as the others. Anger against Beatrice, this heartless woman who had abandoned this vulnerable man once she had grown some self-confidence.

Be business-like, she thought. You were confided in in confidence. You cannot tell what you know but you can help this man in other ways. Give him something to do.

"What about her car?" Joanna prompted.

"It's in the garage. I checked. She didn't like driving. Preferred to walk or use her bike. We're only a little way out of the town centre. It's funny really." He was beginning to relax. "It wasn't so much the driving that bothered her. She said she could never find anywhere to park."

Joanna smirked. Neither could she.

"So she used her bike to go to work. It's still there, outside the library, locked to the railings. So she *arrived* safely. But she never went inside. I've asked her colleagues. No one saw her that morning. So she must have got all the way to work, locked her bike and then walked off somewhere. It's extraordinary. Why would she do that?" His face was a perfect mash of astonishment and grief.

Joanna was silent.

"And I've checked our bank account too. Like you advised. There's no money missing. Not a penny. She hasn't withdrawn any from the cashpoint since last week – just before the weekend. And that was only for a bit of shopping up the High Street. Bits and pieces, you know. She wouldn't have had much on her. Twenty, thirty pounds. No more."

Maybe her lover has enough for both of them. Or maybe she's been salting away some of the housekeeping money each week in preparation for the great day when she would cast off her shackles.

Arthur Pennington consulted a tick-list in a tiny notebook he had kept stowed away in his jacket pocket. "Her passport's in our holiday drawer and I can't see that there's clothes or a suitcase missing. She's just vanished, Miss Piercy."

"Have you spoken to...?"

"I've rung every single friend in our personal phone book and drawn a complete blank."

So Romeo wasn't in this personal phone book. This secret lover was not a mutual friend.

"And your children?"

"There's no getting hold of our son, Graham. He's out on the rigs somewhere. There's no answer at his flat and his mobile's switched off – or at least there's no signal. And Fiona says she hasn't heard from her mother for months. I'm at my wits' end, I can tell you. I don't know where to turn. Where to start looking. It isn't possible for a human being to disappear. She must *be* somewhere. But where? Living another life? I'd say it is impossible. I can't believe it of Beatrice. And there's something else."

He leaned to one side, picked something up from the floor.

She hadn't noticed him carrying a pink carrier bag. She did now when he picked it up. *Ann Summers.* In fancy, scrawly writing. She read the name on the side, looked at the man sitting opposite her and wondered what on earth was coming next.

He put the bag between them on the desk. "Look inside it," he invited.

It was the usual stuff, a black basque, black, lace-sided knickers with pretty red bows, holdup stockings. A black chiffon negligee which would have reached somewhere halfway up Beatrice's plump thighs.

Pennington still looked puzzled. "I've never seen her wearing anything like *this.*"

He hadn't made any conclusions about this merchandise. Certainly not the obvious one.

To give her time to think Joanna fingered the flimsy garments and pictured Beatrice, stout, short, red-faced, puffing her way up a hill, hair greying, roots overdue for retouching, cellulite all the way up her legs, stomach overhanging her cycling shorts. Joanna smiled to herself. Love had many guises. For a brief moment she savoured the image of Beatrice Pennington squeezing into these for her secret lover. And the secret lover adoring her in return.

Then she looked back at Arthur and felt how unfair it was. He was puzzled, distraught. Heartbroken. *The soul had gone out of the man.*

Something in her died. She knew Matthew's face would not look like this if she had disappeared for one night. And now he never would. She could picture him all too clearly as he had looked on the night before he had left. Chin firm, gaze clear, a certain hardness around the mouth.

"The tickets are still on these scraps of material," Pennington continued. "She never has worn them. They're new. All new. And considering what material's in them bloody expensive too."

A little anger was seeping in fed by his native meanness. He was beginning to suspect something. Joanna was learning something now about Arthur Pennington that only his wife had known. A certain petulance that he would not want *her* to recognise. His wife disappearing might break his heart but it was the wasting money which was the greater sin. The one he would probably never be able to forgive. Mentally she shook her head. We all have an ugly side to us.

She ran her finger along the sharp edge of the new lace on the knicker-leg. And felt a new emotion. For the first time since she had heard of Beatrice's disappearance she was very slightly concerned.

These were obviously clothes she had bought to take with her, to wear with her secret lover in nights of passion. *So why had she left them behind?*

In the excitement and tension of the final walk-out had it been an oversight?

It was possible. But these had been very deliberate and expensive purchases and Beatrice Pennington had struck her as a very careful woman – apart from this one, huge impulse – her plan to vanish. Joanna was surprised that she had forgotten this vital ingredient for her Karma Sutra.

Her eyes sharpened as she studied them. Had this really been an oversight?

Or had Beatrice been a different sort of woman? Malicious? Had this possibly been a deliberate gesture? Some little clue for her husband to find and work out where his wife had gone? A poke in the eye for the man she was to abandon without a backwards glance or one single word of explanation or apology?

She jerked her head upwards to find Arthur Pennington waiting for her to speak, his pale eyes, behind the glasses, drooped and sad but fixed on her face with the vaguest glimmer of hope. That Detective Piercy would find his wife and bring her home again.

Joanna felt she must perform. "Your wife didn't leave you a note, did she?"

"No." Said indignantly. "I'd have told you. I wouldn't have kept that from you. I know how important these things are."

Then it was time to take the bull by the horns. "Your wife. I mean – Beatrice..." She was aware she must tread very carefully. *Tiptoe through the tulips*. "There isn't any possibility that your wife has gone away *with* someone, is there?"

The scraps of scarlet and black lace and chiffon lay between them, almost obscenely, on the desk.

Pennington didn't even stop to consider. "Don't be ridiculous." He rejected the idea out of hand. "That's a stupid suggestion. My wife is a *moral* woman. I'd have thought you'd have realised that. Have a lover, you mean?" He tried to laugh. But really he was seething at the suggestion. He began to lecture her. "Inspector. I know it's all the rage now to go on and on about these things but sex. A lover. Well – it doesn't play a big part in our lives. We're far too busy getting on with things. I'd suspect the Pope of having a lover before my Beatrice."

Joanna opened her mouth, clamped it shut again, realised the Pope quip had been an attempt at a joke, smiled and felt a terrible pang of anxiety.

Arthur Pennington was due for a very big shock.

His forehead was shiny with sweat. He mopped it with a hanky he drew from his pocket. An old-fashioned, man's cotton handkerchief, starched, pressed and ironed. All this registered and made her slightly uneasier. She was going to have to play this one strictly by the book, gather all the evidence and confront him with it. Otherwise Arthur Pennington was the sort of man who would virtually camp outside Leek Police Station. He would believe nothing bad about his wife unless she could confront him with her whereabouts. For her to simply disappear was not going to be an option. There was a steeliness about his face, a mulish stubbornness too. "OK," she said finally. "I need to know a few more details about your wife."

And then the petty side of Pennington peeped out again as he mocked her. "What is there to tell? What do you want to know? How often she takes a bath? None of that'll find her." Then he lost it. "Oh, none of this makes any sense." He passed his hand across his brow, wiped the moisture off this time on his trousers as though his standards were slowly slipping.

"Where does she work?"

"In the library." He frowned. "I already told you. She's an assistant there. No one there knows a thing. I've been and asked them. I've virtually done my own investigation. More than you have, anyway."

Anyone who deals with the general public, particularly when they are labelled a *servant of the people,* is on the receiving end of their scorn. They are paying for you. They dish out *your* wages. There was something belligerent about Pennington now. This was going to be hard work with no reward.

"And what does she do in her spare time?"

"Not a lot, Inspector. A bit of gardening, keeps the house, shopping. She reads a lot of books. That's why she went to work in the library in the first place. She has a fondness for reading. She started up a Readers' Group there. It's been going a few years now."

Joanna felt the faintest of tingles in her toes. Readers' Groups sounded fertile feeding ground for a romantic entanglement.

She would find him there. Some quiet, shy man, who loved to dream of romance through the pages of a book.

"We lead a quiet, organised sort of life," Pennington said with pride.

On the surface, maybe, Mr Pennington. But underneath? I suspect otherwise.

Keep mum.

"And what do you do?"

He showed his impatience then. "What has that got to do with it? I work as an accountant. But knowing that won't help you. This is nothing to do with either of our jobs."

"Does she have any brothers and sisters?"

"One sister, Frances. She's a widow. She and Beatrice were fairly close. Not very, you understand, but I thought she might have some idea." *Again he looked acutely lost – bereft.* Then he shook himself so the shoulders of his jacket puckered and smoothed. "But I've already rung her. She doesn't know where Beatrice is."

The little worm of suspicion bored its way through Joanna's mind again. Sworn to secrecy? Or truly ignorant?

"And her parents?"

"They're retired farmers. They're both in their eighties. They live near Brown Edge now, in a smallholding." For the first time she saw Arthur Pennington smile. It was a nice smile. He had good teeth and it was wide and looked genuine. He looked a *nice* man. As had his wife. "They're meant to be retired but they can't be without a few pigs and a couple of sheep. It wouldn't feel right to them, you understand. But I've spoke to all the family this morning. They haven't heard a word from Beatrice for months. I tell you. We live a quiet life."

Not that quiet. Somehow, somewhere, in this quiet life, she has met a lover.

"Friends?"

"Apart from the people at the library and, I suppose the other folk in the Readers' Group, she has really just the two close friends that live in the town." He gave another of his surprisingly sweet smiles. "Been pals since schooldays. Close as skin they are. Once in a blue moon they go out for a bite to eat up the town and I suppose a bit of a gossip."

"I shall need their names."

"I've phoned them too. They know nowt."

"I'll talk to them anyway."

"All right then. Marilyn Saunders. She trained as a nurse. Works up in the Cottage Hospital. Nights. And Jewel

Pirtek."

"Jewel? That's an unusual name."

"Changed it herself, by deed poll," Pennington said in disgust. "Has a Fancy Goods shop halfway up Derby Street."

Joanna took their addresses and telephone numbers, noting that Arthur Pennington had already methodically prepared a list which he handed to her with resignation. Typewritten. As the day clicked by he must be coming to terms that his wife had, wilfully, abandoned him. And he expected *her* to investigate. He had thought no further than this. Certainly he had not considered the consequences. She had better not let him down.

"One last thing, Mr Pennington, does your wife carry a mobile phone?"

He looked excited. "She does. She does. I'd forgotten all about that. She does." At last the policewoman had earned his respect. "I've never seen her use it though. It just sits at the bottom of her bag. I've never heard it go off. It's for emergencies, you know?"

"Do you have the number?"

"It's written down somewhere. I'm not sure where. I have it at home."

"So you haven't rung it?"

"No. No. I simply forgot all about it." He looked flustered. Probably cross with himself for such an oversight. "How strange. How very odd. I'll ring you and let you know. Will that be all right?"

"Fine."

They both stood up together. The interview was at an end.

Joanna touched his shoulder in a gesture of friendship. It was peculiar that she should feel she shared any responsibility for Beatrice Pennington's disappearance. She certainly had had no hand in it. She had hardly known the woman. And yet, oddly, she did feel this was more than a normal disappearance. *"Behind every crime,"* Colclough, her Chief

Superintendent, had once told her, *"lies a story. It's up to you, Piercy, to tease it out. Not to make judgements, just make sure that, when appropriate, the entire story is lain before the courts."*

She shook herself. This was ridiculous. This was not a police case. Beatrice's story was a private affair, something she must square with her husband.

And lover.

"Please," she said, "don't worry, Mr Pennington, Arthur. Statistically your wife is likely to be fine. Just going through a bit of a crisis. A brainstorm, if you like. She wasn't depressed, was she?"

She hadn't needed to ask this. Beatrice Pennington had been a woman who had been happily rediscovering herself. Right at the opposite end of the spectrum to depression.

"No."

"And she wasn't on medication?"

"I've seen her take some pills occasionally but..." He turned around. "She was happy with her life. With *our* life. As I've said. None of this makes any sense."

"And you're sure," she began delicately, "that there is not another man?"

"Oh, no," he said firmly. "No. It isn't possible. It simply isn't possible."

And that was as far as she would get with him now.

He left then, his shoulders slightly more bent than before.

Joanna closed the door behind him very gently.

When she was again alone in her room she realised there had been something fiercely uncompromising in Arthur Pennington's stance.

He would defend his point of view, fail to recognise another's.

In some circumstances this could be a dangerous attitude to take.

Chapter Five

Working in the same room as Korpanski it was impossible to sustain any sort of bad atmosphere so when he returned she launched straight in without preamble and speaking in a way deliberately blocking out previous hostilities.

"I've lumbered myself with this now, Korpanski," she said laughing, running her hands through the unruly hair, as she invariably did when she was embarrassed, "so I may as well see it through. I shall always blame the Femina Club of Leek," she finished ruefully.

"Ladies with bikes," was Korpanski's cryptic comment and Joanna couldn't resist making a sly dig at him. "Safer than ladies with cars?"

He made a face. "Don't remind me. And I'm not really sure about safer the way you rattle around the countryside on your bike, but cheaper certainly." His grin was the usual warm-Mike grin and she felt a quick heat towards him. He was a good colleague, one who would back her all the way. A loyal friend too. Korpanski was the immovable object as far as his emotions went. Once you had enlisted his friendship you could count on it. *Forever.*

She picked her jacket up from the chair. "Well I may as well make a start on this."

"Want any help?"

She stopped in front of his desk. "Not sure at this point, Mike." She laughed again. "To be absolutely honest Arthur Pennington had forgotten she has a mobile phone. He's going to go home for the number then ring it. If she answers it'll all be sorted by tea-time." She was thoughtful for the briefest of seconds.

If Beatrice Pennington had a mobile phone why hadn't she at least put her husband out of his misery? Told him she was safe, left a message – or something. That was the whole point about mobile phones. You could use them any time, any place.

So why hadn't she?

It was that and the *Ann Summers* underwear. So obviously meant to have been packed. But left behind. She'd considered the theory that it had been a deliberate and malicious act and discounted it in the same second. From the brief contact she'd had with Beatrice Pennington she hadn't struck her as a malicious type. She simply *wouldn't* have abandoned her husband then twisted the knife in the wound with such spite.

So, still paused in front of Korpanski's desk, she frowned. "It won't do any harm for you to do a spot of fishing, Mike. I've got the name of Beatrice's two closest buddies. I'll just try and find out the name of this secret lover, maybe even where she's gone off to." She knew she was still frowning. "I'll tell you what though, Mike, just in case there is a hiccup, you could see what you can get on the mobile phone companies. See what was registered to her and then we'll home in on the detail. Whoever this secret lover was, she's bound to have used the mobile to contact him. It'll all be in the printout."

Korpanski tilted so far back in his chair he could look up, straight into her face. "And having wound up the mystery of the missing woman you can spend the evening sorting things out with Levin."

Now it was her turn to make a face. "I'm not sure he'll want to hear from me, Mike. He isn't lonely any more."

Awkwardly he covered her hand with his own, his eyes glancing away. "He will want to talk to you, Jo. I know he will. If he doesn't he's a..."

Now it was *her* turn to feel awkward. "Well thanks for the vote of confidence, Korpanski." She was back to her own, habitual acerbic tone.

Once outside she looked down her list of the missing woman's friends. The one that appealed most was conversely the buddy that Arthur Pennington had appeared to dislike. Jewel Pirtek, the woman who had (pretentiously according to Arthur) changed her name in accordance with her image. Idly she wondered what Jewel's name had been before.

Derby Street was only a stone's throw away so Joanna strode out for what passed as the High Street, but was actually named Derby Street. Bustling with people, busily doing their shopping.

She knew Jewel Pirtek's shop well. It sold handbags and belts, jewellery and perfume. Today the window was filled with bright, flowery beach bags and big, flashy necklaces, strewn with seashells, luring the individuals about to head off on holiday into a late buy.

She pushed open the door. It was a small premise, a tiny counter on her left, huge hooks of handbags on her right – and at the back of the shop were pashminas and scarves. A woman was sitting behind the counter, regarding her.

"Jewel?" she asked hesitantly.

"That's me." A bright, gravelly voice only very slightly tinged with suspicion. "Who wants to know?"

Like many old school friends Beatrice Pennington and Jewel Pirtek were as dissimilar as the proverbial chalk and cheese. Jewel was skinny, a size eight or ten, deeply suntanned, wearing an impressive amount of make-up including heavy, black false eyelashes. She displayed a scrawny cleavage and enough jewellery to sink a boat. She also smelt very strongly of Estee Lauder's Beautiful. And Joanna had a sensitive nose for such things.

The shop-owner treated Joanna to a great view of capped teeth. "Can I 'elp you?" Her accent was pure Leek.

Joanna flashed her ID card. "Does the name Beatrice Pennington mean anything to you?"

The woman blinked. "Beattie? Course it does. We've known each other since schooldays. A few years ago now," she added coyly.

There was no affectation about Jewel – except the name – and that Joanna liked. Particularly when compared to Beatrice; it sounded exotic, exciting, unusual. And it suited this tough-skinned woman.

The sticky eyelashes flickered wide. "What's she done? Parked on double yellows?" There was a throaty cackle.

"No. She seems to have disappeared," Joanna said apologetically.

Jewel did a double-take. "Beattie. Disappeared?" But there was not quite enough incredulity in the word.

Joanna realised that this woman was busily sizing her up, wondering how much she knew.

"Look," she said, settling down on the stool the shopside of the counter. Girl to girl. Woman to woman. "Arthur Pennington has consulted me professionally but I had met his wife on a couple of occasions. She came cycling with us. The Femina Club of Leek?"

"Oh," Jewel said again. "Yes. She did mention it. After getting fit, weren't she?"

"Yes. Why?"

Jewel shrugged. Eyes wide open. "We're always being told, aren't we? Get fit, stop smoking, don't drink too much. I suppose she was just following health advice."

Joanna thought there was something more to Beatrice's sudden desire to change her image but she said nothing, leaving it to Beattie's friend to continue.

Jewel fixed her with a suddenly sharp look. "I can't believe she's gone missing. Since when?"

"Since yesterday morning. She didn't go to work in the morning and didn't return home last night."

"Doesn't Arthur know where she is?"

"No. Have *you* any idea where she might be?"

Instinctively Joanna just knew that on the tip of Jewel's tongue was the phrase, it's for me to know and for you to find out.

She braced herself, daring Beattie's friend to say it but she didn't so Joanna added.

"She hinted to me that there was someone else. And Mr Pennington himself has some *evidence...*" (It seemed inappropriate to call the titillating underwear evidence but that was what it was or what it might become), "that she might be having an affair."

"Oh," Jewel said again. She was giving nothing away.

It was time to play the heavy-handed cop. "Ms Pirtek, Police investigations are very expensive and time-consuming. If this is a simple case of a middle-aged woman going off with another man I'd like to save the state some money. Understand?"

"Oh I do that, dear." Jewel was playing pally now.

"And anything you tell me will be treated in confidence. So?"

Jewel smirked and studied her false fingernails. "I had my suspicions," she said. "I don't know who it was but about six months ago Beattie completely changed. Just before Christmas it were. She had been down. Really down. We was worried about her. But then she changed. She started to look brighter. Much happier. Said she'd met someone. That was all she said, that she'd met someone. But it had quite an effect on her. She joined Weight Watchers. Tried on the fitness thing." The eyelashes flickered. "To be fair to Beattie, life with Arthur was...well...shall we say predictable?"

Joanna bit back the instinct to agree. It was not for her to pass judgement.

"Do you know anything about the man? Do you know who he was?"

Jewel hesitated. "No not really, except that she said this was someone who'd brought her back to life. That she'd never felt better or more fulfilled. That this was what the word kindness meant. She said an awful lot of things."

And suddenly now the flood gates had been opened there was no holding Jewel back.

"Look – I can't hide it, Inspector. To be honest, I didn't really take it that seriously. I didn't listen that hard. You see." She leaned forward, right across the counter. "I've known Beattie all my life, practically. I'm not saying she makes things up but she sort of romanticises. Maybe she reads too many slushy novels and it gives her ideas."

"Like what?"

"Well – someone gives her a bit of a smile and she sort of takes it further, imagines they're eyeing her up – when it's just friendliness. I've known it happen a few times to Beattie and watched her slowly wake up to find out she's been made a bit of a fool of. That's when she needs her friends, Inspector. Me and Marilyn."

"But this time she must have gone somewhere, with someone," Joanna pointed out.

"Aye maybe this time it was for real. Maybe not."

"So how did you feel when she was telling you she'd found a lover?"

"If you want to know the truth, Inspector, at first sceptical. I didn't believe a word of it."

"Later?"

"I started to believe in it."

"And then?" Joanna persisted doggedly.

"Then I was glad for her." Jewel was in defensive, defiant mood. "It was fun to see the old Beattie up to no good. *She'd* always been the stodgy one. *I'd* always been the tearaway. And then of course, Marilyn. Well – Marilyn."

Marilyn would have to wait until later.

"Do you have Beatrice's mobile phone number?"

"Oh – somewhere." Jewel looked vaguely around her. "But she never answers it, you know. Waste of time her having one. I don't even know that she knows what to do with it. And she always forgets to charge it up. It usually has a flat battery so you start talking and then lose her. So frustrating."

"The number?"

Jewel dived beneath the desk, fished out a brown leather handbag as big as a suitcase, delved around inside it and finally produced a maroon leather Filofax. She flicked through it, produced a scrap of paper and handed it to Joanna. Immediately Joanna dialled it on her own phone.

The mobile phone you have just dialled may be switched off. Please call again later.

"Bugger," she said. There was no offer of a messaging service.

It would have been so nice to have kept her promise to

Korpanski and sewn the thing up by teatime.

Jewel was watching her. "No answer?"

Joanna shook her head.

Jewel looked unsurprised. "That's our Beattie," she said pertly. "Mind you – if you'd just gone off with your fancy man you wouldn't want your friends all ringing you up to find out how you were, would you?" She gave a dry cackle.

Joanna put her phone away. "When did you last see her?"

"Last Sunday."

"She didn't come cycling with us that day."

"No." Jewel scratched at a point on the back of her head. "She seemed a weeny bit down, to be honest. We sat in the garden and cracked open a bottle of wine. Cheered us both up."

"You don't know what she was 'down' about?"

Jewel shook her head. "She didn't say and I didn't probe."

"You had no ideas?"

"Not really. I wondered if she was fed up with Arthur. You know – she'd wanted to go abroad again. Back to Italy. They'd been there, camping, a couple of years ago and she'd been hankering to go back but Arthur was having none of it. He hadn't liked it. Quite a stick-in-the-mud, you know, our Arthur."

The two women regarded each other. Jewel broke the silence to voice Joanna's thoughts. "I suppose she was plucking up the courage to finally go. And it's a big step, isn't it?"

Joanna nodded.

"You didn't question her?"

"No. I decided that if she wanted to tell me something she would. I've never been one to pry."

It was patently the truth. For all her sophistication Jewel Pirtel struck Joanna as an honest woman. Now it was Joanna who hesitated. "Do you mind if I ask you something?"

"Not at all."

"Unconnected with the case."

"Go ahead," Jewel said archly. "I can only say no, can't I?"

"What was your name before you changed it?"

"How did you know I'd changed it?" She was quick, indignant and rapier-sharp.

"Arthur Pennington told me."

She chuckled. "Disapproved, didn't he? Well – he wasn't christened Eartha."

"You're joking."

"Aye. Me dad was an Eartha Kitt fan – big-time. And no matter what my mother said he would have his way. *He* registered my birth, you see, my mother being laid up like. The minute I could I changed it to something I really fancied." She crossed her skinny legs encased in tight black trousers and asked archly,

"Answer your question, Inspector?"

"Yes. Thanks." But she didn't move. "Jewel," she said slowly, "who is the man? Beattie lived an isolated sort of life, didn't she? She didn't know many people. If she was having an affair you must have some idea who it was with. Was it someone from the Readers' Group?"

"Oh, you know about that already, do you? Work fast, don't you? I'm sorry, Inspector, I don't know. I honestly don't know."

It seemed a dead end.

Jewel's eyes were the colour of wood bark. A nice, warm, toasty brown. But they were very shrewd too. "Don't worry. And don't spend too much police time looking for her. She'll be back. I know it. With her tail between her legs. She'll have gone off somewhere for a little bit of drama. Have you tried the kids? Maybe they know something."

"She isn't with them, according to Arthur."

"Oh – he's that drippy. If I were you, Inspector, love, I'd do a bit of checkin' myself. Arthur doesn't always see what's right in front of his face."

But Arthur had seen the Ann Summers underwear all right. And read plenty into the flimsy garments.

Jewel touched her arm and with a heavy stare that bordered on psychic, repeated the sentiment. "It'll be all right, Inspector. I promise."

Joanna wished she could be as certain. As it was she continued to fish.

"Has she ever done this before – actually left her husband?"

Jewel was stage-thoughtful, polished fingertip on chin. "No. No – I can't say that she ever has. Not actually *gone*. She's talked about it but no. She's never actually left. She isn't one for action."

"Until she joined the bike club."

"Well – yes – until then. But she's fantasized before. That's one of the reasons why I never took her little confidences too seriously. You see they weren't real. They were in her head. Most of the time." She had tacked the phrase on.

"OK, thanks for your help." Joanna tacked on the traditional policeman's parting. "Here's my number. If you *should* think of anything else…"

Jewel flicked the card on to the shop counter. "Of course. But she'll be back. I know it." She gave a mischievous grin. "Mark my words."

But as Joanna left the shop she wasn't convinced. Beatrice Pennington had appeared quite serious about the effort to make herself more attractive. It had been tough work and the phase had lasted for around six months. Something or someone must have been encouraging her. A real person and relationship, surely, lay behind it. Not pure fantasy. The problem was who? Was it fact or fiction? Or an odd mix of the two?

She wandered back up Derby Street, dubious now that the job would be over by teatime.

Maybe she should have remembered the words uttered as World War Two broke out. *All be over by Christmas.* Even now it conjures up jaunty, cocky faces, in khaki, marching to the battle-drum. For years.

Still – it had been worth the trip up Derby Street. She now had the missing woman's telephone number. She could easily get Korpanski to run a trace through. She walked slowly back towards the station.

It was a hawthorn hedge, thickly overgrown and tall, weeds growing through its roots, embedded in clay, farm land beyond, on a little-used lane between Grindon and Warslow. A couple of tractors passed by once or twice a day. The farmer even caught the scent of rotting flesh, recognised it and thought, badger or fox. Two or three cars rushed passed, too fast for the road, not caring about the mud thrown up into their wheel arches. None of the drivers noticed anything. They were absorbed in their thoughts and their car radios, one tapping the wheel in time with the bass rhythm of his favourite song.

It will be a little while before she is discovered.

Corinne Angiotti had finished her afternoon surgery and was sitting, motionless, for a while, thinking.

The knock on the door was an unwelcome intrusion. Her "Come in", sharper than usual.

"Just a couple of prescriptions to be signed." The receptionist hadn't missed the frown on the normally good-natured doctor's brow – or the failure to greet with a smile.

Her eyes flickered as she placed a small pile of papers on the doctor'sdesk.

"Thanks," Corinne said absently, without looking at her.

"Thanks yourself," the receptionist thought.

Corinne sighed and her hand wandered towards the pile of prescriptions. She hardly read them, as she signed one after the other.

She was supposed to check due by dates, over use and under use of drugs, dates when blood tests should be checked. But she couldn't be bothered. She felt a terrible, heavy lassitude.

Her hand reached out again. A thick envelope.

No. It couldn't be. No. The voice screamed inside her. No.

But it was. Same writing. Same envelope. Same person.

Marked Personal.She tore the envelope open and scanned the words twice.

"Don't think you can be rid of me – ever. I am with you for always, you with me. Our relationship is far too precious to discard. Remember this when you work, when you eat, when you sleep – or not as the case might be. Remember this. We – are – together."

Medics call a faint a vaso-vagal attack. The blood pressure suddenly drops, leaving the brain short of oxygen. And so the person faints.

Corinne slid from the chair and landed in a huddle on the floor.

Korpanski was not in the office. Joanna tried Beatrice Pennington's phone again and got the same recorded message.

It was beginning to irritate her that this silly little problem was sitting at the back of her mind like a computer virus. It was a tease which she wanted resolved because while it distracted her she found it difficult to concentrate on anything else.

She looked at the mountain of work in front of her. There was plenty to do, quite apart from her own, personal problem. For the next hour she worked her way steadily through statements and forms, checking details. The footwork of a detective. She managed to forget about Beatrice and Arthur Pennington.

Right up until Korpanski appeared an hour and a half later waving a fax. "Got it," he said. "Mobile phone details."

It would seem cruel to tell him she had already obtained the number, especially when he had found out so much.

They poured over the list of numbers made from Beatrice Pennington's phone. It was a long list of calls. Evidently Beatrice Pennington *did* use her mobile sometimes to contact people. And one number cropped up frequently. An 01538 number – Leek.

But when Joanna tried it she was connected with the

doctors' surgery. Not what they had expected at all.

"Well, this isn't her secret lover," Joanna said. "She must have had some sort of health problem. Even if her husband wasn't aware."

Korpanski was frowning. "Why use her mobile to ring the doctor," he mused. "Why didn't she ring from home?"

Joanna was less curious. "Some illness she didn't want her husband to know about? Women do like their secrets, you know, Korpanski. Particularly when it comes to their health and personal problems."

"Ye-e-s." He was not convinced.

None of the other telephone numbers cropped up frequently or were prolonged conversations. They'd check them all out, of course, but neither of them was hopeful.

They'd basically drawn a blank. So far.

The last time the phone had given out a signal had been in the Leek area, slightly to the north east. That had been at 10 a.m. on Wednesday morning – an hour after her husband had left for work.

It still wasn't enough evidence to cause concern. Most people nowadays knew that mobile phones were eminently traceable and sent out frequent signals. If Beatrice was really serious about her bid to disappear she may well have dumped her mobile phone somewhere. And Jewel had made a comment about her friend allowing her mobile battery to run down.

So this meant nothing.

Or something.

And it was back to the irritating little question. "So where is she?"

Mike shrugged. "Search me."

"Are you all right, doctor?"

Corinne felt such a fool. She had lifted herself from the floor and was sitting at her desk, dizzy and sick, a pulse pounding in her head.

"I'm fine," she mumbled and knew she had fooled no one and certainly not herself.

Joanna glanced back at the still large pile of papers waiting to be dealt with. She could not afford to waste time on this knotty little problem.

And yet...

She made a small note for herself of people to contact if Beatrice Pennington didn't turn up in the next day or two.

Top was the members of the Readers' Group. They could probably get a list of participants from the library – and speak to Beatrice's colleagues at the same time. Then there were her two children, her other friend, Marilyn, her parents and her sister. Surely *someone* would be able to throw some light on the whereabouts of the missing woman?

There is always a voice inside you which acts as devil's advocate.

Jewel Pirtek had been her confidant. She had been the most likely person to know. And Joanna didn't think Jewel had hidden anything that she *really* knew.

She worked hard until five o'clock. But Joanna still felt fidgety and dissatisfied by the end of the afternoon. She looked up Arthur Pennington's number in the phone book and called him. He was in.

"It's Inspector Joanna Piercy here."

"Hello." His voice was eager. He thought she'd found something out.

"I wondered..."

"There's been no sign of her?" His disappointment was tangible. He was close to breaking point.

"No. I'm sorry. I've tried her mobile number."

"Oh." It was as though he'd just remembered. "I was supposed to... I'm so sorry. It just slipped my mind. I came home. Suddenly everything caved in on me."

"Is there somewhere you could stay?"

"I can't leave here. What if she comes home and finds me gone?"

They all do this, parents of missing children, husbands, wives. All the detritus of the missing. They wait and stay, as a dog guards a bone and just as pointlessly they stand guard inside their homes and wait.

What else is there to do?

Sometimes they expend their energy. They drive round areas where they think their loved one is. They haunt hospital casualty departments or search other places their loved ones felt attached to. Sometimes – in desperation they visit places their loved ones would never have been to – churches, Salvation Army hostels, railway stations.

And each time they leave the house they leave a neighbour or friend on guard or pin a note to the front door, "Darling, if you read this…"

Just in case.

"Is there someone who can come and stay with you? One of your children, maybe?"

She was sure his laugh hadn't meant to sound so dry and cynical.

But it did.

There was a short pause before, "No." The pedant had won. "It wouldn't be fair to drag them in to all this. They have their own lives to live. I'm sure when Beattie comes back she'll have a perfectly rational explanation."

When Beattie comes back.

It sounded an empty refrain.

When Beattie comes back. Not *if.*

"It's been two days now, Inspector Joanna," he said. "I don't know what to do next."

There is nothing, Mr Pennington. Nothing you can do except wait, hope and forgive.

She felt action was expected of her. "Can you give me your son and daughter's telephone numbers?"

"But I've already–" He capitulated. "Hang on. I'll just look them up."

He came back with the numbers.

She asked then for a complete list of the telephone numbers and addresses of all of his wife's friends, family and acquaintances.

It was the least she could do.

But under her breath she was already cursing Beatrice.

Damn you, woman. How could you leave this mess behind you when a short note would have saved so much?

He did not demur but read the list out mechanically.

"If you do hear anything, Mr Pennington, you will let me know, won't you?"

"Of course. Of course." He hesitated. "And if *you* hear anything, Inspector."

"Yes. Yes. Of course."

"And may I ring you again to find out how your investigation is going?"

It was a mistake but she agreed anyway and gave him the number which led straight to the phone on her desk.

Like him she wanted a neat solution to the problem.

She put the phone down then picked it up again, struck with a sudden picture. Beattie's bike, a Dawes hybrid, racing green, almost brand new. She detailed a couple of officers to go and detach it from the railings outside the library – if it was still there. Bikes were popular with thieves.

To herself she was relating the small fable, that it could do no harm for the forensics team to give it *the once over.*

She could have gone home then, back to the empty cottage in Waterfall. It was late; she'd done a full day's work. But there is something of the terrier in all detectives. She wanted answers, just to hear the end of the story. Not this unsatisfactory question mark.

Obviously the library should be the next port of call. And it would still be open.

Leek library is halfway up Stockwell Street, the road that runs behind, and parallel to, Derby Street. It is housed in a Gothic Victorian building called the Nicholson Institute. Marked by its green copper dome and like many libraries more of a cultural centre than a mere book-house.

As Joanna mounted the stone stair case she was reminded of the strange story she had heard about the 'ghost' of Joshua Nicholson, its founder, said to walk here. Listening to her footsteps echoing as she climbed, she could almost believe it was true.

And that was not the only strange story connected with the library. In 1965 the mummified remains of what had been thought to be a child were discovered in a barrel in the loft of what had been the museum. The fact that the discovery had been made on April 1st had not alerted the authorities that it was, in fact, the remains of a carefully dissected orang-utan, until after the National Press had run the story.

Leek has more than its fair share of strange stories and odd legends. Maybe it is the moorland which surrounds it and seals in its people, isolating them from the rest of the world and not subject to its wider laws and rules.

During the ten minute walk from the station to the library Joanna had toyed with the idea that Beatrice Pennington's secret lover was possibly someone at work. In which case would he be there too? Or on a sudden "holiday"?

As she reached the railings outside the library she passed a couple of uniformed lads struggling with a green bike and a pair of stout wire cutters. As she watched they freed the bike and, wearing gloves, she was glad to see, loaded it into the back of a police van.

She carried on in to the Nicholson Institute.

Two women were working in the office, a young, slim woman with poker-straight hair, no make-up and large, lugubrious dark eyes. The other was in her forties, a plump, motherly type, very like Beatrice herself. At a guess she would have been the one Beatrice would have confided in.

Joanna flashed her ID card for the second time today. "We're making enquiries about Beatrice Pennington," she began.

The two women looked at each other. She could sense their speculations. They looked enquiringly at her, waiting for her to speak first.

"Do you have any idea where she might be?"

"She hasn't been at work yesterday or today." It was the younger one who was trying to be helpful.

The older one nodded. "That's right. It really isn't like Beattie. She's normally reliable. Doesn't take time off at all. She didn't phone in sick either." The younger woman agreed vigorously. "We've had her husband on the phone. It seems she's left home."

They exchanged swift glances so Joanna knew they had come to the same conclusion as she.

"It's really odd though," the younger one said. "She must have *meant* to come to work. She's come right to the door. Her bike's locked to the railings. It's still there."

Not any more.

"What time does she normally arrive at work?"

"Well – we open at half-past nine. She generally gets here a few minutes earlier."

"Did you see her on Wednesday morning?"

"No." Again the younger one. "No – I didn't. I was a bit late myself."

"What time did you arrive?"

"Round about twenty-five to ten."

The older librarian turned to her. "It was later than that, Lisa. More like a quarter to."

Lisa didn't argue. Joanna turned to the older librarian. "And you?"

"I got here early on Wednesday – at quarter past nine. Her bike wasn't there then or I'd have seen it."

So between the two sightings the precise time of Beatrice's disappearance was narrowed down to between nine fifteen and nine thirty-five.

"Have either of you any idea where she could be?"

Both women shook their heads.

Joanna drew in a deep breath, thinking quickly. She needed names, a lead, some direction from these two women. Here and the Readers' Group was the best possibility for finding Beatrice's secret Romeo. Once she had confirmed his identity she was still confident that she could satisfy herself the wretched woman was safe and move on to more important things. But this could so easily turn into a difficult and protracted investigation if people stone-walled them. And she didn't know how discreet Beattie and her lover had been. Her colleagues might know nothing. Delicacy, she thought and planned her approach with devious care.

She tried the same sentences which had been so unsuccessful with Jewel Pirtek: that anything they said would be in confidence, that this would turn into a full-scale police investigation were Beatrice Pennington not found, that anything, however seemingly insignificant, could be of relevance.

She drew a blank. The two women gaped at her and said nothing.

She tried a different tack. "Mrs Pennington had recently changed her lifestyle," she commented.

"Oh yes. Into dieting and exercise," the senior librarian said comfortably. "It quite altered her. She'd been so *down* before Christmas. *Something* must have happened and whatever it was it did her the power of good. It seemed to change her into someone else almost. She seemed brighter, more optimistic. Almost as though..."

The two women looked guiltily at each other.

So they did know something.

Joanna waited, knowing what was about to be said.

But they needed prompting. "As though she had a lover?"

"I'm sure she didn't," Lisa said. "She wouldn't. I mean – she wasn't like that." *Joanna glanced at her, amused. She was of the generation only ten years younger than herself who believed that anyone over the age of forty was over the hill and had ceased to have sex or sexual desires.*

"Are you sure?" she asked gently.

"We did wonder," the older woman said reluctantly "You're right. There was something different about her since just before Christmas. She was sort of – lit up – from the inside."

It was as good a description of a woman who had a surreptitious lover as any Joanna had heard. To her this seemed to rubber stamp the theory. But the librarian had something more to say. "I even wondered if the doctor had put her on something for her depression."

It fitted. Joanna recalled the mobile phone printout and the numerous calls to the doctors' surgery.

She tucked the fact away and moved to a different tack. "You run a Readers' Group from the library?"

"Yes."

Remember the game Hot and Cold? Warmer, Warmer. Joanna felt it now. But mentioning the Readers' Group had sent her back into the cold area. Clearly, neither of the two librarians believed the answer was here.

Still – she pursued it.

"How many members do you have?"

Lisa answered for both of them. "Oh, it varied. Somewhere between sixteen to twenty." The plump woman was perfectly comfortable chatting about the Readers' Group.

"Could you provide me with a list?"

"Yes – certainly." It gave them both something to do. They bustled towards a filing cabinet in the corner, help-fully searching together but they found no list.

"We'll have to do a thorough search later for the list. Very much Beattie's little baby the Readers' Group was."

"Who else works here?"

Both the librarians were startled into a response. *Warm, warm now. Getting hot.*

"There are eight staff. We're both full time. Adrian Grove is our chief librarian. He used to be a teacher in another life." There was a distinct flicker through the eyes, an almost disapproving tightening of the mouth.

"I might want to meet him."

"You can't. He's on holiday."

"Where?"

"In Italy. Tuscany. On a walking holiday."

"And when did he go?"

"Saturday or Sunday. He's away for two weeks. He'll be

back on the fifth of July."

Joanna squirrelled the fact away. She recalled Jewel's comment about Beattie's desire to go abroad. To Italy.

But her passport was in the drawer at home.

Besides – Beatrice Pennington had not disappeared until the Wednesday. Three or four days after Mr Grove's holiday had begun. Was it possible he had not gone to Italy but was still here, in the country, and had not set out over the weekend but waited for his lover until midweek to divert suspicion?

Innocently she asked, "Did Mr Grove and Beatrice get on well?"

A swift exchange of glances before the older woman nodded. "Oh yes," she said. "Indeed they did."

Sometimes the explanations are so-o-o simple. "And is Mr Grove married?" she asked in the same, idly innocent tone.

"He's divorced. Has been for ages. I never have met his ex-wife."

"Nor me," Lisa inserted.

"Has he gone on holiday alone?"

"I believe so." Eyes round. "You don't think...?"

But Joanna wasn't falling for that one. She was not some junior police constable to start making public assumptions to feed the gossips.

Even so it was hard not to smile. "We'll wait and see, shall we? Do you know which company he's travelled with?"

"No," the older librarian said. "But I do know he booked it with Wardle's Travel on the High Street."

But in her heart she believed she had teased the entire plot out of them. Beattie was with Adrian Grove, her colleague. Here in the Victorian library love had blossomed. Sometimes explanations are so obvious. Lift the stone and the entire plot comes wriggling out.

One phone call to the holiday company and Arthur Pennington's wife would be found.

Chapter Six

But life is not always so simple.

Metamorphosis.

Each week had wrought a subtle change in Beatrice as though she stepped from a chrysalis to a beautiful butterfly. On the second week she had joined the Femina Club, the week beginning June the 6th, she had definitely looked a size slimmer. She had dyed her hair to an attractive auburn which hid all the grey and took five years off her age. And she was wearing orange lipstick – an unfortunate statement which didn't really suit her – but she'd learn. She'd made a clumsy attempt at eye make-up, clumping her eyelashes with brown mascara and sparkling gold eyeshadow. It reminded Joanna painfully of her own early forages into the sophisticated world of make-up – when she had been thirteen or so – and had slapped on bits and pieces without studying the final effect in the mirror. Women begin their quest for beauty in a clumsy, inept way. But most learn by trial and error. They are not born with the talent of the palette. Some never acquire it.

Unfortunately it reminded her too of Eloise Levin and a certain lunch in a pub at Warslow. And evoked the same emotion of exasperation, pity and affection that Eloise always inspired in her. But without the dislike that had marked the early years of their relationship.

The biggest change in Beatrice Pennington was in her face. She looked radiant – confident, happy with the biggest, hugest grin almost slicing her face in half. Her eyes sparkled and even her skin seemed tauter – younger.

She looked a different person.

Such is the inner light of love.

Friday, June 25th

It had been too late to catch the travel agent on the previous evening so nine o'clock found her and Mike parked outside, waiting for the doors to open.

She was in for a disappointment.

The girl was helpful. Yes, Mr Groves had booked his holiday through them. A fortnight's walking through Tuscany, departing from Gatwick Airport on Saturday afternoon. A quick phone call confirmed that he had been on the flight – travelling alone. She gave Joanna a brilliant smile. "Does that help you, Inspector?"

Actually – no.

With a deep sigh she realised they were no nearer solving the thorny, irritating little problem.

It was to be a day of telephone calls.

Beatrice's daughter, Fiona, was difficult to get hold of. Joanna had two tries and received either an engaged tone or the answering machine. On the third attempt, however, she was connected and made a brief introduction. Fiona was initially frosty and brisk then frankly incredulous. "What do you mean my mother's disappeared?" Joanna could hear the sharp derision in the daughter's voice.

She answered patiently and steadily. "She set off for work on Wednesday morning but never arrived."

"Well, where's her car?" Fiona was still impatient.

"Her car is at home, in the garage. She'd been using her bike recently."

"Her bike! My mother?" This time the derision was frankly cruel.

Again Joanna felt that wash of sympathy for the missing woman. While there was more than a tinge of contempt in the daughter's response she failed to detect any hint of affection or worry.

"That's right. She'd been on a bit of a keep fit drive."

"OK," Fiona said impatiently. "So where *is* her bike?"

She could have been grilling a six-year-old.

"Currently impounded by us. We removed it from the railings outside the library."

"So you're saying that she got to work safely and then vanished?"

"That's right."

"Well surely *someone* saw her lock the damned thing up?"

"We haven't found anybody who admits to that yet."

"Ri-i-ght." Joanna gained the impression of a telephone tucked under her ear, scribbles on a pad and scant attention. "So for two whole days no one's seen my mother?"

"That's right."

"Not even Dad."

"No," Joanna answered patiently.

"Well what about her mobile?"

"It's switched off or the battery's flat. We've called and called but had no response."

"Does my brother know where she is?"

"Not according to your father. I shall be ringing him after you."

"I suppose you've tried her work – and her friends?"

"Yes."

"And my aunt and grandparents?"

"Your father's spoken to them all. We shall be following through with a visit."

"This is all I need."

It was the response of a truly selfish, busy person. To perceive the effect of disaster on you alone without regard for anyone else. Joanna did not trust herself to make a comment.

Fiona Pennington gave an irritated sigh. "She must have had some sort of a break down or something."

"It's possible." It was at least an opening, a suggestion. "Do you know of anything that's been troubling your mother recently?"

"No." Said crossly. "– Well I wouldn't, would I?"

"When did you last speak to your mother?"

"Goodness knows. I don't. Months ago, probably. I can't remember but whenever it was she seemed the same as always."

Beatrice's daughter must have realised she was not responding terribly well to the crisis and even, maybe, wondered how her behaviour was striking the detective. She turned hotly defensive.

"We weren't terribly close, you know. We had nothing in common. I mean – her and Dad. Well – they led such boring lives. Provincial. You know what I'm saying?"

Oh yes. I know exactly what you're saying. Joanna felt hugely glad that she knew about the Ann Summers underwear and suppressed a smug smile. *Your mother's life was not as boring as you think, clever daughter.*

She heard noises in Fiona's background, followed by a reedy voice making shrill complaint. "Look – I'm sorry," Beatrice's daughter said. "I can't help you. I'm really busy at the moment. I have a meeting. I'll ring Dad. See if I need to come home. Though how the hell I'd wangle that with a new advertising campaign about to be launched I don't know. Oh, well," she said brightly. "Not your problem, Eh? I guess your remit is to find my mother."

For the first time Joanna almost warmed to Beatrice's daughter. For all her brisk ways she obviously did work under pressure. Where do you squeeze a missing mother into a frenetic work schedule?

"That's so," she said very calmly. "We just want to find her and make sure she's safe. That's all. And if she does make contact you will let me know, won't you?"

"Oh yes. Sure. Of course. I will. What did you say your name is?"

Joanna supplied it.

"And number?"

Joanna reeled off her direct dial, heard the scratching of a pen over paper and then there was a pause.

She waited.

"You're not. I mean – you aren't. There isn't any suggestion. You don't think anything's *happened* to her, do you?"

So – for all her sophistication Fiona had once been a vulnerable little girl who had wanted her mummy. Provincial or not. Maybe then she had not made such a harsh judgement on her mother.

But that had been before she had grown up.

Joanna was honest. "No-o, there aren't any worrying features but we're really anxious to find her."

"Ye-e-s. I see. I understand. OK then. Byee."

Joanna waited for a minute before dialling the number given for Beatrice's son.

She connected this time with a sleepy-sounding Scot who promised to fetch Graham, "Right away."

A few seconds later she was speaking to Graham Pennington. He sounded gruff, with, surprisingly, considering his Staffordshire origins, a faint Scottish accent. And he sounded as disinterested, initially, as his sister had been. In fact he echoed the very same words. Angrily. "What do you mean, my mother seems to have disappeared?"

Patiently Joanna repeated the story almost verbatim and Graham's lack of concern rose even more to the surface.

"Oh, she'll turn up, no doubt. I shouldn't worry. Some menopausal crisis."

Joanna didn't have a son. But if she had she would have been bitterly disappointed to have provoked this cold response to an unexplained disappearance for forty-eight hours.

"We're not worried, Graham," she said primly. "We deal with many disappearances, but your father is. I think he would appreciate a phone call from you."

"Oh, aye," said the son and she put the phone down. And started doodling, thinking.

Korpanski was eyeing her warily from the other side of the room, waiting for her to speak first, unsure what was in her mind.

"Strikes me," she said finally, "that although Beatrice Pennington had a family she led a very lonely sort of life. No one seems to have cared very much about her."

"Her husband does," Korpanski pointed out.

"Does he?" Her pen sketched a decreasing circle, spiralling inwards to the centre of the snail. "As much as most husbands?"

"I think so. He seems gutted at her going anyway."

"Yeah, maybe."

Korpanski's dark eyes were fixed on her. "What do you expect? Kids get on with their own lives, Jo. The fact that her son and daughter didn't have a lot to do with her and don't seem that bothered that she's beggared off for a couple of days is nothing unusual. I'd say it's more typical. Maybe they think she and their dad had a bit of a row."

"He hasn't said so."

"Yeah – but kids are intuitive."

She was pacing the room. "She wanted more out of life than simply being seen as a nuisance, Mike."

For some reason the vision of Beatrice determinedly pedalling up the hill, her face scarlet with effort, her breath coming in deep gulps, caused her pain. She wished now that they had cycled more slowly on the three occasions she had joined them, made it less obvious that they were so much fitter than she. There had been something so admirably gritty about the firm tightness around her jaw, the set of her mouth. Something which, according to her friends, had been a new ingredient.

So what had changed her?

Answer, the lover.

So who was he, this magic man?

She and Korpanski had a mountain of paperwork to do and plenty of other enquiries pending and the disappearance of Beatrice Pennington was hardly top priority. It was simply a frustration. They grabbed a sandwich for lunch and worked through.

From Arthur Pennington they heard nothing. Every time the phone rang Joanna expected it to be him but it wasn't; to her relief he stayed silent. She resisted the temptation to ring him and almost managed to push the missing woman to the back of her mind.

Until four o'clock in the afternoon.

When she stood up, restlessly wanting an answer to the question. "I think I'll visit Beatrice's other friend," she said.

"See what she's got to say. She's on night duty at the hospital so she should be just getting out of bed. If she's working tonight, that is."

Mike barely looked up. He was checking through some personal details of a man who had applied to be a classroom assistant.

Detectives have so many more responsibilities these days. They are expected to anticipate crime by screening the entire population for evil intent. It makes it easy then, to find someone to blame, if a criminal swims through the net.

The police.

She was in luck. Friend number two was home. As she drew into Harbinger Crescent she could see a white Citroen C3 in the drive of number 54. A woman dressed in a pair of unflattering cotton shorts and a blue t-shirt answered the door. Her hair was tied back, sunglasses pushed to the top of her head. She was wearing no make-up, her feet were in thick-soled red flip-flops, the toenails painted in chipped red nail varnish. She looked in her early fifties and very very bleary-eyed.

The night-nurse.

"Mrs Saunders?"

"That's me." Her response was more of a sigh.

Joanna introduced herself and was invited into the garden.

It was a warm, golden afternoon, peaceful, with a background of chirruping birds and buzzing insects. A soft breeze was moving the stems of the bushes so the leaves whispered their secrets around the flowerbeds and some tall, pink flowers clumped at the end of the lawn performed a slow, elegant dance in the sunshine. French windows opened out onto some green-stained decking on which stood bright blue china pots and some garden furniture – a table and four chairs topped by a jolly parasol. It was obvious someone in the household was a keen and skilled gardener. The lawns were immaculate, bright green, with ruler-straight edges, as neatly striped as the picture on the front

of a packet of lawn seed. A Joanna Trollope novel lay face
down on the table. It is nice to know what people read (if
they read). It tells you more about them than they will tell
you themselves. You unearth the romantic, the intellectual,
the thrill-seeker.

The introductions over, Marilyn settled back down on one
of the chairs and Joanna took the seat at her side.

"Now what can I do for you, Inspector?"

Surely – she must already know about her friend's disappearance?

But Marilyn Saunders shaded her eyes by dropping the
sunglasses. Joanna eyed her suspiciously. Sunglasses are a
great way to conceal your expression. Leek is a small town.
News travels as fast as a forest-fire. And Jewel Pirtek had
struck her as a woman who would find it hard not to spread
gossip, particularly to such a close friend. If she could have
read Marilyn's eyes she knew she would know whether she
was telling her a stale story or hot news. But with the sunglasses in place even this would remain a mystery. As succinctly as possible Joanna gave her the benefit of the doubt
and outlined all they knew about Beatrice's disappearance,
distracted by the dual image of herself mirrored in the sunglasses. Marilyn Saunders listened without giving anything
away, her head tilted to one side. She was a good listener,
nodding and responding with an, "Ah-ha", at all the right
moments without interruption. There was a reassuring balance about her manner and the way she gave Joanna her
undivided attention. She must be an ideal nurse, someone
who would listen, and give a thoughtful, unbiased, professional and informed opinion.

If Beatrice had been tempted to confide in anyone it
would surely have been in this woman who was so patently
close to her in age and outlook and had the stable character
of an agony aunt?

Or was there something more complicated behind those
blocked-in eyes?

Joanna stopped speaking and sensed that the nurse's

attitude had changed.

"I see," Marilyn said quietly. "So she's gone. That is what you're saying?" Her face was turned away. She looked as though she was staring out across the lawn. And now her mouth looked slack, unhappy, uncertain; her hands were draped over the arms of the chair, her legs tightly crossed, her ankles jerking so it looked as though she was tapping out some swift panicked rhythm.

Joanna's answer was set at a deliberate tangent. She wanted to winkle out the truth that she sensed this woman knew but was reluctant to tell. She leaned back in her chair and shaded her eyes from the dazzling sun. "In some ways," she said, watching the nurse from lowered lashes, "this is the sort of disappearance which does not give the police cause for concern. But in others –" She stopped deliberately short.

Marilyn rose to the bait and nibbled at it gently. "Can you explain?"

"This is a middle-aged woman, Mrs Saunders. Not a child or a vulnerable person. There's no history of mental illness – depression or acute anxiety. If anything her recent mental state has been more robust in the last few months than it had been." She noticed that Marilyn did not argue. "She lives a bare mile from her work in a town that is generally considered quite safe. She disappeared some time between nine fifteen and nine forty-five in the morning on a busy market day when there would have been plenty of people around. I don't believe she could have been forcefully abducted in that time without somebody seeing and inter- vening. It was light; the entire area is well populated and she was on a bicycle, which was carefully locked up. It is much more likely that she went voluntarily, either alone or with someone she knew."

This was the perfect opportunity for Marilyn Saunders to volunteer some information.

But she didn't. She simply sat, her face turned towards Joanna, the sunglasses masking her eyes. Joanna felt a strong impulse to peel them away and peer into the depths of her emotion.

"But in other ways there is more to this disappearance than we first thought," she continued.

Beatrice's friend froze and her hand flew up to her cheek. The only other movement in the garden were leaves and petals, stirred by the soft summer breeze.

"Your friend Beatrice seems to have led a very quiet life. None of her family knows where she is. According to her husband no money has been taken from her bank account. Her mobile phone is switched off. Her car is still in the drive. Her passport is not missing. So where is she, how did she leave, what is she living on and who is she with?"

There was no response from Beatrice's friend apart from a guarded tension around her month and a sharp twitch of her shoulders.

Joanna continued. "I'll be frank with you, Mrs. Saunders. The facts are this. In the last few months it has been noticed that she has been making an effort to appear more attractive, to get fitter, to lose weight. She's been happier and she's more or less admitted that she has a lover. I believe she's gone away with someone. I simply want to know who and to check that nothing is amiss. I believe you know who it is. You were close friends, after all."

At last Marilyn Saunders removed her sunglasses and rubbed her eyes. Something very bleak looked out of them then. They looked world-weary. Unhappy. Tired. She made a small, futile gesture with her hand but said nothing. Joanna reminded herself that the two women had had a long and close friendship.

"Why do you think that, Inspector?" Marilyn's voice was low and worried.

"You know Jewel Pirtek?"

Marilyn smiled and wiped ten years off her face. "Oh yes," she said with real warmth and affection. "Beattie, Eartha – sorry – Jewel – and myself were all at school together. We're old mates. The Three Musketeers." Her fist flung up in the air.

We all have these throwbacks. Joanna recalled Cathy and Ruth and smiled too, recalling chalk and biro pens, copied homework, shared secrets and teen magazines and thought how long it was since she had seen them. Friends disunited.

She smiled. "United we stand?"

"Divided we fall", responded Marilyn Saunders automatically. And although it was the inevitable next line it rang a dull thud in Joanna's mind.

Divided we fall. This mantra held menace rather than promise.

Joanna was suddenly fed up with wasting time on this. "Your friend, Jewel, more or less said so. Beatrice herself hinted something on those lines to me when we were cycling together. And Arthur found some new underwear in her drawer."

"What sort of underwear?" Marilyn asked, a note of panic making her voice shrill and sharp.

"Ann Summers."

"Really?" Marilyn smothered a smirk. "Well – what a turn-up for the books." But there was still something wary and guarded in her face. She wasn't altogether happy – even with the tasty titbit of the sexy underwear.

Suddenly she drew in a swift gasp of air. "I think it's my – I think I might have encouraged her to –"

She looked at Joanna.

That was when Joanna first felt frightened for the missing woman. Because Beattie's friend did too.

"Look – it isn't my job to drag her back, " Joanna said, leaning forward, "All I need to know is that she is safe and well. Only that. I promise. I don't need to know *where* she is. Once I have confirmed that she is all right I can cross her off the Missing Persons' Register. It reverts to a domestic affair. She has every right to leave her husband."

Marilyn Saunders said nothing for a brief while but carried on staring towards the clump of pink flowers, her lips moving silently.

Joanna waited.

Sometimes it is better to give your witness space to decide what to say and how to say it.

Finally Marilyn drew in a deep breath, looked up and fixed Joanna with calm, grey eyes. This time there was less worry. More of a sparkle. "You're right, Inspector," she said. "Beattie does have someone. But I don't know who he is. I only know bits." She sat bolt upright, dropped her feet to the floor. "Can I get you a drink, a lemonade or something?"

Joanna nodded knowing the simple action would relax her.

She was back in seconds, tall glasses clinking with ice-cubes and fizzing, cloudy lemonade, sipping for a while before talking.

"I feel responsible," she said.

Joanna let her continue without interruption.

"Beattie was desperate to find herself, to have a bit of fun before it was too late." Marilyn frowned. "To have some adventure and enjoyment." She frowned abstractedly. "You're young yet, Inspector, but believe me. Life is not long."

Joanna made some polite comment, followed it up with, "Do you know how she met him?"

Marilyn shook her head. "I don't even know whether it's someone from work or someone she met elsewhere but she will be with him, I promise." She allowed herself a small smile. "Quite safe. From what she said he is just as passionate about her. She was quite desperately in love and her feelings were reciprocated. They will be together," she repeated. "It doesn't surprise me that she hasn't taken anything with her. Beattie's honest and fair. She wouldn't rob Arthur. She simply wanted a new start. A new beginning. A second chance of life." She lay back again and drank some more of the lemonade. "You've spoken to her son and daughter?" A gentle lift of the eyebrows invited comment.

"Yes."

"Then you know that they couldn't care less about her. They're a selfish pair of buggers if you ask me. And they've never been close. And as for poor old Arthur." She smiled sadly, shaking her head. "He was one of those who was born old. He's never had anything about him. He just plods on, going to work, doing the garden, sleeping, eating. He's never been any different. There's no sparkle about him. And that's what Beattie desperately needs. Sparkle."

A young man wandered in. In his thirties. Crop-haired, muscular, in a black vest and well-fitting jeans, tattoos on both arms. He bent over and gave Marilyn a kiss on the cheek. "Hiya."

Marilyn's face warmed and softened. "This is my partner, Guy," she said, with the self-conscious pride of a trophy-dangler.

Joanna tried not to gape and failed completely. Guy was around her own age, Marilyn an obvious twenty years older. They looked like mother and son.

Guy sat down in the third chair, patently at ease. He grinned at Joanna. "I don't think I know you, do I?"

"This is Detective Inspector Joanna Piercy, Guy. You'll never guess what's happened."

"Speeding again?"

Marilyn shook her head, stroked his arm with her hand. "Silly boy," she said indulgently. "No. Beattie's run off with someone. Or at least – she's vanished."

Guy looked neither shocked nor surprised, but folded his arms behind his head, displaying hairy armpits, blatantly masculine. "Wow," he said theatrically. "What scandal."

"And she's been buying naughty underwear too."

The *Ann Summers* underwear was exposed as though it was strung along a plastic washing line in a dull, urban garden. Just as tawdry and unsexy and inappropriate.

The scenes began to remind Joanna of Beryl Cook pictures because it stripped away so much illusion and left her with a graphic vision of reality yet still marked by this great sense of fun and mischief.

Guy's touching up his partner's leg was simply one of the tableaux; the memory of Beatrice's metamorphosis another.

Guy's hand wandered up towards Marilyn's thigh. "Who's she gone off with, tiger?"

"We – don't – know, Guy. We *really* – don't." A warning was tucked inside the transparent words.

Joanna's suspicions were alerted. This pair of lovebirds knew something. She looked from one to the other and addressed her next question to Guy. "You knew Beatrice Pennington well?"

"Not really," he said casually and without interest. "Not that well. I mean – she came here sometimes. A couple of times."

"What did you think of her?"

Guy shrugged. "Not a lot," he said.

Exactly, was what Joanna was thinking. So what was the secret? Another youthful paramour?

"I don't suppose *you* have any idea where she might have gone?"

"I'm sorry, Inspector. Not a clue." There was a tinge of matey Cockney in his voice, which made Joanna instinctively mistrust him.

Guy grabbed his partner's lemonade and took a long swig before handing it back to her. "She's not with her mum and dad, is she?"

"I don't know," Joanna said. "Not according to her husband. Is it likely she would have gone there instead of going to work?"

"I'm only thinking if her mum had been ill or something. I'm sorry. It's the only thing I can think of." He subsided with a look of mock humility.

Joanna returned to questioning Marilyn. "You never saw the man?"

Beatrice's friend seemed confused by the question. "I don't know," she said. "I don't think so. At least – not for certain. We met for lunch one day. I was early so I called around to the library. She was talking to some bloke. Tall, thin, round-shouldered, bald patch with comb-over. I think he works there. His name's Grove. Adrian Grove. But I don't know if he was the one. They just seemed sort of pally."

What they didn't know was that Adrian Grove was on his holiday, walking in Tuscany – alone. While Beatrice's passport was lying in a drawer at home.

Joanna stood up. She would gain nothing more from here – for now. Besides – Guy's hand was moving with intent towards his partner's upper thigh. Joanna was no prude but it embarrassed her, as she knew it was supposed to. They meant to shock her. She could see it in the demeanour of both of them as they regarded her slyly.

But her thoughts were not as they imagined. What she was thinking was this: Marilyn had her toy boy. So why wasn't she looking as though she was enjoying it more? Why did she have this downtrodden look? And if things were so hunky-dory why did this pair have to rub her nose in their relationship? They had each other. What did she matter?

"Thanks," she said quickly, turning towards the exit. "Her parents. They live in Brown Edge, don't they?"

Neither of them looked at her. "They've got a smallholding there," Guy muttered.

It would be her next port of call.

It was still a beautiful afternoon, full of birdsong and colour. Pollution seemed a million miles away and not for the first time Joanna was glad she lived in this part of the country, this hidden part of England, a small haven cleverly concealed from tourists and crowds alike, quiet and green, pleasant and rural. She would not leave it. Washington DC seemed on another planet, one that Matthew inhabited but that she could not reach. She allowed her mind to flicker across the distance and picture his face without anger and without another woman behind him before schooling it back to Staffordshire, England.

One step at a time, Sweet Jesus.

With the sun full in her eyes she drove up the hill which led out of Leek, towards the Potteries. Known as Ladderedge it consisted of three steps, leaving the town below, in the valley. She drove through Longsdon, passing its pretty, spired church and turned off the A53 just before Endon, forking right up Clay Lake before taking another right turn into Broad Lane, rising to the ridge which marked the southern boundary of the Staffordshire Moorlands. At the summit, marked by a chapel converted into a house, she turned right again to travel along the ridge of Biddulph Moor, towards Lask Edge and Lion's Paw.

Involuntarily she smiled. Years ago she had asked an ancient moorland-dweller where the name Lion's Paw came from and been amused at her answer.

"'Tis where they shot the last lion in Staffordshire."

It was a more poetic explanation than the fact that the lumpy outcrop resembled a lion's paw.

Beatrice's parents lived in a tiny cottage, pebble-dashed-grey with bright green paintwork. There was a chicken run to the side and a couple of inquisitive sheep in a fenced field to the side. As she pulled up a dog started barking. She approached the gate warily. Some of these farm dogs have sharp, aggressive characters.

But the dog was chained up. Otherwise it would certainly have launched itself at her. It growled and lunged at her a few more times before being stilled by its master.

Beatrice's father had arthritis. His back was bent almost double. He looked in his eighties and frail, his face sharpened and wrinkled by a hard life. He stood in the doorway of the cottage, squinting across the yard at her. "Hello. Can I help?"

"Mr Thomas Furnival?"

"Aye. That's my name. What have yer come about, young lady?"

Joanna flashed her ID card. "Your daughter."

"What – our Beattie?" He looked incredulous and again Joanna realised that Beatrice Pennington had never been a source of worry to any member of her family before. Not ever.

"Have you seen her lately? Is she here?"

"No – she ain't. Arthur's already been here. What's it to do with the police anyhow?"

A voice called from inside the cottage. "What are yer doing out there? Shut the door, will yer, Thomas."

The old man turned towards the voice. "You'd best come in," he said grumpily.

She followed the old man through a low doorway into a small room.

The evening was warm. Marilyn might have been sunning herself in her garden. But warmth rarely touched this bleak part of the county. It was too high. Too exposed. They had still lit a fire, probably out of habit. This ridge was well known for its harsh conditions and cold winds that found the tiniest crevice in a house and whistled right through. Added to that the exposed position of the cottage, on the ridge's highest, easterly point, meant that draughts always would find a way in. But such properties have their advantages too. Every few years a heat wave cooks the county. On those days this high point is the most perfect spot on earth. Still cool and green, with the freshest air.

There is another advantage too. At some point, probably during the 1960s, the cottage had been altered and a picture window inserted which ran the entire width of the sitting room to take full advantage of the sweep of the valley down to Knyperseley Pool before rising to the highest point four miles away – the crooked castle of Mow Cop. The view dominated the room. Made a picture window a true description. It was impossible to ignore it.

Mrs Catherine Furnival sat in an armchair. Wispy grey hair, arthritic hands gripping the arms. But her face was strong and she had a very direct gaze through sharp blue eyes. "You'd best sit down," she bade.

Joanna did, on a shabby sofa with a rug stretched across it. "I'm a police officer," she said. "I've come about your daughter."

The husband spoke for the wife. "Aye. We've had Arthur up asking if we'd seen her. She must have took off for a day. Out of character, I admit. But I can't see why he's dragging the police into it. She'll be all right, will Beattie. Just got a bit over-excited. That's all."

Catherine Furnival nodded vigorously. "Aye – she'll be found when she wants to be found. But we don't know where she is. We've not seen her for a week or two. I don't know where she could be now." Husband and wife glanced at each other.

But there was no conspiracy.

"I should try askin' them two cronies of hers," the wife put in. "That Eartha. Right one she is. Tried no end of times to lead our Beattie astray. I should ask *her* if I were you. She'll have some idea if our Beattie's got 'erself into trouble."

Joanna reflected that actually it was more likely to be Marilyn Saunders who had given Beattie the first spark of discontent, made her recognise that her life was unsatisfactory and made her want to step into the pages of her very own Mills and Boone.

But Joanna said nothing. It was not the direction she wanted her interview to move in.

"I have talked to Jewel Pirtek," she said smoothly. "She doesn't know where your daughter is."

Catherine Furnival wasted no time in moving her wrath on. "And that Marilyn? Tekin' up with that young man? Could be her son." The old lady made a face. "Disgustin' I call it. The talk of the town. I'd be ashamed if she were my daughter. Livin' with a…" Not knowing such phrases as 'trophy-man' or 'toyboy' she had run out of words. "…Young lad," she finally managed.

All the time Joanna was learning about Beatrice Pennington she was understanding that, in a way, her disappearance had been inevitable. While her friends might have brazened out any scandal, *she* would have found it difficult. Her own mother would not have forgiven her daughter for causing scandal in the town. Leaving her husband, eloping with a younger or divorced man. Joanna winced. These were Victorian morals that she thought had been left behind in the twentieth century, consigned now to the history books together with other prejudices.

Not so.

The prejudices were still alive and flourishing here, in this tiny cottage.

Thomas Furnival hobbled across the room, to add his disapproval to his wife's. "Left her husband and three fine daughters she did to go off with that *thing*."

"And them brazen enough to go get a house together right in the middle of town."

Their venom was as potent and visible as when you milk the fangs of an adder.

Joanna left the house believing she understood some of Beatrice Pennington's motives. Even that she could move into her state of mind. But while she sympathised with the missing woman the different attitudes intrigued her. While her parents would condemn her, her son and daughter were indifferent, her husband despairing and puzzled. Only her friends seemed tolerant.

Therefore it was back to her friends that Joanna must search.

Briefly she wondered about Beatrice's sister. If the missing woman didn't turn up over the next couple of days she might be worth a visit.

At this point all seemed clear.

It was only later that the fog would descend.

What we see is not always what is. Being rational people we rationalise.

What we believe we see is sometimes what we want to see. Not always the truth. Purely wishful thinking.

Chapter Seven

Cycling home had given Joanna the chance to ponder.

Secrets between partners are not always a good idea.

What can be concealed can be found out.

And misconstrued. They needed truth and clarity.

Corinne kept opening the drawer and reading through the letters. Days had gone by now and there had been no more. But instead of feeling relieved she missed them. *"You are my reason for living, my life, my love, my only true romance."* Because she had felt threatened she had not realised before how beautiful the words were. *"No one in my entire life has ever touched me the way you did."* They had a sort of...reverence. *"A respect for my body, for who I am, for what I am. Therefore our love is complete. A full circle. A perfect sphere."* She scanned the page.

"I daydream about the life we will have together, the home we shall buy. Maybe a little further south from here. We should both be able to get work to pay for it. I cannot rob Arthur for what is, in effect, the result of my traitor heart. I remember once I broached the subject with you of what a woman should do if she fell in love with another. I recall your answer so clearly. "She should follow her heart," you said categorically.

"To its ultimate conclusion?"

With your eyes fixed on mine you moved closer. "Most definitely," you said. "What else can a person really do?"

What clearer directive could I have had? You were telling me exactly what to do.

"Tosh."

The thick sheet of paper, blue, smothered in violet ink, was scrunched up and flung into the waste-paper bin.

But less then ten minutes later a hand retrieved it, smoothed it out and fatally she put it in her handbag.

Maybe it should be preserved.

Why?

As evidence? To prove that this bad dream really had

happened and was not simply a disobedient nightmare, one which inhabited daytime thoughts too or simply because the sentiments expressed were a manifestation of pure affection?

Joanna tried to convince herself that she could forget about Beatrice Pennington, or at least relegate her to the back of her mind. Okay. So there was a murky little story behind her disappearance but it was not a police affair. A woman has the perfect right to go with whom she chooses. As does a man. Matthew? Yes. She answered her own question without flinching. If one elects to leave one's partner one may do so. And vice versa. This is a free country and it is a domestic affair. Not one for her. She should take a leaf out of Beatrice's book, sort her own life out, spend the evening writing the letter to Matthew.

She felt a sudden surge of happy energy. It was in her nature to be clear about situations. To take positive action. She *wanted* to tell Matthew. Everything. Everything? Yes – everything. Right from the beginning. All that had been in her mind. At least then for the first time their relationship would be based on the sure ground of truth. Not an affair, not a deceit. He would get the letter within the week. And then he could decide where his future lay. She would not try to influence him, but would show him the same courtesy he had awarded her. She would merely let him have the full facts. Then all would be clear – and honest.

Joanna, whispered the voice. Life is not like this. It does not move towards clarity and honesty but hides behind corners, waiting for the opportunity to jump out and surprise you. This is what life is like. Full of nasty surprises.

Watch out for them. Life is not a meadow full of butterflies and wild flowers always in bloom.

As she inserted her key into the door she had a sudden vision of Matthew, standing in the doorway to the living room, tall, slim, fair, with that faintly quizzical smile he often wore, the smile which was half greeting, half question. The smile which gave her an ache in her heart.

But once inside the cottage the scent of him was gone, that tangy, male, spicy smell. The place smelt feminine, of perfume and cleaning fluids, washing powder, fabric conditioner. Nail varnish. And acetone remover. Joanna breathed in and smelt only herself. Lemons, lavender. Chanel. Coffee. There was not the slightest hint of Matthew. His desk in the corner of the lounge was tidy, his laptop gone with him. This was the room of a lone, single woman. She felt restless. She wanted settlement, a finality. If he wasn't going to live here then he should go. She would remain in the cottage and adapt it as her single home. Otherwise he should come back. Not remain in the States. In limbo.

All the time he had been gone she had not allowed herself to think so deeply. In the early weeks she had been too damaged. But now she felt fit. Stronger than before. It felt like time to fight.

She dropped onto the sofa, recalling a particular night, one of the many, when they had been teasing and flirting and the phone had rung. Eloise, sensing from more than a hundred miles away, that her father and his mistress were enjoying themselves perhaps a little too much.

Did she want him to return?

Joanna sat bolt upright. Did she want him to return?

She could not stop her face from curling into a smile. What sort of a question was that? Of course she did.

Did she?

Did she really? Was that the truth? Or did Matthew make her just a little too uncomfortable with his demands?

With Eloise? With...

She should face it. One thing or the other. Commitment or split.

Life without Matthew, whispered the voice? Having him not even on the periphery of your life? Not even for brushing encounters or surreptitious dates, meals at little-used restaurants?

Affairs.

So her mind turned full circle, back to Beatrice

Pennington's affair.

The family had gone quiet. Maybe they too were putting two and two together and working it all out for themselves. Possibly they had guessed that there was more to this mother, wife and friend than they had thought and realised that in the end it had been *she* who had left *them*.

Again she mouthed, *Good For Beatrice*.

But she would have cheered louder had there been money missing. Or a passport gone. Her car or even her bike gone too. Something that fitted in with her theory.

And she wished Beatrice had remembered to pack the Ann Summers underwear.

She yawned and glanced out of the window. If she didn't move now she'd miss the evening.

She took the road south towards Waterhouses, riding fast and furiously. It stopped her thinking and forced her to concentrate on movement. Her lungs, her legs, her skin. Alive. A light drizzle had sprung out of a moist, grey sky. It cleaned her skin so it felt pure and freshened. She never felt fitter, happier or better than when she was pedalling her bike around the moorlands. She took her eyes off the road with its moss-smothered centre (some of these lanes were little used) and stared to the left and to the right at the grey-stone walls which divided the fields up, sheep from cows, corn from hay. The evening was punctuated by the plaintive sound of sheep baa-ing. Think she must. But in manageable sound bytes. Not all at once, in unpalatable chunks. She could not allow her mind to flood with the idea of life with or without Matthew Levin. The void. Not life. Because it would not be life without him somewhere. It would be a void. An unimaginable void.

They had been together for almost all the years since she had arrived at Leek.

The first post-mortem she had watched had been performed by him. She pictured herself, Sergeant Piercy, seconded from Stoke, puking noisily in the corner during the post-mortem, Matthew's hand on her shoulder, the offer of a cup of tea quickly followed by a dinner invitation. An invitation she had accepted – and been damned.

When you lose a lover you lose a small part of yourself.

Her first case as an Inspector had been solved through his skill and knowledge.

At Waterhouses she swung left, passing The Old Beams restaurant, and entered the Manifold cycle-path, quiet today, as it was a weekday, tracking the River Hamps until she reached the village of Grindon. And now she had accepted the truth about Matthew she slowed her pedalling down to a steady rhythm, knowing she could keep this up for hours.

Like many areas isolated by geography and the lay of the land, the villages of the Staffordshire moorlands are full of strange myths and tales. Grindon is no exception. Marked by hikers by the tall spire of the church peeping over the brow of the hill. The winter of 1947 was especially hard with a deep fall of snow, which cut its villagers off from the outside world. On February 13th, 1947, in that hard winter which came so close on the heels of a hard-fought war, an RAF Halifax and its crew flew over the village, detailed to drop food to the hungry villagers who had marked a safe spot with a sooty cross on the snow. But the Halifax dipped too low. A wingtip of the plane caught the ground and it crashed in a ball of flame, killing its entire crew, in front of the eyes of the horrified villagers they had been trying to help. To add a terrible poignancy to the incident, on that very day, the road between Leek and Grindon was re-opened. The people of Grindon never forgot their would-be saviours. In the church a memorial has been erected, In Grateful Remembrance.

Only two years after the end of the war the horrors had been re-enacted in front of people who had thought they were as far away from violent death as it was possible to be.

Stories and legends are an integral part of these areas.

On the narrow lane between Grindon and Butterton she

passed by a hedge, tall, hawthorn, white with late May blossom and as she rode passed she caught the scent of rotting flesh and thought the same as the farmer. Dead fox or badger, rabbit or stoat.

We never think it could be a person.

Joanna sped by, through the villages of Butterton and Warslow, Hulme End and Flash, back passed the Mermaid's Pool, across the bleakest, highest part of the moor, crossing Royal Cottage and finally, through Thorncliffe and Bradnop then home for a shower.

And then...

She felt wonderful. Empowered.

Ready to act.

This time around the right words came easily, the Dear Matthew note, an honest account of events and her feelings. Not too baldly factual nor over-emotional. If Matthew did not understand her after reading this he never would. And she may as well face it. For all their attraction they were simply not compatible.

She put the letter on the table, ready to post the following day, opened a celebratory bottle of wine and watched one of her favourite old films,

Room at the Top.

A story, as much entertainment is, of the cruel trick nature can play and the resulting conflict when the person you *should* love is not the one you do.

As she watched the film she made another resolution. If, after the weekend, Beatrice Pennington had not turned up she would speak to her sister, and then try to contact Adrian Grove – walking holiday or not.

She was at peace.

Until the film had almost finished and the phone rang. Her "hello" was answered in a low, voice, female and young. One she recognised instantly.

Eloise.

"Hello, Joanna."

"Hello, Eloise."

"I just wondered how you were."
"I'm OK. How are you?"
"Up to my neck in exams."
"Well, good luck."
There was a brief, awkward silence between them before
Joanna said, "I'm missing your dad."
"Me too. Have you any – cases on?"
"A missing woman. Nothing much. She'll turn up."
"Oh." Another awkward silence. Then, "Look after your-
self."
"You too."
"Goodbye."
Joanna put the phone down. This was puzzling her.
She sighed. Love comes in many guises.

He'd been in her bag.
Corinne Angiotti was pacing the room, trying not to lose
her temper with her husband who was holding a piece of
paper in his hand.

"Smutty, " he said.

She was instantly defensive. "That it isn't."

"So what do *you* call it then?"

"I call it sad," she said, stupid, traitorous tears rolling
down her cheek, making her angry with herself. Their marriage was unravelling and she powerless to stop it.

"You must have encouraged it." The note of accusation
made his voice hard and unsympathetic.

Pointless to shake her head.

"It's obvious to me that you did."

"Don't be so silly, Pete."

Peter Angiotti was not a big man. Around 5 foot 8 and
quite slim. But he had some power in his manner. Perhaps
power is the wrong word. Maybe the correct word is threat.
Certainly Corinne did not take her eyes off him, as though
if she did, he would steal a blow against her.

It was odd that she feared him physically. He never had
hit her.

It was more the threat. Maybe she was a coward.

She believed that he was capable of it. But he was, in fact, a weak man, both physically and psychologically, with an unfortunate speaking voice, a slight Cockney accent laced into a high-pitched tone. There was no menace in his physical appearance either. He had rather pale eyes, a slim build and sparse brown hair. When he wanted he could be funny. Very funny. Side-achingly funny. And charming too. The shame was that Pete Angiotti rarely bothered to exert this talent these days.

Since the Wandsworth business he had fallen into the habit of complaining.

Corinne had wanted to believe that he had settled at Westwood High School. He had been lucky to have landed the job as geography master after the fiasco of his last couple of years in London, the hearings and final disciplinary action.

It had taken her a while to realise that her husband was one of life's victims. The children had initially teased him – as they probably do most teachers. But the teasing had turned nasty. Dangerous even. Pete had played into their hands by involving the headmaster and then taking time off sick when he could not face going in. After the trouble it had finally become quite impossible for him ever to return to his post and he had left – the fourth job since he had graduated.

Corinne was looking in his direction but not at him. More through him. She was wondering. Why did married life have to be like this, saturated in mistrust, a permanent competition between the two of them. Why *should* she feel permanently wrong-footed, or that she should apologise for being content in her life as a GP, a high-earner. When he was not even working for half of the year. He worked short hours she would love to have, had long holidays and time off sick with a multitude of small complaints. What was wrong?

She put her hands to her face and gave a small, panting laugh. "Huh."

Pete looked enquiringly at her.

"I was wondering..."

And she realised how very pointless it all was.

This was her husband, the man she had married.

"Like it or lump it, my girl."

Her father, the military gentleman.

And her mother?

Her mother had departed when she was two. Departed?

Our dear departed?

Funeral words?

Her mother was not dead. Yet it was the word her father invariably used when referring to her mother's absence. It had never struck her as strange before. But now she wondered. How abnormal is it to abandon your two-year-old daughter and never attempt to make contact?

Her father had given her no explanation. The military are like this. Hard. In permanent denial of their emotions.

But her mother was not military. She had been a secretary. And that was all she knew about her.

She had one photograph that had escaped her father's destruction. Of a plain, dumpy woman with anxious eyes who stared into the camera and held on to her baby as though she was frightened someone would take it from her.

But it had not been like that but the other way round. Hadn't it? Hadn't it?

When Corinne had been a teenager she had often stared into the mirror. Not to search for spots or blackheads or perceived ugliness but to stare at her mother's eyes and wonder whether she looked like her and where she was now. And something in Beatrice Pennington had struck a chord. She and her mother had been of the same type.

"I don't even think you're listening to me."

It was an earth-shattering realisation. Enough to numb her. She was vaguely aware of her husband talking in the background.

"I am, Pete," she said firmly. "But I don't think you're being fair. I didn't invite this sort of attention. I found it embarrassing and tiresome. Besides." She grew suddenly fierce. "Hasn't it occurred to you that this could endanger my job? Relationships between doctor and patient are scrutinised by the Medical Council. If there is the slightest hint of impropriety... (*how strange and old-fashioned a word – impropriety'*) it will be rigorously investigated, I can tell you. And the General Medical Council seem to come down hard on the patient's side. No one will believe me. As you don't."

She spoke the last sentence more vehemently than she had meant to. She had meant it to be an appeal. Not a challenge. Her husband reacted as he usually did. By growing pale and quiet and thoughtful. Pete at his most dangerous.

"I see," he said softly.

And he reminded her even more of her father so she wanted so scream out at him. Or appeal to him to be kind, show some emotion. Affection.

She smothered her mouth with her hand.

We are all damaged goods.

Grandparents? Paternal grandparents had seemed in awe of their son, slightly fearful. She had never met her mother's parents. They must have known of her existence because they sent her money at Christmas and birthday time and even when she set off for university. Her father had thrown the cards at her with a growl and now there was not so much as a note or a card. They had made no attempt to make contact for years and had not been invited to her wedding. Her father's choice. She knew only that they lived in Reading.

Nothing else. And her father never spoke about them.

Peter Angiotti scrunched up the letter into a ball of paper. "And you keep them," he sneered. "How touching. How very touching."

Corinne stared at him, thinking bitter thoughts.

Saturday morning dawned bright and hot. Joanna woke and within seconds was out of bed, throwing back the curtains and staring up at a Wedgewood blue sky.

Perfect.

She would ring Pagan and Pat and they would plan a long ride through the moorlands, ending up at a country pub.

But we cannot always plan our lives so.

The telephone ring was insistent – and early.

Her heart skipped once, twice.

Matthew?

But it wasn't. It was Caro. Caro, her journalist friend, who had married Tom, a local solicitor, before scurrying back down to London. They had an apart marriage, she had haughtily said to Joanna, before laughing and saying that was the only way Tom could stick her – part-time – and then told the truth. That they would spend what time they could together, knowing that their separate jobs meant they must spend most of it apart.

"Where are you?"

"With my husband." Caro sounded light-hearted and happy. "Can't stick London in the summer so I'm here for the weekend, in Cheddleton. And Tom wants to know if you can come across so we can do the canal walk and then have an evening at the pub. OK?"

"What do you think?"

So the day was spent differently from how she had planned. But none the less perfect. Joanna smothered a smile as she greeted her friend. Caro looked so much the London week-ender in her pale cotton trousers and designer t-shirt with pink loafers. And Tom. How little he had changed from the early days. However casually he dressed – in a polo shirt and chinos – he never looked anything other than a country solicitor. Maybe it was the glasses, Joanna reflected as she hugged them both.

"It seems ages." Caro adopted her London-talk.

"It *is* ages. You haven't been up for months."

"Blame the West End," she said, shrugging her thin shoulders. "There's so much going on. I've bought a flat which has room enough to swing two cats at a time. So Tom has been coming down a lot."

She linked her arm through Tom's while he grinned good-naturedly. "You've got an open invite," he said.

"In fact, I'm trying to persuade him to come down and join me permanently."

Tom gave a mock shudder. "No way," he said. "London's OK but here is better."

And Joanna agreed with him.

Caro waited until they were on the towpath, almost at Cheddleton Flint Mill, before she asked about Matthew. "Have you heard from him?"

And suddenly Joanna had had enough of the shadow hanging across her. "Look," she said. "I'm sorting it out. OK? There's a lot to explain and so on. I've written to Matt and posted it on the way here. He'll get it middle of next week."

"Why didn't you ring him?"

"I did."

"And?"

Caro was a typically tenacious journalist.

"Someone else answered his phone and I didn't really want to talk to *her*."

"Oh."

And for once her dainty mouth closed – and stayed closed for a few minutes.

Tom, always quiet, and supportive, merely smiled at her. "It's great to see you, Jo. It really is. I can't tell you how much I miss having you for a next-door neighbour."

"I can imagine."

She felt at home. Among friends.

June days are long. It was very late when she finally let herself in through the door. And the first thing she saw was the answering machine winking at her. One message.

As always she hoped it would be the one message she wanted it to be.

But it never is, is it?

PC Hesketh-Brown's stolid voice delivered his message.

"Really sorry to trouble you, Ma'am, on your weekend off but I thought you'd want to know Arthur Pennington's been ringing the station every half an hour. We've told him you're not in till Monday, but he's really makin' a nuisance of himself. We'll fend him off if you like. Enjoy tomorrow. I've heard it's goin' to be a scorcher."

She replaced the phone slowly, wishing she had not been so curious as to pick it up.

Because now, despite the hot weekend, the perfect weather, the two friends with whom to go cycling, her mind was firmly fixed on Beatrice Pennington again.

She met Pagan and Pat in the market square in the centre of Leek early on Sunday morning and mentioned the disappearance of their cycling buddy. Like her they smiled and joked.

Beatrice was with her lover.

They could relax.

It was a day when everyone seemed to be enjoying the Staffordshire moorlands. Even so early the roads were busy. Not so good for cyclists so they headed out towards Flash, taking the smallest lanes and cycling fast. They stopped for drinks beneath the Winking Man. Inevitably the conversation turned towards the strange disappearance of Beatrice Pennington.

They were two widely different women, with different life experiences. But they both came down firmly on the side of Beatrice Pennington. They liked the thought that she had gone to find a new life – somewhere.

But it reminded Joanna too much of the end of the rainbow. Where was Beatrice?

Somewhere else.

Simply not here. But always in another place. Somewhere else.

For some reason the idea frightened her.

Chapter Eight

Monday, June 28th, 8.30 a.m.

The cycle ride in had exhilarated Joanna but as she entered the station she knew perfectly well what would be lying in wait for her on her desk. Two things, to be precise. One, a summons from Superintendent Arthur Colclough of the bulldog jowls and the piercing eyes. Surely he should have retired by now!) But Colclough was a typical old-fashioned copper, married to the job. Liked to have his fingers in every single pie and was as nosey as a net-curtain-twitcher.

Two – a memo left by the weekend desk sergeants detailing every single telephone call from Arthur Pennington.

She was right on both counts. The only thing she hadn't guessed at correctly was that Korpanski was late in. His chair was still neatly tucked underneath the desk with no jacket hanging over it; all the papers were cleared and the final giveaway – his computer was turned off.

Joanna smirked. She loved it when Korpanski was later then her, even though he lived in the town and drove in while she had to cycle in from Waterfall *and* she had to shower and change out of her cycling things which delayed her by at least ten minutes.

She dialled Colclough's extension number first and he barked nicely down the line. "Ten minutes, Piercy. I want you here."

"Yes, sir."

It doesn't do to argue with senior officers when you're in the police force. Better to buckle under.

Her second phone call of the day was, of course, to Pennington, who provoked the usual mixed feelings of pity and exasperation.

He was, initially, aggressive. "Didn't you get my messages?"

"They've all been delivered to me this morning, Mr

Pennington."

"But I've been ringing all weekend."

"It was my weekend off."

There was a brief, pregnant silence before Pennington finally exploded. "But you *knew* my wife. She wasn't just some stranger to you. And she's *missing*, for goodness sake. *Anything* could be happening right at this moment. Don't they care? Don't *you* care?"

"Mr Pennington, as I've explained, there isn't any reason to believe that something sinister's happened to your wife. We're not worried about her. She's a grown woman, in good health. Able to make free choice."

"What exactly are you saying? You think I'm dreaming that she's gone?"

"I'm saying that we're not concerned for her safety."

"*You* may not be concerned." Pennington's tone was definitely chilly. "But I am. I'm *very* concerned. This is not in her character therefore I can only come to the conclusion that she has been abducted against her will."

The pompous words should have sounded funny. Possibly sad. But they struck a chord deep inside Joanna. And the chord was in a minor key. She was beginning to realise that this case was going to stick by her side as close as a shadow. It was cornering her. Why?

Nothing. No reason. Except that Beatrice Pennington's disappearance was untidy, full of loose ends and anomalies. It felt *wrong*.

She drew in a deep breath. "Mr Pennington. I thought I'd speak to your wife's sister later on today and then I do have a lead I intend following up."

"Oh – right." The wind was nicely snatched out of his sails.

Korpanski had entered the room. Grinning broadly with a good-natured wave. She smiled back at him, twitched her shoulders in half a shrug, meant to inform him who was on the other end of the line.

There was no colleague in the world better than

Korpanski – when he was in a good mood. The day boded well. She felt quite cheerful.

He slung his jacket on the back of his chair, sat down behind the desk and switched his computer on.

It was time to wind up Pennington. "I can't tell you any more at present but I will be in touch the moment I have any news." She replaced the phone.

"So what's put the smile on your face?"

"The Insurance company have stopped asking questions. That's what," he said. "The car's mended, they've agreed to pay up."

She grinned across the room at him. "So next time Fran tells you something wants fixing...?"

"Don't push your luck," he warned.

"Fancy a trip to Italy, Mike?"

"You serious?"

"I don't know," she said. "I just wish Beatrice would turn up so we can put all our energies into this little lot." She indicated the pile of forms in her In tray."

Korpanski broke out into song. "Just one cornetto..." Then he stopped. "I take it that *was* her husband on the phone." He paused just long enough to think. "We'll never ride a trip to Italy out of the tax-payer," he said, "when her passport's still in Leek."

"Oh – who knows," she said impatiently. "All I know is I've got the usual interview with Colclough this morning."

Korpanski blew his cheeks out in a useless attempt at impersonation of his senior officer.

But she had misjudged Colclough. He had remained as one of the senior officers in the town for good reason. He was fair. And popular. And he knew his job.

He looked up as she knocked and entered.

"Ah – Piercy." There was no hostility in either his face or his voice but the warmth of the long years between them of an old, faithful dog. But like a Staffordshire Bull Terrier Colclough was tenacious and it was a great mistake to underestimate him and treat him as too close a friend. She was wary and waited to be bidden to sit down.

He eyed her over the top of some half-moon glasses. "How are you?"

It was not what she had expected.

"I'm fine, thank you, sir."

"And Levin?"

"Still in the States, sir."

"Ah."

A brief word. A wealth of meaning.

"I suppose you'll be making some big decisions soon."

"Sir?"

"Whether to join him or creep a little further up the career ladder." He gave a rusty smile. "*Chief Inspector Piercy.*" He cackled. "Sounds good, doesn't it?"

She didn't know. Chief Inspector Piercy, Mrs Levin, Mummy. What did sound good?

She liked where she was, Inspector Piercy, the woman, who had worked hard when confronted by a succession of murders, which had all been difficult to solve – in their varying ways. Each one an individual story with suffering and unhappiness behind it. Both tragedies and comedies. Sometimes both at the same time.

She met Colclough's eyes without flinching. "I don't know, sir," she said.

"Right." As usual his perception was beyond the average senior officer. Colclough understood people.

"Now then, Piercy." He continued briskly, without giving further thought to the subject. "The desk sergeant has informed me that a Mr Arthur Pennington is anxious about the whereabouts of his wife. Would you care to enlighten me?"

As succinctly as she could she filled Colclough in on the bare details of the case and watched his pupils sharpen as he took in her concerns.

"So you think she's having an affair."

She nodded.

"Of which her husband, I take it, is completely unaware."

She nodded again.

"And yet..."

She nodded for the third time.

"I see," he said. "Well, may I say you've had experience of these sorts of cases as have I. I think it perfectly possible that if Mrs Pennington doesn't want to be found we never shall find her. But you should go through the motions. Keep her husband happy. Let him see that the police are takin' his concerns very seriously. We are, after all, community police, are we not?"

"Yes, sir."

"And we don't want any hostile headlines in the *Post&Times* about us being uncaring or unhelpful, do we?"

"No, sir."

"Right then, Piercy. Get on with it then."

She walked back along the corridor wondering whether the interview had been to sound her out about her career prospects or to learn about the Pennington case.

Answer – she didn't know. One often didn't with Colclough.

Beatrice's sister, Frances Sharnell, lived in a small, terraced, mill-worker's cottage in one of the back streets of the town. With a front door which opened straight out to the pavement and just one window to the side, two above, it had an old-fashioned, Victorian feel to it. But the electronic doorbell which played *Für Elise* was bang up to date.

Joanna had a shock when the door was pulled open. She was staring at the missing woman. Same round face, same surprised eyes, same plump body and anxious expression.

"Excuse me."

"Can I help you?"

She exhaled. The voice was different. Flatter. Without the spark that had lit her sister up like a candle.

"Are you Frances –?"

"Sharnell."

The voice was snappy now. Irritable. She glanced behind her, anxious to return to whatever it was she had been doing.

"I'm Detective Inspector Piercy," Joanna said. "Leek Police. I've come about your sister."

"Aye."

Something else hinted at now. A resentment, dislike. Certainly the anxiety had melted away. So it had been for the intrusion of a stranger rather than concern for her sister.

"So you've come about Beattie, have you? Well there's nothing I can do to help you, young lady. I don't know a thing about it. Arthur's been pestering me like a ruddy gnat. Up here all the time, bothering me."

Joanna found herself, unexpectedly, bound to defend Pennington. "He's very worried."

"Well there's no use him bothering me. I can't help him. There's nothing I know."

Joanna looked up and down the street. "Can I come in?"

Frances stood back, grunted and allowed Joanna to pass.

The room was small, stuffy, and stank of cigarette smoke. It was filled by two armchairs and a television set which was switched on without the sound. Perhaps Frances had switched it down when the doorbell had rung.

Joanna sat down. "When did you last see your sister?"

"A week or two ago. Market Day anyway. I bumped into her in the town. We exchanged a few words. Nothing more."

"Which was it, a week or two weeks?"

Beatrice's sister thought for a moment. "It were the 16th," she said finally.

"You're sure?"

"'Course I'm sure. I had a doctor's appointment in the afternoon," Frances snapped.

"How did she seem?"

"Her usual self." Joanna studied Beatrice's sister. Now she looked closer she could see differences. Frances was marginally thinner. Her face was more wrinkled, its expression sour and shrew-like. Joanna studied her. The two sisters were not really alike at all.

What makes this woman tick? What makes her laugh or smile?

She looked at the walls for inspiration. Photographs of friends or family?

One reproduction of Van Gogh's *Sunflowers*.

Nothing there.

Somewhere, deep inside this woman, is a trigger which will explain how Beatrice's sister came to be like this, why she is so guarded. Does she hate her sister? Is she jealous of her?

"Who is older, you or her?"

"What's that got to do with it," Frances snapped. "How is that going to find her?"

"Just answer the question," Joanna said coldly. She did not like this woman.

"I am. By three years. Now I suppose you'll find her somewhere or other. Drawing attention to herself."

Frances fumbled down the side of the chair and pulled out a packet of cigarettes, lit one and stared boldly at Joanna.

Was it then purely sibling rivalry which had made the three-year-old Frances jealous of her baby sister?

Only that?

Joanna stood up. Even if there had been antipathy between the sisters *she* could not expect to find the trigger. And she did not have the right to ask Frances whether she had disliked her sister. Besides – much as she hated to admit it, Frances was right. It had no bearing on this investigation. The solution lay away from Beatrice's family.

Joanna strolled back to the station and sat down at her desk.

Korpanski was out of the room.

The golden rule of policing is check, check and double check.

She picked up the phone. Walking through Tuscany.

Or so he said.

Telecommunications are a wonderful thing. Within

minutes she had spoken to a very nice girl who worked for Explore Holidays and confirmed that Adrian Grove was indeed walking in Tuscany. Once she had allowed the same girl to ring back and confirm that she was, indeed, talking to a police officer, things got even easier.

She had faxed through a copy of the other people on the same tour. No Beatrice Pennington. Grove had booked alone and there was not another single woman on the walking tour. There were other women but they were either married or with other partners. Joanna stared at the list and felt uncomfortable. Nothing more powerful. A simple discomfort. Like indigestion. Or the beginnings of a tension headache.

This was the sixth day that Beatrice had been missing. Almost a week. From the first Joanna had assumed that she was with her secret lover, her invisible man.

OK, she reasoned, so the missing man is not Adrian Grove.

It is someone else.

But Beatrice had led a quiet life. She met few people, she reasoned. It must be one of an inner circle of friends or acquaintances. And something else puzzled her. How had Beatrice kept the identity of this mystery man secret? Her husband admitted she rarely went out – to work, to the Readers' Group, few social occasions. So how come, in such a small town as this, no one had ever seen them together?

Adrian Grove had been the natural suspect but he was in the clear.

So who was it?

Korpanski barged back in, kicking the door open as his hands were full of two mugs of coffee. He set the cup down in front of her.

"Do you know your lips twitch when you're thinking out loud?"

She laughed, brushed her hand across her mouth and slid the papers across her desk in his direction.

"Take a look at this."

It took him moments to come to the same conclusion as she had.

"It must be someone else."

"There is only one other potential area in her life with any possibility," she said. "It has to be someone from the Readers' Group. I need a list."

"You going up the library?"

She nodded.

"I'll come with you."

They walked companionably up Stockwell Street. "Mike," Joanna asked hesitantly. "You know all this business about Beattie trying to look more attractive – and everything else?"

"Yep." He was striding ahead.

"What does it tell you, as a man?"

Korpanski stopped, turned and started laughing. "Oh it's the old one, isn't it? You know – woman finds man, wants to keep him. Gives them a bit of a spurt on, you know?"

"We are talking romance then. I'm not just imagining it."

"Well – she told you as much."

"I know."

"So why are you doubting it?"

"I don't know. I don't know."

But she did. And now she could put her finger right on it. It was the dizzy excitement. The almost maniacal joy with which Beattie had told her about her future. Her lover. There had been something…something not quite real about it. It had been more like when she, Joanna, had been a fourteen-year old leggy teenager with braces on her teeth and she had fancied the captain of the school rugby team. She had dreamed and imagined every single time he looked at her it had been with adoration, with love. Yet when she had finally plucked up courage to speak to him he had stared at her and said. Oh mortifyingly he had said, "Do I know you?"

It had been the adoration of a stranger.

Or was she simply jealous? Having watched her own joy evaporate in front of her eyes, was she now infected with

with the green-eyed monster herself, like Frances, envious of another's simple happiness?

Possibly. Possibly. It is all possible.

There were a few different staff on at the library today.

And they were happy to give her a list of the people who belonged to the Readers' Group.

It was to be an afternoon of telephoning.

With some success. Many of the people who had belonged to the Readers' Group were retired. And on a fine Monday afternoon many of them were digging the garden. Joanna and Mike ticked their way down the list.

And were left with half a dozen names.

She glanced across at Mike. "I suppose there is one theory we should consider."

"Suicide," he said without looking up. "In a few words," he said, "no reason, no note and you know as well as I do it's hard to hide your own body. They almost always turn up – and quickly."

It was almost six. If you ring people at seven, most are at home. Back from their work.

"Mike," she said. "You go home. I'll hang on a bit here." She indicated a mountain of paperwork connected with the other myriad of cases they were supposed to be concentrating on. The trouble with this was it might lead somewhere. It might lead nowhere. But police time was being spent on it when there was plenty of work to be doing.

"You sure?"

"Go and play footie with your lad," she said. "Or take them all out to a country pub for a drink and a meal."

Why was she doing this, in her situation, painting this idyllic portrait of idealised family life. In all probability Korpanski would go home, have a few beers, go up the gym, bawl out his wife, argue with his son and daughter.

She looked up to see him eyeing her with that look of concern she hated so much.

"Don't get married to the job, Jo," he said softly. "It would be a bloody waste."

And then he was gone through the door before she could think of a witty answer.

Maybe she never would.

Chapter Nine

Tuesday, June 29th, 11 a.m.

And then, quite simply, the body was found.

Many people must have walked, driven, ridden past Beatrice Pennington's body. Within inches. If they had breathed in the unmistakable scent of decay they had probably assumed the same as Joanna had on her peaceful cycle ride – that an animal had died and its body was slowly decomposing. If they thought anything at all.

But one hiker, a bank manager from Leek, was interested in the badger population. He had been involved in badger watching years ago when a student at Endon High School and had never lost fascination for the creatures.

So when he smelt the scent of decaying flesh he wondered whether a badger had met an unfortunate end. Curious, he pulled away the undergrowth and peered into the thick branches of hawthorn.

And saw a naked foot.

A human foot is unmistakable. It looks like no part of any other animal.

Although he recognised what it was he stared at it for long moments, feeling sick but still curious. Then slowly he backed away, sat on the opposite verge and, just as slowly, pulled a mobile phone from his rucksack.

And dialled 999.

"Police," he said. Then he was sick.

Within ten minutes two police cars arrived. And in the first them sat Joanna Piercy and Korpanski, together with four other officers.

Joanna's heart sank as she stared down at the partially clothed body. Beatrice Pennington lay on her side, one arm outstretched. Her legs were bare, the skirt of her dress pulled down modestly over her knees, the bodice hardly disarranged. Joanna touched the cold cheek. She'd been dead for days. Probably the entire week since she had vanished. So now the next priority was to preserve all the evidence, seal off the scene. And wait for the police surgeon.

He was brisk, efficient and swift. "When was she last seen?" he asked once Joanna had explained that she knew who it was. "Last Wednesday morning."

"She almost certainly died later on the same day," he said.

"And was her body left here soon after her death?"

"I can't tell how long the body's been here," he said. "We'll know more both when we move the body so can look at the vegetation beneath it and when we look at signs of hypostasis."

Joanna dropped her gaze to the crumpled body. So no holiday, foreign or native. No elopement with a secret lover. No need for a passport or the Ann Summers underwear. Beatrice had simply been murdered. It was almost an anticlimax.

"Manual strangulation," said the police surgeon, a young GP from Leek. New on the job. He indicated an area of dark bruising on the front of Beatrice's neck, either side of her windpipe.

Strangely, there is often room for relief in a case like this. Joanna's apparent inertia would have made no difference to Beatrice Pennington's life or death. She had not died because Joanna had failed to instigate a full police investigation. By the time Joanna had learned of her disappearance she was already dead.

Joanna glanced around, at the thick hedge, the quiet road and the cunning way the body had been concealed in long grass, at the base of a thick hawthorn hedge which would not now be touched until autumn. It had been no mere chance that she had been hidden here. It was lonely and remote. Only local people would have used such a hiding place.

But – although it was a clever hiding place it was also quite stupid. There was opportunity for a wealth of trace forensic evidence. In the soft verge there were a few tyre tracks and some nice, sticky mud. Above Beatrice's body were the spiny branches of hawthorn, reaching out to gather evidence – hair, material, fibres and pieces of skin. And cling on to them. In yet another way it was a good forensic scene because there was so little sign of human visitation. Few people came here ergo *any* evidence was potentially of significance. It was not like the back of a Liverpool taxi, a rich scene, full of false trails and red herrings.

Also this was a remote spot. It was conceivable that *someone* had noticed a solitary car in such an isolated area.

Already she was mentally rubbing her hands together. Killers imagine that a remote area is a good place to leave a body; somewhere where they will not be evident. This is not true. Better to bury your signs in a mountain of evidence than out here where each cell can be discovered and identified.

She rang the coroner.

He kept his comments to a minimum. The post-mortem and the police investigation would all be orchestrated by him. But for now he merely had to be kept informed.

Beatrice's body was put in a heavy-duty, dark grey plastic bag with a zip up the side and loaded into the black police van for transportation to the mortuary. Joanna contacted the crimes scenes officers and then rang Colclough.

"I'm afraid we've found our missing woman," she said without preamble.

"Oh?"

"It looks as though she's been strangled."

"Oh, dear." Said with a wealth of meaning and a hint of grief too. "That *is* bad."

"The SOCO team is on its way. We're moving the body now. I suppose I'd better go and tell Mr Pennington that his wife's no longer missing."

There was a momentary silence between the two police. Most people know that in cases of murder forty per cent of the time it is the partner who is to blame. The police make jokes about this. "Put your hand on the collar of the chief mourner," they jest, "and you've a forty per cent chance of being right."

But there is a very ugly side to this. Think about this. How insensitive it can appear. A grieving man, such as Arthur Pennington? To be *interrogated* about the death of his own wife? It is even worse when it is a child who is missing. Particularly when people will talk and gossip. And there is no shortage of clichés to support their suspicions. How mud sticks, No smoke without fire. And so on...

"Kid gloves, Piercy."

Inevitably in the car, alone with Korpanski they both voiced the same question. "Did he do it?"

Mike hadn't even started up the engine. Joanna moistened her lips, shook her head, turned to look at him and shrugged. "I don't know, Mike." Then, "He could have. It's not impossible."

"Why?"

"Well – that's obvious. The old story. He found out about her secret lover. It wouldn't be the first time a husband lost his rag for that and committed murder. It could have been like that. Come on, Korpanski. Start the engine. Let's at least get down there."

So when they drove up to the neat house on the estate they sat and considered it for a minute or two.

It is silly this, to imagine that you can recognise the house of a murderer. Killers live in all sorts of places. Condemned flats, millionaire's mansions, council houses and yes, neat and tidy homes just like this. Because people who are, by nature orderly, dislike having that order upset.

It was June. The sky was predominantly blue, with a few woolly clouds bouncing around. The scene was bright – almost surreal, the green, the white, the blue. The grass was perfectly clipped and short and looked more like Astro-turf than living, breathing vegetation. No weeds sprung through it. The weeping cherry tree in the dead centre of the lawn was the right size, in perfect harmony with its surroundings. The flowers borders too were orderly. Lobelias, salvias and alyssums planted in red white and blue rotation.

The house itself was in good order. Nothing needed doing to it. The paintwork was brilliant white. The bricks were neat and red. The windows were polished and set in hardwood frames. As Joanna watched she saw a pale face swipe across the downstairs window.

Their arrival had been noted. She and Korpanski left the safety of the car and covered the four paces to the front door threading passed a dark green Ford Focus and behind it a red VW. Arthur Pennington pulled the door open before they'd had a chance to knock.

He said nothing initially but stared, first at Joanna then at Korpanski. She eyed him too – and read nothing there.

Still without speaking Pennington jerked his head back towards the inside and they followed him through.

Whatever her suspicions Joanna felt she must go through the motions – at the very least.

"I'm sorry, Mr Pennington."

A flash of panic lit his face before he said, very carefully, "You've found her, haven't you?"

There was a clatter of dishes from the kitchen.

Someone was washing up.

"Is someone else here?"

Pennington looked impatient. "Only a neighbour," he said. "She'd come to cook me a meal."

How swiftly the vultures fly in.

"I am sorry, Mr Pennington. You are right. We *have* found your wife."

He blinked. "You wouldn't believe me," he said softly. "You thought I was being... You thought I was worrying. Dreaming it all up. But I knew."

He knew *what* exactly?

Joanna felt she must get this one in first. "She was already dead when I learned of her disappearance," she said – very clearly. There was to be no room for misunderstanding. "There was *nothing* I could have done whatever action I might have taken."

"Where did you find her?"

"Her body had been hidden, (it is a kinder word than dumped), under a hedge."

The clattering in the kitchen had stopped. The kindly neighbour was eavesdropping.

Joanna anticipated the next question correctly.

"How did she die?"

"A post-mortem will be carried out later on today."

"I said, how did she die?"

"We think she was strangled. We'll know more – later."

"Can I see her?"

"We'll drive you down there now, if you like."

He stood up. "I'll just…"

He stumbled towards the door. Joanna met Korpanski's eyes and again read in there the same question that she was asking him. *Guilty? Or not?*

Neither had an answer.

"Kerry."

A woman poked her head round the corner. "Arthur?"

She looked accusingly at the two police.

"They've found her, Kerry. Someone's…"

And interestingly in the neighbour's blue eyes they read the very same question. She was very slightly unnerved.

"Oh, Arthur," she said quickly. "I am so very sorry."

"I've to go down now and identify her."

She didn't offer to accompany him but pressed her lips together.

"Oh, I am sorry," she said again. "But I'd best be going now. Sean'll wonder where I am."

Sean? Husband? Son?

"I'll come over and see you later on."

Pennington managed a martyred smile. "Thank you. You're very kind."

He was quiet in the car. Joanna sat on the back seat next to

him, with a part-view of Korpanski's cynical eyes in the
rear-view mirror. She may as well prepare the new widower
for what would inevitably come next. "Mr Pennington."

He put his hand over hers in a slightly creepy, intrusive
way. "Arthur. Please."

"Arthur." He had not realised this would not do at all. *He*
was the chief suspect.

"Your wife's death will be the subject of a full police
investigation. We will spare nothing to discover the truth."

"Well – she's been killed, hasn't she?" Pennington's hand
lay back on the seat, still uncomfortably close. "It's a murder investigation now, isn't it?" There was a touch of a sneer
in his voice.

"Exactly."

Korpanski was still eyeing her in the rear-view mirror.

There was a brief, awkward silence before Joanna continued. "We're going to need you to be more specific about
your movements on last Wednesday morning. About the
last time that you saw your wife."

Arthur Pennington swivelled his scrawny neck around
very slowly to stare at her. "You surely are not suggesting
that I was, in any way, involved?" *Did he not know the ugly
facts about murder?*

Joanna sucked in a deep breath. "We will explore every
single avenue, Mr Pennington. This will be a major investigation and we take it very seriously."

"I see." He turned, ever so slightly, away from her.

It was a long and difficult drive to the mortuary. The traffic was heavy and there was a diversion from the A53 at
Stockton Brook. Pennington was now silent and Joanna not
in the mood for chitchat. Pennington would have to be
asked all the awkward and difficult questions in a police
interview room, and the entire episode recorded onto audio
cassette. Anything he said in the back of the car, witnessed
only by the two senior investigating officers, would be
classed as hearsay and inadmissible.

She preferred her facts on the record. And well docu-
mented.

Korpanski had warned the mortuary assistant in advance that they were on their way so Beatrice was neatly laid out and covered very decently with a purple cloth. They would perform the post-mortem later on this afternoon. Pennington stepped towards her and Joanna lifted the sheet from her face.

She got her confirmation of identity. "Oh, my Beatrice," Pennington said. "What have they done to you?"

Joanna tucked the words away in the back of her mind. They seemed strange.

What have they done to you? They? There was nothing here to suggest there had been more than one killer. So why had he used the plural?

"Just for the record," she said.

"Oh yes," Pennington answered, understanding quickly. "It's my wife all right."

Joanna waited until they were outside the mortuary before making a polite request that Arthur accompany them to the police station. And from the blank look in his brown eyes she knew that he was still unaware of how police minds work in such a situation.

There were formalities to be gone through, obvious questions to be asked, the answers to be recorded.

"When did you last see your wife?"

"Around half eight on Wednesday morning. I was just setting off for work."

"At what time did you arrive at work?"

"I was there for ten to nine."

They were going to have to examine his car, take it to bits if necessary, scrape the wheel arches in the hunt for vegetation, mud and other trace evidence.

"You drove in, I take it?"

Pennington nodded.

"And your wife's car remained in the garage?"

"That's right."

"While she cycled to work."

"Yes."

Did anyone see her locking the bike to the railings?

"How would you describe relations between you and your wife?"

"Excellent." And now Pennington's eyes flickered from one to the other. At last he had realised he was a suspect.

Chapter Ten

Wednesday, June 30th 7.30 a.m.

This very morning Matthew would read her letter. It would arrive and be put in the post-box in the hallway of the flat where he was living. And then, maybe, he would read it before he went to work.

Her bit was done. From the moment when Joanna awoke she felt cleansed. She ran downstairs and boiled the kettle, made two cups of coffee then went back to bed to drink them and to ponder.

She must put her own problems to the back of her mind and concentrate on Beatrice Pennington's death.

By 8.30 she was in her office, reading through the post-mortem report. The police surgeon had been right. Cause of death: manual strangulation from the front. The pathologist had put forward the opinion that it was probably a man's hand as it was too large for the average woman. There were clear thumbprints around her windpipe, just below her larynx and finger-marks around the back of her neck. The hyoid bone was broken – a common finding in strangulation

There were also some signs of a struggle. A bruise between her shoulder blades. It looked as though someone had thumped her from behind. And evidence of her last cycle ride: her dress had been torn in places, the full skirt had caught in the wheels, (traces of bike oil) the dress had been torn at the shoulder, one cap sleeve practically ripped off. There was a fresh bruise to her scalp. Another blow? There was bruising on the upper arm.

Joanna read on. There was no evidence of sexual assault. Her knickers were undisturbed, her pink Marks and Spencer's bra still fastened up. There was no evidence of semen anywhere on the body or the clothes. Therefore the motive was not sexual. Again the pathologist had ventured an opinion, that it had been a while since the deceased had been sexually active. There was evidence of peri-menopausal atrophy. Joanna frowned and wished Matthew was around to explain some of the medical terms.

Next she turned to the heading, Time of Death. As usual the stomach contents were the best indicator. Beatrice's breakfast was partially undigested. Her last meal had been an unspecified muesli-type breakfast cereal. The pathologist surmised that Beatrice had probably died within an hour of eating it. According to Arthur he had left her eating her breakfast just before nine, which fixed her probable time of death as Wednesday morning some time before ten.

In some ways the worst comment was the bottom paragraph of the report.

"There are clear signs of insect and animal activity."

Joanna dropped the report back on her desk. Face-to-face strangulation suggested murder by an intimate rather than person or persons unknown. It is a fact that people will not willingly stand close enough to a stranger to be grasped by the neck. A survival instinct.

Beatrice had trusted her killer sufficiently to move within the magic circle of his killing span.

Joanna picked up the police photograph of the railings outside the library where Beatrice's bike had been so carefully locked. They had had to cut the lock with wire-cutters as the key had been missing; presumably it was still in Beatrice Pennington's handbag which had yet to be found.

Joanna studied the background of the photograph. The street behind was busy and full of traffic – as it would have been last Wednesday morning. And to the front, the library and Nicholson Centre with its hosts of students from the Leek College of Arts. A forceful abduction from there would surely have been impossible. It was too public a site. Which left her with the option that Beatrice Pennington must have gone voluntarily with her killer.

Either walked or been picked up in a car.

Joanna leafed through the pictures of the body. Beatrice's

dress had been of a popular fashion this year, a throwback to the fifties, white background, large, red poinsettias. Conspicuous. Deliberately so? Surely many people must have noticed her that morning,? Did she always dress so well for work – or was this unusual? If so why? Had she had an assignation that day? With her mystery lover? The one with whom she was, apparently, not sexually active?

So who *had* picked her up? Her husband? Certainly Arthur would have had a motive for the murder if he had found out about Beatrice's paramour.

But this left her confused as she remembered his words.

"What have they done to you?"

What had he meant?

She twiddled with her pen, rolling it to and fro, trying to work out a rational explanation for the phrase – and came up with nothing so she picked up the phone.

The police are like this. They cannot see enough of the people they suspect. They think of any old excuse to make contact with them. Harass them. She wanted to keep him close. So she dialled up Pennington's number and came right out with her question.

"Why did you use the phrase, what have they done to her?"

"I don't rightly know why I said it," He sounded confused.

She didn't believe him. He must have had something running through his mind. It wasn't the type of phrase you pluck out at random – without thinking. "You said *they*. Who are they, Mr Pennington? Why did you say *they*? Do you think more than one person is involved in your wife's murder?"

She was trying to rattle him, to provoke a response. Find out what had been lying in the back of his stodgy little mind to produce the plural. Drag it out of him – if need be.

"I suppose I meant those two buddies of hers."

"You mean Miss Pirtek and Marilyn Saunders?"

"I suppose I do."

"But in what way? How can they have had any *possible*

bearing on her death? Are you suggesting they're *responsible*?"

To her it seemed an illogical, heinous idea. They were her *friends*.

"Look," Arthur said. "I'm not a fool."

So she had succeeded, deliberately tipped Pennington into defensive mode. On the whole she was pleased. Anger might make him drop his guard and careless talk is what solves cases.

"I'm not suggesting they actually killed her," he said petulantly. "But I do know that there's things about my wife that I am not fully aware of. I can only surmise that these two women – my wife's old school pals – had something to do with it. They led my wife astray. Suggested all sorts of silly things she might get up to. Maybe they even said unkind things about me. I'm not one of these toyboys, you know Inspector."

Joanna smothered a smile. Pennington was about as far from being a toy boy as the Queen is from being a pole dancer. But she quickly wiped the smile from her face. Telephones have eyes. Your voice changes if you smile while you are speaking on the telephone.

"I'm not sparky and exciting. I'm just an ordinary man. I've little get up and go and not a lot of imagination – as I expect you've guessed. But I am steady and reliable. And that's worth a lot in these troubled days. Beatrice was quite happy with that until recently." He sounded aggrieved.

Joanna nodded. Pennington had a point but...

She thanked him, put the phone down, sat and thought.

She pictured Beatrice Pennington puffing her way up the hill, determination toughening her up.

There was something obviously wrong here somewhere. Beatrice Pennington had known Marilyn and Eartha or Jewel since she was a child. Pennington had to be mistaken. It hadn't been them. At least – not primarily. They might have encouraged it but the seeds had been sown elsewhere. By someone else. The "X" beloved of detective novels.

She was relieved when Korpanski kicked the door open

and walked in carrying a sheaf of papers in both hands. "I've managed to make contact with everyone except two of the Readers' Group," he said. "Angela Bold and Christopher Snelgrove. Angela is a social worker from Rushton Spencer. I asked Hesketh-Brown to pop over there. A neighbour says she's away on a course until tomorrow. And Christopher Snelgrove is a retired bus driver who, again according to a neighbour, takes frequent trips to Spain. Otherwise all present and correct." He grinned and looked pleased with himself.

"Have either of these two been particularly linked to Beatrice Pennington?"

"Phil Scott interviewed one of the librarians – Lisa – and she said both Angela and Christopher had had a drink together with Beatrice once or twice but always as part of the crowd, with others of the class. And they'd enjoyed a giggle. Nothing special, I suspect."

Joanna swivelled her chair away from her computer screen. "How do you feel about Arthur Pennington?"

"He has to be in the running, doesn't he?"

Joanna nodded. "He certainly does."

She yawned. Staring into the computer screen was making her eyes tired.

"What have we got from forensics?"

"It's early days yet, Jo."

"Sit on their shoulders," she urged. "Bully them a bit. I'd really like this case wrapped up quickly. It isn't complicated."

Korpanski picked up the phone.

Maybe that was her mistake – had been from the beginning – to underestimate the complexities of both woman and crime.

She pushed her sleeve up her arm to peep at her watch. 11 a.m. At what time would Matthew read the letter? Not yet. Not in the middle of an American night. More importantly what would be his response?

It was as though her brain was split in two, like a walnut. One half was working through Beatrice Pennington's life and death, the other on hold, hardly daring to wonder when she would hear from him. At work Matthew was a fading face, a ghost-smile, a pale and insubstantial memory. At home she could feel him all around her, see him, smell him, taste him. All but touch him.

She sighed.

Back to her case.

One never really knew whether it was worth putting a board up to appeal for witnesses. Statistically it rarely produced results. But if there was even the slimmest of chances that someone had seen something it could save police time. And as Colclough was always reminding them, time *was* money.

In the end Joanna decided to produce two, one for outside the library and the other for the spot on the moorland road where they had found Beatrice's body. This one she volunteered to drive across the moors herself.

She took the flat Ashbourne road for a few miles before turning left at Winkhill and rising in the direction of Butterton, passing the millstone which marks the entrance to the Peak Park. Just before Butterton she turned right towards Grindon Moor, pulling up when she reached the parked cars of the SOCOs and the white tent protecting the area where Beatrice's body had been found.

Word had got out. Bunches of flowers had been laid against the grey, dry-stone wall, almost filling the narrow grassy verge. The public have soft hearts.

In bygone years the SOCOs were serving police officers. Her favourite had been "Barra", Sergeant Barraclough, an experienced officer who had combed almost as many crime scenes as he had his own sparse hair. But a few years ago it had been decided that civilians could do the job cheaper and just as well. And so the work was put out to tender. But Joanna had never quite trusted these civilians to the same degree as her old SOCO colleagues. And she missed Sergeant Barraclough who had been moved to the Potteries

Motoring Division.

It was a waste.

But such is progress.

Mr Mark Fask was in charge today, a good-looking Potteries native with dark brown hair and very pale skin. A trifle paunchy round the middle maybe. The obligatory white paper suit wasn't flattering to his figure. As he walked towards her he reminded Joanna of a pregnant penguin. But he was a pleasant guy who had worked with her a few times before. He was already walking towards her when she opened the car door.

"So what have you got for me?"

"Plenty," he said. "It's a rich crime scene. Bit of a treat, really."

She glanced at the hedge and saw fresh wounds where the branches had been lopped away. "I thought it would be."

"Hawthorn. Nice and prickly, see." He touched the thorns with an experimental forefinger.

She nodded.

"Anything interesting?"

He jerked his thumb behind him. Bags of evidence were stacked neatly.. Maybe she had done him an injustice. Even "Barra" couldn't have gleaned more evidence than this from such a small crime scene.

After all – by a process of deduction Beatrice's body had almost certainly only been dumped here. She hadn't been wearing shoes when her body had been discovered. One had been found at the crime scene but her feet had not been muddy. Ergo it was unlikely that she had been killed here.

"Fibres, hair. We got a cigarette stub with a bit of lipstick on."

"DNA?"

"It's always a possibility, Inspector." He waved his hand vaguely behind him. Some paper, what looks like a till receipt..."

She smiled. *A till receipt. As good as a signed cheque.*

". . . the wrapping from some chewing gum. We got

footprints and tyre prints."

Joanna nodded. "We've decided to put up a board, just in case a motorist or someone else saw anything."

Fask nodded slowly. "Seems like a good idea."

"The tyre prints," she said. "I don't suppose you've any idea what car they could have come from?"

"Not so far. Looks to me like an ordinary saloon car but we'll take the pictures in to the garages and get them identified."

"What about the soil samples?"

"Promising," he said. "But you know what the soil's like round here. Clay, clay and more clay. Difficult to pinpoint as specifically as some other locations."

"How much longer will you be?"

"An hour – two hours. Then we'll get this lot to the labs and seal off the scene." Fask looked around at the landscape, the tiny fields bordered by dry-stone walls, the isolated cottages, the animals grazing quietly. "It just doesn't seem right, does it?"

The worst thing was that she knew exactly what he meant.

It was too pretty round here for the ugliness of murder. It was an affront. Worse – as sacrilegious as peeing in a church. It was an outrage to bring urban murder out here.

This was the desecration of traditional England.

But traditional England is an illusion. Like personal happiness or safety. You can only ever know you *had* it. Never that you *have* it. Do not take it for granted because it is transitory.

She stopped scanning the landscape and turned, reluctantly, back to her car.

She had a briefing in half an hour.

What did she have to tell them?

She had ten officers at her disposal. It was up to her to make good use of them.

Fingertip searches, house-to-house enquiries. These are the expected ways to solve major crime.

But this was not a major case. In her heart she still believed this would turn out to be a "domestic".

The difficulty was sustaining the morale of the officers who, she knew, probably shared the same view as herself.

The only real breakthrough was from Bridget Anderton who had been detailed outside the library with the second board to ask anyone if they had spotted Beatrice locking up her bike. Surely in the flowered dress she would have been conspicuous.

"A woman called Sue Radnor was taking her children to school late because they'd had a dentist's appointment. She saw Beatrice Pennington locking her bike to the railings." Anderton was reading from her notes but she looked up then. "She specifically remembered the dress because she'd seen it in Monsoon and had liked it herself."

Joanna nodded. "I don't suppose she noticed the time?"

"Nine thirty on her car clock which is always showing the right time according to the radio."

Joanna felt almost hopeful. "Anything else? Did she notice anyone approach Mrs Pennington?"

Anderton shook her head regretfully. "Unfortunately not."

"Anyone else get a sighting?"

Phil Scott produced details of a few sightings of her wobbling her way to work. The times all tied in with her journey ranging from nine fifteen to nine twenty.

Scott was laughing. "We got some descriptions," he said, "of that big skirt billowing out behind her like the sail on a windsurf."

"With an hour or two left to live." Joanna spoke more sharply than she'd meant to but the room quietened. She cursed herself. She should know as well as anyone that levity was often a good way to cope with the nastier side of life.

Korpanski touched her elbow. So lightly it could almost have been an accidental gesture but she knew it wasn't. He was both checking she was OK as well as reminding her that these were junior officers who needed encouragement – not criticism. She resented both reminders and turned to scowl at him. But he was grinning blandly and she found her mouth twisting into an answering smile.

If it hadn't been for Korpanski she would have found the last couple of months even more tough.

She owed him one.

The briefing broke up soon after with officers detailed to watch Arthur Pennington and chase up the two people not yet interviewed from the Readers' Group.

"You go home, Mike," she said, when the room was again empty.

"And you?"

She shook her head. "I've got a couple of leads I wouldn't mind following up."

"Anything I can help with?"

She shook her head again. "I don't think so. Don't worry. I'll keep you up to date."

She had her own plans.

Was there any real point in speaking to either Jewel or Marilyn again? They had both denied that they knew the identity of Beatrice's secret lover. But in some ways Joanna agreed with Arthur Pennington. They *were* a key. They must know something more. Maybe the fact that Beatrice had been murdered would loosen their tongues.

Besides – they were the only leads she had. The family, son, daughter, sister and parents had never really known the person Beatrice Pennington was. Certainly they had never known the Beatrice Pennington, passionate woman, who wore Ann Summers underwear and had fallen so desperately in love she had decided to change her entire life for it. The safe, comfortable habits of the woman had been shed, like the cracked, dry skin of a chameleon. And from underneath had stepped a different person. One the old family had not known and now never would, maybe because none of them had really cared. But the bright, shining person had just begun to exist – as Joanna herself had almost witnessed.

The only other people who might have had some insight into the metamorphosis would have been her two old cronies. She hoped they might be a bit more co-operative now.

It was half past five. Jewel would be locking her shop up. Time to walk up Derby Street.

Joanna was right and satisfyingly perfect in her timing. Jewel was just turning the key as Joanna touched her on the shoulder.

She let out a shriek. "Oh my goodness," she said, when she saw it was Joanna. "You gave me a shock!"

It had been deliberate. She had wanted to test for a reaction. And she had got one.

"Sorry." It seemed polite to apologise before diving in. "I take it you've heard about your friend?"

"Oh yes." There was real fear there. But then we *should* fear a killer. Kill once and the second time around is easier. All serial killers say this. But fear didn't make Jewel talk. Rather the converse. She was pressing her lips together to stop herself from speaking carelessly.

Which annoyed Joanna. "Give me a break, Jewel – or Eartha," she said cruelly. "I don't care what I call you but your friend was strangled and her body dumped on the moors and I think you know a bit more about it than you're saying."

Jewel put a hand in front of her face. "Don't. Please don't." Her fingernails were long and squared, painted blood-red. Probably false.

"Just give me a clue," Joanna appealed. "He probably did it. By keeping silent you're protecting him. You said she was sometimes deluded. Maybe this time she simply went too far." She appealed again. "Who is he?"

Jewel gave a bitter smile which wrinkled her face up and made her look suddenly older. "Look – I don't know who it is. Beattie never said and I didn't pry. I thought she deserved a bit of excitement in her life." She paused. "I just never thought it would lead to this." Her face twisted into raw grief. "It shouldn't be hard to find this person. Beattie didn't exactly have a huge circle of friends or much opportunity of meeting new people. And you should be able to eliminate most people she knew from your enquiries quite quickly."

She was telling her something. Goodness knows what but those heavy-lidded eyes were hiding a secret.

Joanna had the bit between her teeth now. She walked back to the station, picked up her car and drove straight round to Marilyn Saunders' house.

It was a different evening from the last time. The sky was sick and heavy with the threat of a thunderstorm. The air was full of biting flies. Not a night for a barbeque or sunbathing but an evening to watch the dusk arrive too early and peer through the window for the relief of the storm. Impending doom is always worse than the manifestation.

She was in for a disappointment. A Vauxhall Astra was in the drive. Marilyn's car was missing.

She rang the doorbell anyway.

And wasn't surprised when Guy opened the door, smoothly dressed in cream-coloured jeans and a navy polo shirt. He gave her a cool, appraising stare. "Well hello," he said. "If it isn't the Inspector. If it's Marilyn you want I'm afraid she isn't in right now."

"Then maybe I can talk to you."

He hung on to the door. "What about?"

"The hunt for a murdered woman, Mr Priestley."

He snorted. "I don't see how I can help. I hardly knew…"

"Really?"

"You're surely not suspecting me of…"

"Of what, Mr Priestley?"

"You don't think *I* was."

In fact it hadn't even occurred to her. But if the cap fits, Priestley. After all – one older woman, another one. Once you've tasted the mature delicacy. What is the difference?

"All I know is that I would like to find her killer. She had done nothing wrong. She was an innocent."

"How do you know?"

"I beg you pardon." Joanna had that tingling feeling – as though she had walked, unconsciously, right into an electric fence. "What do you mean?"

"How do you know she was an innocent?"

"Excuse me." She narrowed her eyes.

"Why don't you come in?"

She followed Guy into a small sitting room with cream walls, one large abstract painting which she would have titled *Turmoil* the sole adornment. It was black and swirling reds, guaranteed to disturb.

Apart from *Turmoil* there was a linen-covered three-piece suite and a huge TV set in the corner. Glancing round the room she could see speakers and a woofer. At a guess Marilyn and Guy's favourite hobby was watching movies.

He motioned her to sit down.

"How well did *you* know Beattie?" He asked the question in a mocking way, a wide smile showing perfect teeth.

"Hardly at all. I met her a couple of times when she came out cycling with us. Apart from that not at all."

"Quite."

"Say what you want to say, Mr Priestley."

"What did you see?"

"A middle-aged woman who felt that life was passing her by and wanted to do something about it. I admired her," she finished.

"Really?" His eyebrows pointed upwards in the middle. "And do you know what I saw?"

She shook her head. "No," she said curiously. "But I'm sure you'll tell me."

As I am also sure that it will be unkind.

"I saw a jealous, envious woman who watched others' lives from the sidelines and dreamed. More dangerously she was deluded. In her own eyes she was a *femme fatale*. An irresistible woman, a siren. She believed she could lure any man onto the rocks."

"Are you trying to tell me she tried to..."

"In the most clumsy, inept way, Inspector. Are you beginning to understand now?"

"I'm not sure."

"Look – she tried it on with me and I just fended her off. But what if she tried it on with someone who wasn't so – tolerant?"

"And then he –"

"He gets mad and the next thing is he's killed her. Understand?"

She needed to take stock. She was seeing Guy Priestley in a different light. Not as a cliché, toyboy lover to a woman more than twenty years older than himself but as a man.

Why do we do this when we see a disparate relationship? Focus on the sex instead of the person?

Guy was a perceptive and intelligent man. Oh yes, he was vain and conceited and arrogant too but he had put forward a theory which fitted this death like a glove.

The absence of sex, the face-to-face throttling.

They sat and appraised each other, neither of them speaking.

There was the sound of a key in the lock.

"Guy."

Marilyn's voice floated in from the hallway. "Oh." It became brittle when she saw Joanna. Joanna stood up, embarrassed for no reason. "Actually," she said, "it was you I came to see."

Marilyn had been to the hairdresser's. She had that unmistakable look of crimping and setting. Added to that, her hair was now striped, like marbled chocolate, cream and beige. It was absolutely and perfectly straight, as shiny as oiled silk. And she looked tired.

She flopped on the sofa next to Guy and pressed her mouth to his. "Hiya, lover-boy. Missed me?"

Lipstick was smeared all over her teeth.

Joanna, for some reason, felt angry. "It's all right," she said coldly. "I think Guy's answered my questions – for now."

As she drove between the fields towards home she saw the cows, sheltering beneath the trees, the sheep clustered towards the lower end of the field. They were all waiting for the storm.

So was she.

It broke just as she was driving across Grindon Moor, having taken a detour through Onecote specifically to pass the murder site.

There it was, in the dingy, sheeting rain.

A serious crime took place on the morning of Wednesday, June 23rd. Please contact Leek Police if you have any information.

An 01538 telephone number was on the bottom.

The question was: would this bear results?

She was almost at Waterfall when she knew it was not the storm which was giving her the prickly feeling at the back of her neck. It was the word *deluded*.

She believed Guy Priestley had put his finger on the throbbing pulse of this murder case.

It was late when she finally let herself in to the cottage. Exhausted yet exhilarated, her mind buzzing with questions, her skin tingling with the aliveness of working again on a murder case. The telephone answering machine winked at her. 1 Message. 1 Message.

Matthew.

She played it back. "Hi, Jo. Expect you're at work. Got your letter. Thanks (pause) for the honesty. Umm. I'll be home on the 16th. Let you know exact times. Don't meet the plane. I'll get a cab. Bye. (Another pause before the softest, sweetest message). I love you, Jo."

She played the message through again. "Hi, Jo..." Right through to, "I'll be home next week..." Then finally, "I love you, Jo." And again. And again.

She slept a deep, dreamless sleep.

Chapter Eleven

Thursday, July 1st, 8 a.m.

Enough inertia.

Jewel Pirtek was up early. Well before her husband. She glanced across at the hump next to her in bed. What she wouldn't give for such peace of mind. She slipped out of bed, padded to the bathroom, showered, pushed a white towelling alice band around her hair-line and sat in front of the bathroom mirror to cream on her age-perfecting moisturiser. But as she massaged her face it was not her own small features she was seeing but Beatrice's podgy face. With that dumb appeal.

"O-o-h." She gave a sound, part animal, part exasperation, part grief. The number of times Beatrice had tried to emulate her, trying a face cream, an eye shadow, a style of dress. None of it had ever altered her appearance. Until.

She dropped her face into her hands. It was no good. This was just too awful.

She glanced at the bathroom door. Locked. Then she drew her mobile out of her dressing gown pocket and tapped out the well-known numbers with the tip of her artificial finger-nail. It was answered almost at once.

"Marilyn."

"What?"

"You know what I'm going to say. She was our friend. We can't do *nothing*."

"We don't know anything. We're just guessing."

"I know. But that detective. She isn't even close. We should at least…"

"Jewel, we don't know *anything*," Marilyn said again. We're almost making it up."

"At least we should point her in the right direction."

"Call in here on your way to work."

"Will anyone be there?"

"Not if you come after half-past eight. He'll have left for

work by then."

"OK. See you then."

Joanna woke with the luxurious feeling of happiness flooding her from head to toe even before she opened her eyes properly. Matthew was coming home. Soon. She threw the duvet off and almost bounced the three steps to the bathroom. She stood under the shower, her face up-tilted and hummed some aria from an opera. She didn't even know which one. She didn't care. It wasn't important. They were all about love anyway, weren't they?

And yet, sitting behind her happiness, was the niggling worry of what Matthew's attitude would be. It wasn't her fault she had lost the child she had been carrying. The doctors were consoling, offered her counselling without knowing she did not need it. One in four pregnancies, they had explained, ended in what they called a spontaneous abortion. A miscarriage to the non-medical. An abortion to the lay mind, is something quite different, something deliberate. But hers had been an accident of nature. Even at the time she had wondered how many of those one-in-four had been as exultant as she. How many had never wanted a baby in the first place?

The trouble was that she knew that Matthew would know she would have been pleased. The encumbrance had been removed. Lucky her.

Then, quite unexpectedly, one week after she had left hospital following the minor operation to clean up any *"retained products of conception"* she had suffered a sudden attack of depression and guilt. Simply hormones? Or had nature known the child would not be welcome and dealt with it in her own wise way?

So what now?

Firstly Matthew must come home. She had been honest enough in her letter, explained that though she had not wanted a child she had taken no part in its destruction.

He would know she would not lie to him.

So again the question. What now?

"No, Joanna Piercy," she whispered, "enough inertia. You are a Detective Inspector and a woman has been murdered. This is what you do now. You work. When Matthew comes home you can see. In the meantime, one step at a time."

Work – work – work
Till the brain begins to swim;
Work – work – work
Till the eyes are heavy and dim.

Again the Hood poem steered her in the right direction.

She had a briefing at nine and had better make good use of it. She started planning the deployment of her officers.

From her wardrobe she selected a raspberry coloured cotton skirt with a black t-shirt and some wedge-heeled sandals. She had the feeling she'd be on her feet for most of the day so she may as well be comfortable.

She was always cursory with her make-up, a smidge of mascara, a smear of lipstick and her hair brushed into submission. Temporarily.

Downstairs she swigged down half a pint of apple juice and grabbed an Alpen breakfast bar. She was even more desperate to move forward in this case than usual.

She had enough energy to solve six murders.

No time for the bike this morning which was a shame as the day was hot, airless and perfect for cycling. But she would need to be mobile. She backed the car down the narrow track that lay at the side of the brick-built cottage and accelerated down the single-track road towards the main A523 and Leek.

Corinne Angiotti, on the other hand, had hardly the energy to chew her piece of toast. She felt drained, listless as she stared her husband with something approaching dislike. "I thought I might have counted on your support," she said softly. "Don't you understand how much I need it now?"

Pete concentrated on spreading his butter thinly, his head bent low over the knife as though he was very shortsighted. He was slightly neurotic about his food, watching calories obsessively, measuring fat content, comparing the saturation in different margarines. It was all part of his self-absorption.

Corinne watched him, gritting her teeth. "I've given *you* enough. All that trouble in Wandsworth... We simply left." There was a slight vibrato in her voice.

"I was innocent," her husband said defiantly. "The girl made the whole thing up. It was a lie. A bare-faced lie. She was simply trying to destroy me. I'd worked hard to get where I was, Corrie. I was up for deputy head. *And* I'd have got the job. Had it not been for that malicious little cow."

His eyes were bulging, the veins on the back of his hand, distended blue ropes. There was a film of sweat over his face. She thought how physically unattractive he was. Intensified by the note of self-pity in his voice.

"Pete," she appealed.

"*Now* look where I am. Buried away up here in Staffordshire. Teaching geography to kids who are lucky if they've been to London in a lifetime."

"Pete, that simply isn't true. Youngsters aren't like that these days. And you've said yourself that they behave well."

"I don't like being manipulated," he said. "I've been pushed here. It wasn't my choice. I didn't want to be here."

"Well, you're here now. You might as well get on with it."

"Thanks for the sympathy."

When it had been *she* who had been seeking sympathy.

They glared at each other, beaming across hostility, dislike bordering on frank hatred.

Domestic arguments are like this. They escalate into belligerency without warning. And yet – how often do they skirt around the real issues? Because real issues are simply too dangerous, aren't they? She had loved her life in London, liked the proximity of friends and family, the amenities and the shops, the West End, the galleries and exhibitions. She hadn't wanted to come up here but they had both felt the need to bury themselves, to hide and lick their wounds. Away from headlines,

"Teacher assaults pupil".

But now that she was here she loved this town too. Loved the people, enjoyed the countryside and the rawness of the weather.

They both sensed they had reached the edge of the precipice and drew back.

She reached across the table to cover his hand with her own. "You're right, Pete. The girl was a troublemaker. Only the year before she'd..."

Pete sneered at her. "Nice of you to mention that, Corrie."

She froze. She knew that tone of voice, that cold, nasty way he'd spoken.

She sighed and moved away. When had her marriage become so difficult?

At what exact point?

The honeymoon? The wedding day itself? The day *she* had graduated? The day *he* had graduated? Who cared? Now she simply felt ever so tired.

Pete put his face very near hers so she could smell tooth-paste and toast. The scent of marriage. "You are bound to me, Mrs Ever-so-perfect Doctor wife. You and I will always know things about each other, which it would be safer for us not to know. Understand? And if I provoked unwanted attention so have you. And out of the two of us I believe mine was the less abnormal and the less deserved." He nar-rowed his eyes at her. "What I shall always wonder is what did you *do* to invite such worship?"

"Nothing." Without warning, from somewhere deep inside her abdominal cavity Corinne felt the stirrings of some energy. She stared back at her husband through unfo-cussed eyes.

Didn't he understand how dangerous this was, how love and hatred are next-door neighbours? Did he not see that it was not safe for him to provoke her like this when she could so easily trip?

She moistened her lips and tried to warn him. At the

same time she recognised what the source of her energy was. Hatred. Such an energising force.

Joanna reverse-parked her car into the space left for her. Korpanski's estate was in the adjacent lot. She threw the door open, pressed the remote to lock it and walked very briskly in through the station doors. Even the desk sergeant caught a waft of her energy as she passed and winked to his colleagues. "Piercy's on the scent," he said.

She grinned at him and moved on.

The familiar buzz was in the air.

They were all ready for her, the entire team. Lounging around, sitting on tables, some scribbling into pads, others simply standing around. The doors swung wide as she marched through, straight up to Korpanski. "Morning, Mike," she said gaily.

He turned around. "Jo?"

She felt a sudden wave of affection for the bull-necked sergeant with whom she'd worked on such a number of police cases. Surprising for a small, largely quiet moorlands town. One would almost think she attracted violent crime.

Korpanski had very dark eyes which he turned on her now – full glare. He had been bristly and hostile during the first few cases they had worked on together but between the two detectives had sprung firstly respect, then, more danger- ously, a fierce and loyal affection. Hopefully it would never be put to the test but Joanna knew Korpanski would risk his life for her. She knew she could never work as comfort- ably or as closely with another police sergeant. There was no one she would trust with so much. To add to that Mike Korpanski knew more about her emotions, her personal life, her loves and hates, than any other man alive. Almost more than Matthew. Sometimes, with a shock, she acknowl- edged that she was almost closer to Mike Korpanski than Matthew Levin.

This was one of those flashing moments of realisation. She flushed.

He was standing very close to her but bent even nearer so he could speak quietly – to her alone. "You've heard from Levin?"

She nodded, knowing the joy would be clear in her face.

"*That* good, is it?"

Again she smiled and nodded. "He's coming home, Mike."

Korpanski raised his eyes then let out a soft chuckle. "So – you want this case wound up nicely so you can have a few days off."

"Holed in one, Sergeant," she said lightly.

He laughed with her now and a few of the officers standing near glanced across and made their observations. This was an unusual duo. Even for the evolving police force with its encouragement of sexual equality.

Joanna moved to the front of the room.

It was a fact that, although she didn't know it, she had the respect of most of her junior officers. They had learned a lot from her clarity of thinking as well as from her intuition. The truth was that she never stopped thinking about the case until it was wound up, whether asleep or awake, eating, talking, bathing, it was always in her mind. Her psychology degree had taught her a lot about the criminal mind, motivation for the crime and its eventual solution. She was not afraid to ask for advice nor to admit when she was wrong and the relationship between her and the Polish sergeant was a matter of endless speculation in the ranks. It staved off boredom.

So the moment Joanna stood at the front of the room and pulled down the white flipchart the officers fell silent and gave her their attention. All of it.

She drew a circle dead centre. "Beatrice Pennington," she said. "Killed, we believe, by an intimate."

There was a general hum of assent from the gathering.

"Husband." She drew Pennington as a satellite joined by a thin line then quickly added others. "Colleagues, friends, secret lover, members of the Readers' Group, acquaintances."

Korpanski was leaning against the wall, to her side. She knew he would shift if she said anything he disagreed with.

"Evidence that Beatrice Pennington had a secret lover? She spoke to me about it, mentioned it in passing. There was the attempt at glamorising herself. There is the evidence of the Ann Summers underwear. Not bought, we think, with her husband in mind."

She scanned the room, gauging their response but they were all simply watching. Not judging – yet. There was little movement in the ranks.

"We must look within these life-satellites for her killer. Only if we cannot find him *within* these parameters should we extend them.

We know that she moved from her usual circle of life into the circle of death early on Wednesday morning, the 23rd of June. We have not yet established precisely where and when this took place but we have sightings of her cycling to work and her bike, as you all know, was locked to the railings outside the library at around nine thirty. We are not yet sure whether this was a planned absconding or a spur-of-the-moment decision." She hesitated. *Except for the frock.*

"Except for the frock she was wearing. Remember she rode her bike into work." She frowned, knowing her next statement could provoke ridicule. "I know this is hardly evidence but I would never cycle in a dress. Impractical and uncomfortable as well as downright dangerous. A full skirt, like that, could so easily catch in the spokes as indeed it did. There is more than one tear and oil stains on the skirt."

She'd known it. She caught a few smirks and knew they were contemplating the Lycra shorts she habitually rode in. She saw that she did not need to emphasise the point.

"Phil?" She addressed Phil Scott, young, blonde, capable PC. "Can you go back to the library and find out whether Beatrice normally cycled in a frock? When she joined us she wore cycling shorts. But maybe for work... Also do a bit of digging around this Readers' Group thing, can you? I wonder whether it was a specific book which sparked off Beatrice's awakened sex drive."

"Sure." PC Scott smothered a grin. She waited for his punch line. "You mean like *Lady Chatterly's Lover?*"

She laughed. "That is *exactly* what I mean, Phil."

It was one of the things which endeared her to her junior officers. Not only allowed but encouraged their jokes. And laughed at them. She was one of them.

"Bridget."

PC Anderton. One of the foot-soldiers. Plump, brown-haired. Korpanski always made the comment that she had "milk-bottle legs". In fact there was something of Beatrice Pennington about her. She would win no beauty contests but she was a valued worker. And in a case like this it might well be one of *her* observations which pointed the rest of them in the right direction.

"Get to know the family a bit better, will you? I wonder – are we missing something right underneath our noses?"

"Did you have anything special in mind?"

"Not really. Just get in there, Bridget. Speak to them."

Korpanski shifted his weight from one foot to the other. He hated these vague directives, these ill-defined pointers. His style was to bash a couple of doors down, dawn raids, stakeouts. But she knew this softly softly approach was the best chance they had. So far nothing of any real value had turned up but they would inch closer.

It was all there. It *must* be. Like tea leaves at the bottom of the cup the case was simply waiting to be read.

"And as for you..." Hesketh-Brown's head jerked up. It didn't seem more than a couple of months ago that Hesketh-Brown had been an idealistic young rookie from the Potteries. Always wide-eyed, sitting in the front row, scribbling something in his pad right through the briefing. Now he was having trouble keeping his eyes open. Ah. She remembered now. His wife had recently had a baby.

Disturbed nights.

"Forensics. Get every single result on every single piece

of forensic evidence gathered at the place where the body was dumped. Thread it all together. Work on it, Heskey. Comb it through very precisely. Use your instinct. And try not to fall asleep," she tagged on kindly.

Hesketh-Brown gave a sheepish smile and nodded.

"And I think we'll take a closer look at Pennington's car, Ruthin. Get that sorted out, will you? I don't suppose we've anything back on the bike?"

The rim of faces looked suitably vague.

"Oh well. Another area then."

She dismissed the officers and they filed out leaving her alone with Mike. "And we, Korpanski, are going to sit on Arthur Pennington's tail until he squeaks and we're also going to harass those two old school friends and lover boy, Guy. It might also be an idea to make the acquaintance of *Mr* Pirtek – if there is such a person. Come on, Mike."

He caught up as the doors swung behind her.

Chapter Twelve

Pennington worked in a small accountant's office situated above a furniture shop in a small shopping mall. The Smithfield Centre sounds as though it would be an attractive part in the centre of this largely picturesque town. But nothing could be further from the truth. It is a Sixties concrete slab with about eight featureless shops and wouldn't be out of place in the gulags of Moscow.

Pennington's office was as bland a premises as you would expect, reached through a frosted glass door at the top of a steep wooden staircase lit by one pink, flickering fluorescent tube. His name was written in modest black lettering beneath that of the senior partner, Robert Astley. In spite of the Sixties exterior something about the grained oak reminded Joanna more of the Victorian age and Scrooge's junior clerk. She knocked and they walked straight in. A secretary glanced up and immediately straight down again as she checked her computer screen, presumably for appointments.

"How can I help?" The offer was made with scant interest.

Joanna flashed her ID card in front of her stuck-up little nose. "I'd like to ask you a few questions before I speak with Mr Pennington. If that's all right," she added sarcastically.

The girl's eyes flickered from one to the other. Inspecting them before she responded.

"I expect. I mean... You don't have an appointment."

"It'll be OK, love," Mike butted in.

The girl obviously warmed to the tall detective. She positively simpered back at him.

As Korpanski was already doing so well Joanna let him lead the questioning, leaning across the desk, his face a foot away from the girl.

"Last Wednesday, love, what time did Mr Pennington

turn in to work?"

"He always comes at..."

"I didn't ask what time he *always* comes in. I asked what time he came in last Wednesday."

"Do you keep a diary?" Joanna interrupted.

The girl's eyes flickered back to Mike. "It's all on the computer."

"Then flash it up."

The girl fiddled proficiently with a couple of the computer keys, pressed return with a bad-tempered bang and announced, "He was in for nine," she said sulkily.

"Thank you," Joanna said sweetly.

Without warning Pennington's door burst open, taking Joanna and Mike by surprise. It was hard to say who was the most shocked – Pennington, Joanna or Korpanski. All three simply stared at one another while the girl at the desk regarded them all with poorly disguised prurient curiosity, her face flushing slightly pink. It was Joanna who recovered her equilibrium first. "Good morning, Mr Pennington. We just needed to check up on a few facts. I hope you don't mind. We realise we don't have an appointment but we were passing anyway."

But Arthur Pennington wasn't taking a lot of notice. He merely looked confused. "They've taken my car," he said. "I've just had a phone call from one of your colleagues. They're taking *both* our cars."

"We'll provide you with a replacement," Joanna said smoothly.

"But why?"

His high forehead was wrinkled with puzzlement. "Why? What on earth have our cars got to do with my wife's murder? How is depriving me of my car going to help you find Beattie's killer?"

The girl behind him was having a struggle pretending she wasn't listening. She was staring fiercely into the computer screen, faking absorption. But her fingers were still, hovering over the keys as though suspended on air jets. On her face was a fixed, wooden smile.

"Mr Pennington," Joanna said patiently. "You know as well as I do that in a case like this we often follow leads which appear quite unrelated to the case."

"Leads?" His head tilted to one side and he was frowning. "What leads? I don't understand. Why follow them if they have nothing to do with it?"

To her shame Joanna ducked behind the police's classic statement. "We're just following lines of enquiry."

But instead of this allaying Pennington's fears he looked even more worried. "I don't know if I can allow…"

Joanna looked steadily back at him, resisting the temptation to gloat and thought, *You don't have the right to refuse.*

"As soon as we've finished looking at them we'll let you have them both back."

"Looking at them? Looking? What for?"

"Anything which might help to find out what happened to your wife."

"Oh well," he said with resignation.

And then he lifted his hooded eyes, read her mind and stared straight back at her. "I don't suppose I've the right to refuse, have I, Inspector?"

She shook her head. "Not really." Again she felt that unexpected wave of sympathy for the man. His wife had, after all, just been murdered.

"Can we have a more private word with you, Mr Pennington?"

He nodded, gave an anxious glance in the direction of the door marked Astley and led the way into his office, Joanna and Mike threading between the desks, following the bowed shoulders. The girl behind them all but left her chair as she craned her neck to watch them through. She would be popular at lunchtime today, full of the story of the morning before it reached next week's headlines.

Man helps police with wife's murder enquiry.

Joanna waited until the door was firmly shut behind them and drew out her notepad. "I just wanted to go over the morning your wife disappeared."

"But I've already told you. I left her at the breakfast table," Pennington said in his flat, nasal voice, "eating her *muesli*."

"Just remind me of the time." Joanna was still being patient. "So I can be absolutely sure."

She knew what she was doing, setting a trap, criss-crossing branches over a deep pit lined with sharp spikes on which to impale him.

Fall in, Arthur.

"It was at about half-past eight," he said firmly.

"And then?"

"I came straight to work."

Joanna stopped writing to look around. It was exactly the sort of office she would have expected Pennington to work in. Small, square, bland, a desk facing the door, computer on it. One tiny window and a fire escape. Piles of files, all of the same, uniform grey lined the shelves. He didn't even have a picture of his wife to look at.

"How did your wife seem that morning?"

"I don't understand," he said. "What do you mean, how did she *seem*? Same as always."

Joanna had a vision of Beatrice, sitting at the table, stolidly chewing her way through her dish of health-giving cereal.

"She didn't seem excited or apprehensive?"

"No, she didn't."

"Was she dressed?"

The question startled him. "She always gets dressed before she eats."

"So was she already dressed that morning when you left?"

"Yes."

"What in?"

Pennington was visibly intimidated by Korpanski's manner. Quite apart from the detective's physical presence his tone had been cultivated to sound truculent and threatening. It was one of the reasons why Piercy and Korpanski worked so well together. Mr Hard and Miss Soft. Sergeant Cruel and Inspector Kind. Except sometimes Joanna wasn't quite so kind. She too could show her claws. And use them.

"What was your wife wearing?"

"I can't remember."

But the frock, with its splashes of colour on a white background, was memorable.

"Think, Mr Pennington," Joanna said kindly. "When she was found she was wearing a dress." She described it. Pennington blinked rapidly. "I have the feeling," he said slowly, "that she was wearing something a bit more ordinary." A brief pause. "I think I would have remembered had she been wearing something so –"

They all waited for the word.

"Flash."

Joanna nodded and heard Mike's irritated intake of breath.

She knew what he was thinking, that this was leading them nowhere.

"But you can't be sure."

"No," he said slowly.

"Had you noticed a change in your wife's mental state?"

Again he looked startled by the question. "What do you mean?"

"Friends have said your wife seemed a bit down before Christmas."

"It's the time of year," he said comfortably. "She always gets herself in a state round that time, frets whether Fiona and Graham will make it home – and all that," he finished lamely.

"And did they?"

"No." He must have felt an explanation was necessary. "Graham had to work and Fiona had a lot on – parties and all that. We were on our own for the festive season this time around."

Joanna could guess it was typical of all their Christmases in the last few years.

Arthur Pennington gave a ghost of a smile. "You do ask some funny questions, Inspector," he said.

The worst was Joanna knew he was right. They were fishing around in muddy water, searching blindly for something that would lead them towards the truth.

It encouraged Joanna to take a jump into the unknown and ask something that *was* relevant. "Who do you think killed your wife?"

Pennington sniffed in a long, sighing breath. "I think. I believe," he started, finally settling on, "it would seem likely that my wife had someone else. A lover." The words cost him. His face looked crumpled and upset and he was deathly pale.

Again Joanna had this odd instinct to console him. "I'm so sorry," she said kindly.

Pennington drooped in his chair. "Have *you* any idea who he might be?"

There was no animosity in his voice. Not hatred for this unknown man who had cost him so much. Not only his wife's fidelity but also her life. "No," she said. "But we will, Mr Pennington. I promise you. We will find him."

Korpanski waited until they were outside before he exploded. "Offer him your condolences, why don't you," he mocked. "Poor bereaved Arthur. You're taken in by him, Jo."

She squared up to him. "I've told you before, Korpanski. He is a bereaved husband until proved otherwise which warrants our sympathy as well as our respect. Understand?"

There was something approaching disdain on his face. "It's the way you get so completely hoodwinked, Jo. It's pathetic."

She knew she didn't deserve this. "Not pathetic, Mike. Professional. I'm not hoodwinked by him. I'm simply giving him the benefit of the doubt."

Mercurial as ever Korpanski's face creased into a grin. "I still bet you he did it."

Mike's moods were as changeable as the weather.

But for once she pulled rank, "I think it would be better, Mike," she said acidly, "if we concentrated on finding our mystery lover rather than taking bets on whether Arthur Pennington is innocent or guilty. Understand?"

It was the sort of priggish statement which should have earned her a mocking "Whe-eh." But in this suddenly-found good humour Korpanski was not to be suppressed. He merely grinned at her, showing a wide expanse of white teeth.

They faced each other for a moment on the busy street before he shifted his feet. "So what next, Ma'am?"

She ignored the jibe of formality. He knew she hated being addressed as Ma'am. It simply wasn't her style. "I don't know. Maybe we should trot up Derby Street and speak to Beattie's two cronies again." She hadn't stilled her curiosity about Jewel Pirtek, Marilyn and Guy. Something here didn't feel quite right. She couldn't see how Beatrice Pennington had fitted into the friendship. They were different types. What had been her role? Maybe their lives and relationships would not lead her straight to Beatrice's killer but they knew more than they were telling. And this "more" would prove helpful to the case.

"Maybe we should get a couple of officers to tackle the loving children again too. Surely kids know more about their parents than this?"

Korpanski made a face. "They were a fat lot of good before."

"I know. That's what makes them so interesting."

He grinned again. Another wide, warm gesture. "I despair, Jo, of the things that you find interesting."

She laughed too. Together they rounded the corner towards Derby Street while she reflected.

What intrigued her about Fiona and Graham Pennington was the sheer detachment they had achieved from their parents. This cold moving on as though their childhood was of no consequence. Was it possible that they really didn't care what had happened to their mother? Was there no instinct to come and comfort their father? At what point do parents stop being solicitous towards their children? At what point – if ever – do the children take up the reins and become solicitous towards their parents? Is this what is meant by the term *growing up?* A detachment to the point of cruelty? At the same time she frankly acknowledged that behind the idle questioning was relevance to her own recent circumstances. Had her own child lived for twenty years instead of dying seven months before it was due to be born would it have learned to cut her out of its life?

Korpanski, ever-sensitive to her own deep moods, stood by silently and helplessly, waiting for her to move on.

"And we can't ignore the people from the Readers' Group either. We should keep the investigation wide until we're more sure."

But Mike wasn't quite so ready to leave Pennington himself behind. He jerked his thumb behind him. "We're leaving the best one behind there."

She turned to face him. "Then how did he do it? He left his wife at home and came to work. She was seen cycling through the town at nine thirty, more than half an hour after he'd left. We've got scores of witnesses now who saw her riding her bike, locking it to the railings." They continued walking until Joanna stopped and frowned. "What do you make of the fact that Pennington didn't remember what his wife was wearing on that last morning?"

Korpanski shrugged. "Not a lot," he said. "I couldn't tell you what Fran's got on in the morning."

"You would if she was wearing a flashy frock."

"Maybe," he said, non-committal to the last.

They walked steadily along Derby Street, passing Strawberry Fields and the hardware shop which sold everything from spanners to doormats, when on impulse Joanna turned right into Market Street. Korpanski winced. This was the scene of his wife's embarrassing affair with the car.

Joanna only realised it when they reached the dry cleaners. "Is this where...?"

From the puce colour Korpanski's face turned it was obvious she was right. He tugged at his short collar as though to loosen a stranglehold.

"Is it all settled now?" she asked kindly.

"Getting there," he muttered. "I've just paid up the excess. Fran's stumped up half. We'll survive."

Woman-like she couldn't resist it. "And the handbrake?"

"Fixed," he said through gritted teeth.

She resisted her next impulse to quote. *For want of a nail.*

Sneaking a look at his face her colleague wouldn't thank her for that particular philosophy.

"Good." She stopped. In front of them was the doctors' surgery. Name plate clearly displayed. It was as though her feet had led her there, directed by her subconscious mind.

They stood in front of the black-painted door for a moment. She could feel Mike's scepticism seeping towards her but it did nothing to suppress the tingling feeling that iced her spine. From her neck right downwards. A feeling she knew Mike wouldn't either share or sympathise with. And she was right. "We're not going to get anything from there, Jo."

"No?"

She pushed open the door.

The receptionist looked tired and fed up. She was a honey-blonde with a centimetre of dark and greying roots. She was wearing very black mascara which had run slightly into the crow's feet at the corner of her eyes. Her mouth, bright with nicely applied pink lipstick was pursed up with tension.

The reason?

In front of them was a plump woman berating her for not being able to make an appointment for the following day.

"I'm sorry," the receptionist was saying. "It's very difficult these days with this forty-eight hour access."

"Which – you're – denying me." The plump woman in large jeans and a loose, white cotton shirt thumped her fist hard down on the counter, bouncing the vase of silk flowers into the air. "It's my right. If I need to see a doctor I can see one."

The receptionist cast around for help, found none and consulted the computer. "You can see Doctor Morgan at nine thirty in the morning."

"I want to see Doctor Angiotti in the afternoon. Look – Doctor Angiotti is my doctor. She understands me. She knows my history and sympathises with my problems. It's her I have to see."

"It's her afternoon off tomorrow."

The plump woman moved forward. "She'll see me. Just ask her. I know she will. When can I see her?"

Joanna watched the receptionist curiously. She was in a difficult position. She was not going to please this customer whatever she did.

Finally the woman accepted an appointment for two days' time, grumbling all the while, and the receptionist wrote the time down on a card. As she turned from the desk, the patient spoke loudly to the waiting room in general, "You'll get no joy here."

Joanna met her disgruntled gaze. *I wonder.*

The receptionist's face was tight with anger as she continued staring at the computer screen. "Can I help you?" It was an automatic politeness.

Joanna flashed her ID card. "I'd like to ask you a few questions."

The receptionist immediately brightened up.

Strange how anything out of routine can rejuvenate, banish tiredness. Call it energizing curiosity, if you like, but all humans thrive on variety.

"We're investigating the murder of Beatrice Pennington. I believe she was a patient here?"

The receptionist had very bright blue eyes which looked uncertain. "I don't know whether I'm. I mean – it's confidential information."

"It's connected with a murder enquiry," Korpanski repeated.

The woman was visibly flustered. "I'm sorry. Could you wait a minute?"

She picked up the phone, spoke to someone. The door behind the desk opened and a woman walked out.

"I'm Corinne Angiotti," she said briskly. "I believe you wanted some information about a patient of mine?"

Joanna's impression was of coolness. That and a determined control. Doctor Angiotti was small and slim with blonde hair, prone to curliness. She wore no make-up and was about thirty. She had a smooth, olive complexion. Her eyes were brown. Not as dark as Korpanski's but nearly there. Her lips were thin to the point of hardness and without lipstick. She wore the status badge of a doctor around her neck, a stethoscope.

Joanna took all this in with interest. She responded equally coolly. "I'm Detective Inspector Joanna Piercy, Leek Police. We're investigating the murder of Beatrice Pennington whose body was found last week on Grindon Moor." She tried the appeal. "To be honest, doctor, we're floundering a bit. We're trying to find out a bit more about Mrs Pennington in the hope that it might help find her killer."

The doctor leaned across the reception desk and spoke in a low voice. "You haven't any idea who killed that poor woman?"

Joanna shook her head. "Not yet," she said.

She sensed that Mike, standing behind her, almost close enough to feel her body warmth, was scrutinising the doctor. She felt the strength of his gaze – powerful.

"Would you like to come into my surgery? I can't spare much time but she was a patient and I would like to help."

They followed her through into a pleasant room, children's toys in the corner, an examination couch, a swinging curtain, a large desk and three chairs.

Corinne Angiotti sat in one, Joanna in the other. The doctor looked up at Korpanski, standing in the doorway. "Do you ever sit down?"

"No thanks," he said abrupt almost to the point of rudeness.

Doctor Angiotti gave the slightest of nods and smiles – little more that a softening of her thin mouth but it improved her features one hundred per cent. "All right then," she said. "How can I help?"

"Mrs Pennington was a patient of yours?"

"That's correct, Inspector."

"She consulted you frequently?"

"It depends what you mean by frequently. Certainly I have seen her a few times this year."

She pressed a few keys on the computer and deliberately turned the screen away.

"Confidentiality," she said with a smile.

"Friends have mentioned that Mrs Pennington was depressed before Christmas."

Corinne Angiotti gave them a cool look.

"I wouldn't say depressed," she said. "She had simply reached a certain stage in her life."

"Can you explain?"

Corinne Angiotti gave a sad smile. "It's a stage many women reach in their fifties," she said. "Maybe you'll reach it one day, Inspector. Children left home."

Not me, Joanna thought.

"It was a sort of dissatisfaction. A worry about losing attractiveness. She didn't need antidepressants, Inspector."

"So what did she need?" Korpanski asked roughly.

"Just a chat. A change of life style. Reassurance. That sort of thing."

"Well it seemed to work," Joanna said, still watching the doctor's face very carefully. These professionals. They gave little away.

The doctor gave another smile. "Yes," she said.

She wasn't afraid of silence.

"Look," she said. "I don't mean to be rude but I do have a busy surgery ahead of me. I don't think I can tell you anything. I'm sorry. She was a decent woman. I was very shocked."

It was a dismissal.

Outside Korpanski was almost mocking. "Solve your case then?"

Joanna shook her head. "No. But you never know."

"Waste of bloody time," he muttered.

"Well – for one who started the day so well you're a bit tetchy."

"We seem to be going round in circles," he grumbled.

The worst was – she agreed.

She didn't even try to defend her conduct of the investigation. Except that underneath she knew full well that something, at some point, would lead them to Beatrice's killer.

They had returned to Derby Street and walked in silence until they reached Jewel Pirtek's handbag shop. Through the window they could see Jewel waving her arms around and talking on a mobile phone. But the traffic was noisy behind them and they couldn't make out what she was saying.

Korpanski regarded her with tangible suspicion. "I'd love to know who she's talking to."

Joanna gave him a queer look. "Can't you guess?"

Nothing irritated Korpanski more than her implying superior knowledge. "No I can't. Because I'm not psychic."

Joanna continued to watch. "I'd lay a guess that she's speaking to best friend Saunders."

Mike nodded slowly. "Maybe."

They pushed the door open and registered Jewel's appalled surprise. "I'll have to go," she said quickly into the mobile. "Customers."

Korpanski simply couldn't resist it. "Except we're not."

She eyed Joanna's scuffed leather handbag. "You might be," she said. "In fact you ought to be." She chewed some gum slowly with an open mouth. "Special discount."

She unhooked a bag from the wall hooks and handed it to Joanna. "Now this one," she said. Joanna took it from her. Jewel was right. It was a lovely bag with a £70 price tag dangling from the handle. But the leather was soft. She sniffed it. Looked at it. The right size too. She sensed Korpanski watching her and could read his mind without looking across. *Shopping! When there's a serious crime to solve.*

Reluctantly she handed it back to Jewel. "It is a nice bag," she said. "But I didn't come here to buy a bag."

"I can do it for fifty quid."

It brushed too close to bribery. She shook her head.

Joanna settled down on the bar stool; Korpanski took up his usual stance leaning against the wall, arms folded, feet apart. Guarding the exit like the genie of the lamp. Blocking the entrance too.

"Come on, Jewel," Joanna coaxed. "Spill the beans."

Jewel had sharp little eyes. However much makeup and false eyelashes she applied she would never be able to disguise this fact. Also that when she was rattled her voice rose an entire octave in pitch. "Beans. What beans?" Her eyes moved around the shop, deliberately skipping over Korpanski.

"There are little..." Joanna tried to choose her words with care, "titbits you've been leaving out about your friend. You three have been pals for years. You must have shared every confidence – every secret. You and Marilyn think you know who her secret lover was, don't you? You think you know who killed her."

For a second or two Jewel Pirtek went so pale Joanna braced herself to catch her when she fainted. But she didn't. And she'd recovered within a minute to declare her innocence. "I don't. I don't. Neither of us knows. I promise you. We don't know who it was. You're talking about someone who's killed my friend. It wouldn't be safe to know. Not safe."

"We'd protect you from this person. If you proved to be

right he'd be locked up. Put away. And if you're wrong you have nothing to fear." Joanna produced the most powerful argument of all. "If he's not convicted he'll go on to do the same to some other poor woman."

"I honestly do not know," Jewel said, still in a panic. "There were things she said – admitted." She was twisting the big gold ring on her middle finger. "I – we – got the feeling she wasn't too proud of herself. Not sure, you see. In spite of what she'd said we wondered. We sort of –"

What was she talking about?

"She was a bit ashamed. At first she was very flaunty. But then, we thought, maybe it wasn't a man."

It took Joanna a minute or two to grasp. "You're saying that Beatrice was a lesbian?"

"We – no – at least – we don't know. Me and Marilyn – we just wondered it."

"Why? What evidence did you have?"

Jewel went pale again. Joanna could read her mind. She'd said too much. Given away a confidence. She was going to need bullying. "Come on, Jewel."

"Just things. She'd say general things. About woman having softer characters, being kinder, that she'd had it with men." She couldn't resist a swift bitch. "Not that she'd ever got it together with men. Except Arthur." Beattie's friend couldn't resist smiling. "If you can call him a man, that is. She just kept saying things like that it was women who had all the kindness and things like that. But I promise you. Me and Marilyn just thought it. We didn't *know*."

"Did you ask her?"

"I sort of hinted at it."

"And?" Korpanski barked gruffly.

"She just said the less we knew the fewer lies we'd have to tell. We couldn't budge her. She wasn't going to tell us. We thought in the end she would. Beattie was like that. She'd keep quiet but in the end she'd always tell."

Joanna tried hard to flick back to the few bike rides they'd shared and tried to piece together all that Beatrice

Pennington had said. Had *she* picked up on the fact that Beattie's secret love was a woman?

No. Because we all make certain assumptions.

Perhaps Marilyn Saunders would be able to shed some light on it.

Or Guy.

Chapter Thirteen

Marilyn was peering through the window as they drove up. She didn't look at all surprised to see them.

She'd opened the door before Joanna had even lifted her hand to knock.

"Well, Inspector," she said with a touch of bravado. "Nice of you to drop in." Her manner bordered on the flirtatious but it reminded Joanna of a night watching a famous actress in a play, performing desperately. A few nights later it had become public knowledge that this actress had been diagnosed with inoperable cancer. It had been a brave performance but full of pathos.

"Coffee anyone?"

Joanna wanted Marilyn to be at her ease so she accepted the coffee and they waited while the kettle boiled and it was made. Then they settled in her sitting room and Joanna took a good, appraising look at Beattie's friend.

Maybe she'd had a couple of good nights' sleep or maybe she'd simply come to terms with her friend's death but there was something newly confident about her.

She looked good, her hair glossy. Still benefiting from the hairdresser's attention. She'd probably been sitting out in the garden. Certainly her face was lightly tanned. And she was dressed not in casual clothes but a white cotton shirt-waister and some low-heeled pink sandals with toenails to match. Around her clung a haze of expensive scent which Joanna couldn't identify. Not one of the classics, she decided.

Korpanski was staring at her with a mesmerised expression. And the nurse was not only aware of it but took full advantage. She tilted her head back and crossed her legs provocatively, displaying a good expanse of plump thigh.

"Now then," she said, eyes wide. "What can I do for you."

"We've just spoken to Jewel."

"I know."

And suddenly Joanna knew too. Knew all. This was all learned behaviour. Behind the professional smile, like the actress who had learned she had weeks to live, was a frightened woman. A woman who would fight tooth and claw for what was hers.

A cornered tigress.

Joanna stole a swift look at Korpanski to see whether he shared her sudden perception and almost ground her teeth in frustration. He was taken in completely. And *he* was the one who always accused *her* of being hoodwinked by a guilty party. When all it took was a selected outfit and some war paint to fool him.

Well he might explode in exasperation and say, *shopping.* She would always be irritated by this in men, that they were so easily taken in by the superficial gloss of the opposite sex.

She turned her attention back to Marilyn. "Jewel told us that you believed Beattie's secret romance was with a woman."

Marilyn swallowed and evaded their eyes.

Something not quite right here.

"We wondered," she said. "She hinted, you see. She said all sorts of things about how women were so much better. Things I'd never heard her say before. Personal things, about a woman's skin and hair. About them being softer, more understanding. She spouted this sort of stuff for months. And it was so alien coming from her. Beattie had always been..." Marilyn affected a high-pitched giggle, " well – like her name. Sort of stodgy, you know. Old-fashioned. Easily shocked. When she first started saying this sort of thing Jewel and I simply ignored it." A little toss of her head reminded Joanna of a wilful pony. "We thought it was just Beattie being Beattie."

Her eyes strolled from one to the other.

And again Joanna was blessed with a flash of understanding. A little peep through the peephole show that was these three friends' lives. Two of them had been attractive extroverts. Expecting and receiving all the attention. Beattie had fulfilled the role of necessary audience. Always the listener. When the listener had stopped listening and begun, instead, to talk, no one had, in turn, done her the courtesy of listening.

Joanna drank deeply from the coffee while Marilyn chatted on, brightly unaware that she was drawing pictures in the detective's mind.

"We thought it was just her being silly – that she'd read something in one of those daft magazines and sort of thought she'd shock us. To be honest, after Guy and I got together she was always sort of odd. And then after Christmas she started spouting all this sort of nonsense. Adolescent we thought it. Talking all about the higher emotions and inner self, quoting from that book about Men from Mars and women from Venus. Different planets sort of stuff. We just couldn't be bothered..."

Joanna completed the sentence for her...to listen.

"So who was it. This mystery woman?"

"We didn't know that."

"Didn't she say?"

But of course, if Beattie had said, they would not have heard, would they, these "best" friends.

Korpanski was frowning. He shifted his bulky thighs. "Was it someone from work?"

"I don't think so."

"Someone from the Readers' Group?"

"I don't know."

But there were only three areas in Beattie's life – her home and family, her work and these two friends with whom she had socialised. Joanna was suddenly regretful and felt a vague colour-wash of guilt. Because *she* had not listened to Beatrice Pennington either but had regarded her as wallpaper. Background. Had she made some effort to listen to her she might have had a clue to the killer's identity.

Her husband, her lover or even her lover's partner. Because this new knowledge had taken the lid off the box and exposed not a can of worms so much as a bucketful of writhing snakes. Relationships are rarely simple and when they cross such boundaries of convention forces are unleashed.

Joanna was quiet for a while, content to let Mike continue with the questioning about names, dates, and so on. They had this subliminal method of understanding one another and instinctively he knew she needed to sit on the sidelines for a moment and think. To superimpose Beatrice Pennington over that of her best friend.

Joanna was struggling to recall *something. Anything* that the woman had said to her.

Something about a new life, about not needing money, about moving away from Leek, about the tacit understanding that existed between lovers. Something about *Take my breath away* ...

Korpanski. "Were *you* a member of the Readers' Group?"

Marilyn laughed merrily. "Not my cup of tea," she said. Her eyes fixed boldly on Korpanski. "You could say," she said, shaking the chocolate-striped hair self-consciously, "that I have other fish to fry."

Right on cue they heard a skid outside. A car door slamming. Someone humming. The metallic chink of a key being inserted in the door. The door slamming.

They listened silently.

"Hi, tiger."

"In here, darling."

Guy Priestley sauntered in, throwing his keys carelessly across the polished occasional table. Spiky hair, jaunty and grinning broadly. Very over-confident. "Oh, hello you," he said to them both. "I wondered whose the car was."

There was neither welcome nor hostility in his tone. He crossed the room, bent over Marilyn and gave her a noisy, smacking kiss then a suggestive pat on the breast.

Joanna rolled her eyes towards Mike. This overt sexuality was just a bit too obvious, too public and too demonstrative. In fact it didn't wash. She decided that she didn't like

Guy Priestley. Neither did she trust him.

At last the lovers drew apart and Guy took up his seat next to his partner though it wouldn't have surprised Joanna if Marilyn had perched on his lap. Priestley shot her one of his super-confident looks and performed a theatrical stretch. *Hairy armpits.*

Her mistrust for Priestley was growing by the minute.

What was *his* game?

She observed him with an impassive face and waited for him to speak.

He did.

"And where are you up to with your investigations, Inspector? Ready to put a hand on a collar and say the magic words, 'you're nicked, my boy'?"

Joanna met his eyes for no more than a split second but it was long enough for her to read mockery and contempt clearly etched. What she hadn't realised was that Priestley wasn't over-fond of her either. In fact... She toyed with the idea before fitting it together. He despised women. All women. He was giving his 'beloved Marilyn' much the same look. She leaned forward on the sofa. This was interesting. She buried the knowledge deep. She always took pains to hide her personal instinct from suspects. It bore sweeter fruit if she affected sugariness.

So... "Guy," she said with a honeyed smile, "I can't remember whether we've asked you this." (Korpanski was eyeing her with complete surprise. He knew she wouldn't have forgotten what she'd asked Priestley – or his answer.) "Where were *you* on the morning of Wednesday, June the 23rd?"

"I beg your pardon."

His surprise sounded genuine.

Time for Miss Tough to emerge. "You heard." Mentally she added, *Lover Boy*.

"I was probably at work."

"We need to know."

Marilyn looked affronted. "Why? You can't think Guy

had anything to do with Beattie's death."

For answer Joanna looked pointedly at the young man and had the reward of seeing him flustered.

"Where do you work, Guy?"

Again Marilyn intervened. "He's a machine operator at McNaughton's Engineering. They make disc brakes for cars."

"At what time does your shift work?"

Yet again Marilyn spoke for him. "Six till two or two till ten."

"And what shift were you working on *that* day?"

Interestingly Guy began to bluster. "I hardly knew the woman."

At her side Korpanski shifted slightly. Without even looking at him Joanna knew he would be suppressing a smile. He was right. Even with her imagination she could-n't quite see Guy and Beatrice Pennington *getting it together*. She agreed with Mike. It was bordering on ridiculous.

Except that Beatrice Pennington was dead and her killer still at large. And they had not one sure lead; not one con-crete fact; not a single piece of evidence to lead them to him – or her. "Mr Priestley," she prompted coldly.

"It was my two-till-ten week," he said sulkily.

"So what did you do in the morning?" *She was really hav-ing to tease this out of him.*

The first sign of tension between the couple bubbled to the surface. They exchanged glances. Again it was Marilyn who spoke. "He was probably sleeping off a hangover," she said icily. "He will have climbed out of bed at about twelve o'clock, had a bath and eaten the meal *I* had cooked for him."

"Is this what happened on that particular Wednesday?"

He shrugged.

Joanna turned her attention to the nurse. "Did you work on the night of Tuesday the 22nd?"

"As it happens no," she said. "I was on a night off – away for a day or two, on a course in Brighton."

"So you can't vouch for Guy." It was a statement of fact; not a question.

Joanna rose to go, again feeling she had gained the upper hand in this interview, inched forward towards a solution. She would get there – eventually. Of that she was sure.

In the drive they passed a car. A gleaming red Audi A4 convertible which Korpanski's eyes stroked longingly. Priestley had a new car. A reward for being a good boy? Or had he worried his Astra had contained evidence?

"For a small engineering firm they must pay very well, Joanna observed drily.

"Well – he probably lives with her for nothing, hardly pays expenses. I wouldn't be at all surprised if that nursey friend of his foots the bills while he squanders his money on this."

"You're just jealous, Korpanski," Joanna laughed. "Just be glad you didn't have the bill for *this* when your wife left the handbrake off."

Korpanski sighed. "True…true. But…" His head was still turned as they unlocked the squad car. Joanna could read the naked lust a man feels for a beautiful car. It is a different, purer emotion than that which is stirred by a beautiful woman.

"We'd better track down that old car of his."

The briefing was set for 6 p.m. They spent an intensive few hours combing through statement and faxes, reading reports and making notes. By the end of the afternoon Joanna still felt they were missing some very big facts which would bear down on the case.

She fetched two cups of coffee, closed the door and faced Korpanski. "Let's go through this piece by piece, Mike," she said. "What do we know about Beatrice Pennington?"

He sighed, leaned right back in his chair, put his arms behind his head. "She was brought up by a farming family," he began. "Married young. Two children. Husband local too. Couple of good female friends. Librarian, ran a Readers' Group. She was plain, not particularly attractive."

Joanna leaned forward. "And then unaccountably she starts trying to change her life. Gets fit, takes real trouble with her appearance."

"Mid-life crisis," Mike suggested helpfully.

"But what was the trigger factor?"

"Does there have to be one? I thought it was just something that kind of hit you in your middle forties."

"I think usually something triggers it off. Some life event."

Korpanski's dark eyes regarded her with interest. "Go on," he prompted.

"Murders are not the story of one person but two, combined with a set of circumstances."

"Such as?"

She tried one of her ideas on him. "What if it was the other way round? What if it was Guy Priestley who made a pass at *her*?"

He stared at her. "I can't see it, somehow."

"Look at the person he is. Swaggering, self-assured, loves to think he can turn women on and off. What if he did it just for amusement?"

"What's your point, Jo?"

She smiled at him and wagged her finger. "Patience, Mike."

"But we've just had the theory put forward that this secret lover was a woman," he objected.

"Beatrice started all this get-fit thing back at Christmastime. It wasn't until a couple of months ago that she started suggesting it was a woman who was interesting to her."

Korpanski chewed his lip, unimpressed.

"What I find interesting is her rejection of men. She was comparing them and finding women infinitely preferable."

Korpanski continued to look unconvinced.

She tried again. "Open your mind, Korpanski. Try this for size. What if Guy made a pass at her and because she was fairly naïve she took it seriously, not realising that he's just a toe-rag and was playing with her. She thinks he really fancies her instead of, just for once, her friend. But he's just playing around. What happens next? She takes him seriously so he then has to let her down. And knowing the little I do about Guy Priestley I would imagine he wouldn't do it very gently. She's disillusioned and turns to female company. Making a fatal mistake."

"It's a bit of a jump, Jo. I'm not too sure."

She stood up. "If you think about it logically it fits with all that we know about the dead woman. It is a succession of events. Break one link and the chain is broken. Had she had a less sheltered and more sympathetic upbringing, had her husband been a different character, had she been paid some attention by children and friends, not had her head buried in romances and mysteries, had she not been so gullible and lonely. Had her friend not changed her name from Eartha to the romantic Jewel, or her other friend not had a torrid affair with a much younger man. If she had had *someone* apart from this wrong person, Beatrice Pennington would still be alive."

She left the room before Korpanski replied. Something in the previous sentences had sparked an idea off which unsettled her. The Femina Club of Leek. Beatrice had joined in late May. Had she, perhaps, either already known someone in the Club or got to know them after she had joined? Joanna cast her mind back to that chilly May morning when she had first watched Beatrice Pennington push her bike bumpily over the cobbles towards them. Had she recognised anyone?

Joanna didn't think so.

Korpanski caught up with her.

"Let's bring Priestley in for questioning after the briefing We can find out if my theory holds water."

But halfway down the corridor she wavered "Do you see Priestley as a killer, Mike?"

He was nodding. "Potentially, yes."

She didn't offer her own opinion. "Mmm. The problem is, why would he? There isn't a shred of a motive."

Briefings are important from a number of viewpoints. For her, as the Senior Investigating Officer, it was a chance to collate her thoughts, gather in the bright ideas her junior officers might have. For them it was a chance to recap all they knew, pool their own knowledge with their colleagues. And last but not least it was a morale booster.

And they needed it. She took in the rim of faces, took in the fact that they were flopped in their chairs, perched casually on the edges of the table, drinking coffee and looking tired – as though they simply wanted a night off in front of the television with a couple of beers. She read the unmistakable signs of boredom, the lagging eyelids, the fidgeting and the glancing around the room – different from the alert stares at the beginning of the investigation.

So she gave an extra-bright smile and started off with a few words of encouragement which took even Korpanski (who knew her methods only too well) by surprise.

Sometimes it is important to act the part of success with a wide smile and a look of confidence.

"First of all, I want to thank you all and reassure you. I'm so pleased with the progress the investigation is making."

She ignored Korpanski growling in her ear, "Progress?"

"We're piecing together the last months of Beatrice Pennington's life and it is bringing us close to her killer. Before we start I would like to say that Beatrice's two friends are both of the opinion that her secret lover was a woman." There was a surprised reaction around the room but it was muted. She continued. "Sergeant Korpanski and I have our own opinions on this but as it really is pure conjecture it's pretty pointless even putting it in front of you, but suffice it to say that we have the intention of bringing in Guy Priestley to..." She couldn't resist a smile," help us with our enquiries."

She took in the smiles of pleasure that rippled round the room. "For once it means what it says," she said. "We're nowhere near making an arrest. He isn't really a suspect but we do think he may have information which he has, so far, suppressed."

Her eyes alighted on the copper hair of PC Ruthin.

"Paul," she said. "You were detailed to look into her family. What have you got to report?"

Paul Ruthin stood up, puzzlement making his shortsighted eyes flicker. "You asked me to interview the family again. I spoke to Graham and Fiona, both by phone." He frowned. "To be honest, Inspector, they weren't much use at all. They hardly ever see their mother. And when they do," his frown deepened, "they couldn't remember anything specific their mother had said. I asked them who her friends were." He looked around the room. "She's had the same two pals since school and neither of them could even remember their names."

Joanna smiled. "That's helpful."

Ruthin sat down. "I don't see how," he muttered.

But it bore out Joanna's picture of Beatrice Pennington's life. It was building up the same picture that she saw in her own mind.

"It's like they didn't know her," Ruthin added and Joanna nodded in agreement.

Phil Scott stood up next. "You were right about the dress, Ma'am. She didn't usually turn up on her bike like that. She generally wore trousers and trainers and if she was doing anything special she'd get changed."

She'd thought so. Cycling in a skirt is next to impossible. Even as short a distance as from Beatrice's home into her work – a distance of less than three miles. Skirts get tangled up in the spokes. They fly up, giving anyone and everyone a view of your underwear. And compared to lycra cycling shorts, padded in the right places, they are positively uncomfortable. So Beatrice had dressed up specially, chained her bike to the railings outside work. And then what?

She'd been meeting someone.

Slowly she shared her reasoning with the assembled work force.

The questions were, who had Beatrice been meeting, had

she been intending going to work at all or had this been the moment her fantasy had been about to become reality?

"Any luck with the Readers' Group?"

The net was wider now. They had previously looked at men. Now they needed to look at the women.

PC Scott went through every name in the group, men and women. "Teams of us interviewed everyone from the group. We didn't come up with anything. I mean – everyone seemed above board. They expressed their shock at Mrs Pennington's murder and that was that, really. No one had picked up on anything that seemed suspicious or odd. They couldn't shed any light on it. Mrs Pennington's name hadn't been linked to anyone specific in the group either male or female. A couple of them went to *The Quiet Woman* for a drink afterwards sometimes but it was always in a group and Mrs Pennington would talk to any of them."

"What were they like, in general?" Joanna asked curiously.

"Mainly retired people, a couple of young housewives who had children of school age and there was one guy who wanted to be a writer but most of them were very ordinary."

And this, Joanna thought, was the nub of the case. It was the story of everyday folk. Its very ordinariness was what made it so very frustrating but somewhere, amongst the people who had been interviewed, sat a killer.

The phrase wouldn't budge.

An ordinary killer.

And now another direction to take the case had occurred to Joanna. Now the net had widened to include women surely they should be speaking to the two female librarians, Beatrice's colleagues?

She waited until PC Scott had finished speaking before speaking to Mike. He agreed with her.

They'd earned themselves another trip to the library.

Chapter Fourteen

Tuesday, 6th July, 7 a.m.

For Joanna there was one way to clarify her mind, think clearly and shed some light on this case. On a bright morning, early, when the cows are just being led in for milking, the world is still asleep, or drinking coffee and fresh orange juice, when everyone else is listening to breakfast-radio or watching TV a.m. To wake, shower, pack your smart clothes into a pannier and cycle into work. Joanna felt her brain start to put everything in order as she pulled up the hill towards Leek.

Today they must interview Guy Priestley before doing anything else. It would do him no harm to know he was under suspicion. He'd struck her as a cowardly sort who would babble under pressure and he was wise enough to know he would be under suspicion; he'd had the opportunity. The fright might well loosen his tongue. She sighed. But then they would have to release him and search for evidence to support her theory. And then, lastly, there was a task that Joanna didn't want to do. She knew she must speak, informally, to her two cycling buddies, Pagan Harries and Lynn Oakamoor. It was possible that during their cycle rides one of them might have picked up on something which she had missed. Cycling in a group is like that. You ride alongside someone then one of you peels off and you speak to someone else. Everyone is concentrating on their own conversation. People rarely eavesdrop. They are too busy simply keeping up.

A lorry was close behind her and she needed to turn right.

Joanna put her hand out and took a wary glance behind her. She had had one bad encounter with a vehicle, which had left her with a broken wrist, and she was not anxious to repeat the experience. Cyclists run the gauntlet, almost unprotected, of motorists' bad humour or poor driving.

They are terribly vulnerable. When riding her bike Joanna regarded a car-driver as a combatant: she the unarmed gladiator, they wearing a full suit of armour. She negotiated the right turn safely and the lorry roared on.

Luckily the traffic was light and there weren't too many encounters. It was too early for schoolchildren and well ahead of the rush hour. The journey was almost too short and it was with a sense of regret that she turned into the police station. But at least now she had a clear idea of the day ahead.

There were a couple of cars in the car park but no sign of Korpanski's estate. She locked her bike to the railings and went inside.

She had a swift shower and changed into some black trousers and a white shirt with high-heeled black leather boots. She ran a comb through her thick, unruly hair and grinned at herself in the mirror. Today she felt lucky.

Korpanski turned up at eight thirty and he looked good too. He took in the fact that she was already at her desk and gave her a wide grin and a mock, arm-stretching yawn. "You're looking smug," he said, "for so early in the day."

Joanna swivelled her chair round to face him. "I feel smug," she said. "I confess. I'm looking forward to interviewing Guy Priestley."

"Oh?"

"Yes. The thought of making him squirm is positively exhilarating," she said.

Korpanski's eyebrows rose. "So how are you going to play it?"

She leaned forward, chin resting on her fingers, giving Korpanski the full benefit of her clear gaze. "By letting him believe we think he's guilty. I want to scare him into describing his encounters with our dead woman."

Korpanski looked troubled. "You're sure there were some?"

"Oh yes. I'm sure." She jumped to her feet. "Come on. On your feet, Mike. Let's go and haul him in."

Fifty-four, Harbinger Grove looked asleep, with its curtains still drawn. Obviously Priestley was still having his beauty sleep. Joanna smiled. That suited.

"Let's begin this as we mean to continue," she said.

She banged loudly on the door and shouted through the letterbox. There was no response so they walked around the back, through the neat garden with its sets of furniture, across the decking, still damp and slippery with morning dew, and hammered even louder on the back door. They were rewarded by the sight of Guy Priestley in a knee-length towelling dressing gown, peering bleary-eyed through the patio doors. He slid them open.

"Marilyn isn't back yet," he said, squinting at them. "Sometimes she stops off at the shop."

"It isn't Marilyn we want to see," Joanna said calmly. "It's you."

Priestley was anything but calm. He was rattled. "Me?" he squeaked. "Why? What for? I don't know anything. I hardly knew her."

"I suggest you come with us in our car, down to the station."

The first tinge of real panic touched Priestley. "I can't get led away in a *police* car. What'll people think? I haven't *done* anything. I don't *know* anything. I can't help you."

Joanna said nothing. Sometimes it is better to allow the imagination to run free.

Priestley tried again. "How long will I be there?"

"I can't answer that, Mr Priestley."

Standing, half in and half out of the patio doors Korpanski was enjoying the spectacle. He was tensed up, ready to grab Priestley if he made the slightest movement towards resisting arrest. Joanna knew how much he would love to have an excuse to fell him with a rugby tackle.

Priestley scowled at both of them in turn. "Just let me put some clothes on then. Have a wash. Clean my teeth."

The police have the perfect right to stay with a person while they change. Either Joanna or Mike could have accompanied him to the bedroom and the bathroom but Joanna resisted the temptation. They would soon be goading Priestley enough to satisfy both of them. So she merely jerked her head towards the hall and staircase. "Get on with it then," she said. "Don't take too long."

As he ran up the stairs she called after him. "And you might want to leave a note for Marilyn."

For answer Priestley slammed the bedroom door shut.

She watched Priestley in the rear view mirror sitting uncomfortably at Korpanski's side on the back seat. He met her eyes and quickly looked away.

She smiled to herself. She was rather enjoying this.

An interview room was free so they booked it, switched the sign to *In Use* and went through the formalities for the tape recorder. The only fact that was a surprise was Priestley's age. Given as thirty two. She'd thought him younger, particularly with the spiky blonde hair artistically gelled.

It is strange how a person who initially appears handsome can seem to change when you really study their face and watch their confidence evaporate. Never more so than with Guy Priestley. With the light on him and less confidence than a bridegroom on his wedding day his chin seemed to shrink, his mouth harden, his eyes become smaller and less clear and his hands prematurely old, calloused and wrinkled. His accent had slipped without his "tiger" around to impress and as he spoke Joanna began to realise that he had needed the adoration of his lover to boost a fragile ego: an older woman for whom his youth had elevated to the status of super-stud. Oh yes, Joanna reflected. Marilyn Saunders had suited him down to the ground. He was, basically, a very average local boy with dubious looks and a manual job.

What interested her now was what had been in it for her. Sex? A certain spiciness at having a partner who was twenty years younger than herself?

She could have thought about it all day but here was Priestley, waiting for her to begin.

Once she had checked his details for the benefit of the tape recorder she began to direct her attention on his relationship with the dead woman.

"Beatrice was a very close friend of Marilyn's, wasn't she?"

"*She* was. *I* hardly knew her."

"But she must have come round your house sometimes – for a drink or a chat?"

"I suppose so."

"How often?" Mike growled.

Give him his due, Priestley squared up to him admirably. "Dunno," he said, shrugging slightly. "Once or twice, I suppose."

"Oh, I think more than that," Joanna put in quickly.

She was rewarded with a wary look from her interviewee. "It might have been. I don't know."

"How long have you and Marilyn been together?"

"Just over a year. A year and a half. Somewhere round there. I don't know exactly."

"How did you meet?"

Priestley's mouth was dry. He tried to produce some saliva and failed, licked his papery lips with a dry, rasping tongue. Working his mouth then finally rubbing his lips with his fingers. "She was up the pub with a couple of mates. We was on the next table. I chatted her up." He grew suddenly truculent. "What's this got to do with anything?"

They both ignored the outburst. "Fancy older women, do you?" Korpanski said with as much offence as he could muster and a creditable leer.

"Sometimes," Priestley said guardedly. "What's it got to do with you?"

Joanna couldn't stand the sight of him licking the cracked lips. She crossed the room to the sink and filled a plastic cup with some cold water, was tempted to throw it over Priestley but simply handed it to him. He downed it gratefully and Joanna registered the act on the tape recorder. *"The suspect has been given a drink of water."*

With the water Priestley had found a sliver of confidence. He put the cup down deliberately on the desk and dragged in a deep breath, as though drawing in a lungful of smoke from a much-needed cigarette. "Look. What have you brought me here for? I haven't done anything. You can't suspect me of doing away with that old bag?"

"That old bag was the same age as the woman you're shacked up with," Korpanski said brutally.

Priestley blinked. "She was nothing like Marilyn," he said, scowling. "They were poles apart. She was a complete bumpkin with not an ounce of sex appeal about her."

Joanna had waited for this opportunity. "Then why did you make a pass at her?"

"What?"

"You heard. Why did you make her think you fancied her?"

Priestley simply gaped for a full minute before turning a vague shade of puce. It didn't suit him. "What do you mean," he asked slowly. "I didn't..." He looked from one to the other, trying to work out exactly what they knew – and how. "It was her."

Joanna simply regarded him steadily, her head on one side.

"It was just a game," he said grumpily. "Marilyn put me up to it. Old fatty hadn't had a man after her in years. Not since old-fart-Arthur had proposed."

Joanna felt a deep distaste for the fact that Beatrice Pennington's so-called *friend* had been the one to suggest the malicious trick. "So it was a blood sport to you, Guy?"

Priestley didn't even attempt to give an answer. Korpanski's muttered "cruel" gave him the clear message he was outflanked.

Joanna decided it was time to play at being an adorer of Guy Priestley's.

"Tell me," she said, opening her eyes very wide and staring at the young man. "Did you find Beatrice attractive?"

Priestley struggled to decide whether she was mocking him or whether it was a serious question. He looked back at her suspiciously.

"I – um." Then the truth burst out. "You must be joking."

"So tell us exactly what happened."

"I told you. Marilyn put me up to it."

"So?"

"Beattie came round a bit early one evening. Marilyn was tired. She was still in bed. I went and woke her up and she said, *'Give old Beattie a thrill, lover-boy'*.

So I did."

Joanna simply raised her eyebrows as a prompt. The thing was she could imagine Marilyn Saunders saying the exact words. Even picture her expression as she said them. Half casual, half spiteful.

"So I came back downstairs again, said that Marilyn was still asleep. Beattie was sitting on the settee so I go and sit right next to her, really close. I started fumbling her, said things to her, about always having fancied her like mad, but that Marilyn was always watching. Really I was in stitches inside. I couldn't believe she'd take it seriously but she did. Poor, dumb Beattie with her podgy moon-face and stupid ways. She couldn't see that I was just mucking around. I even started snogging her like she was Britney Spears or someone. *And* she fell for it all. The whole bloody lot."

The arrogance of youth.

"And then?" Korpanski asked roughly.

"Then nothing. Marilyn came downstairs. She acted sort of suspicious and I kind of acted guilty. But when we were in the kitchen later on together me and Marilyn had a laugh about it. A really good laugh."

Joanna felt slightly sick.

"And then what?"

"It got embarrassing. She started ringing me up. Sending me letters. The old fool." The contempt in his voice was cruel. Joanna would remember this if she, in turn, was expected to show Priestley any mercy. Her dislike was deepening by the minute.

"Then she started being a real nuisance. She came round a couple of times when she knew Marilyn'd be at work. I had to fight her off. It was horrible. It got really disgusting."

"When was this?"

"Round about Christmas-time. She sent me this really stupid card about Santa could come up *her* chimney any time. I chucked it in the bin. It was getting beyond a joke."

"And then?"

Give Priestley his due – he did look regretful now. "Some time early in February, it was getting ridiculous. She was writing me letters, really silly ones, all about waiting for someone like me all her life. Complete rubbish." His disdain was absolute. "She'd come round in the most saucy outfits, red satin stuff and..." Priestley gave a genuine shudder. "I couldn't hack it. I had to tell her that I'd been having her on, that it was a set-up, that I didn't fancy her."

Joanna could picture the scene all too well. "What was her reaction?"

Priestley did look ashamed now. "She started crying, saying I'd been really cruel and that she'd loved me and that she thought I'd loved her. It was awful. I felt..." He shook his head slowly, kept his eyes down. "I felt terrible. I couldn't believe she'd been so taken in. I ended up putting my arm around her and kissing her, telling her she was a lovely person. And then Marilyn walked in on us."

"And took it seriously?"

Priestley nodded, shame-faced.

This was interesting – a new angle to the story which neither of them had anticipated.

"What was *her* reaction?"

Again Priestley shook his head. "She was really silly about it. She thought I really had been up to something. I can tell you, Inspector, she threw a wobbly at me. She bloody hit me, started screaming."

"Was this witnessed by Beatrice?"

"Yeah. She saw Marilyn weren't pleased. She bolted."

"And then afterwards?"

"I couldn't seem to convince Marilyn." Priestley suddenly realised what he was saying. "I mean – I don't think she had anything to do with it. She just... She just didn't believe me," he finished lamely.

Joanna glanced at Mike. Here was someone else with a motive for wanting Beatrice Pennington dead. They had seen the way Marilyn Saunders had doted on her young lover. It had given her a status and mystique. But at the same time this aspect made her vulnerable. Her humiliation in such a small town would be public and cruel if he left her – particularly if it was for another woman of her own age who had previously been counted as one of her best friends.

She was silent while both Korpanski and Priestley watched her.

At last she lifted her head. "Tell me, Guy, how much do you love Marilyn?"

He studied her back. "That's a funny question," he said. "I don't know how to answer it."

"Honestly, I suggest."

"I'm happy enough with her for the time being."

"And then?"

"If it didn't suit I wouldn't be there." He swallowed. "Look – if it was a guy with a younger bird no one'd bat an eyelid. Just because it's the other way round people think it's weird. It's no big deal. Understand? It's no big deal."

Joanna nodded. She had not read Priestley wrongly but correctly. Moving in with Marilyn Saunders had seemed like a good idea at the time.

She watched him keenly. "Did you kill Beatrice Pennington?"

Priestley looked really scared now. "No, I didn't. Please believe me. Why would I?"

She kept her eyes trained on him then stood up, terminating the interview into the tape recorder. "You're free to go," she said, "for the time being."

Priestley looked suspicious at his freedom.

He stood up quickly, almost knocking over the chair, gave a swift glance at the door, then at Korpanski who was staring him out.

Then he bolted. Towards the door, threw it open and was gone.

Joanna couldn't help smiling. He was so like a frightened rabbit. "So what did you think of that, Mike?"

"Interesting."

"My feelings exactly."

Chapter Fifteen

So they had learned the answer to one anomaly at least. They knew now why the Ann Summers underwear had been new, left in the drawer and forgotten about. Beatrice had bought it for the benefit of Guy – who in the words of Rhett Butler – couldn't give a damn.

But for now it meant another trip up the High Street, calling first at the library. They climbed the stone steps with a distinct feeling of déjà vu. Who would have thought that one simple murder would have proved such a tricky nut to crack?

They pushed open the library doors and left them swinging behind them, started climbing the stone stairs. At the top stood a thin, middle-aged man who reminded Joanna vaguely of Arthur Pennington. Same type. He watched them climb with an air of involvement, his eyes stuck on them. Instinctively Joanna knew he must be Adrian Grove.

"Excuse me," she said as she reached the top, "you're not Adrian Grove, are you?"

Pale blue eyes focused on her. "That's right," he said. "That's who I am." He was one of those men who have a prominent Adam's apple in a skinny neck. His hair was mousy, thin and wispy across a bright pink pate. He must have caught the sun on his holiday.

Joanna introduced herself and Mike to him and Grove gave a tangible sigh of relief. "I'm so glad *you're* looking into it," he said. "I've seen you on the television a year or so ago. When the little girl disappeared from the school. I thought you were..." He blushed. Joanna felt sorry for his acute embarrassment.

"Is there somewhere private we can talk, Mr Grove?"

"Yes. Yes. Of course. Let me just go and tell the girls."

He scuttled off through the double glass doors. They caught a glimpse of Lisa Chorley and Kerry Beardmore staring at them then Grove bustled back out and ushered them through a side door into what was obviously a staff room.

It was barely furnished with drab walls but the furniture was cheery, two pale sofas and an ash coffee table. In the corner was a sink and tea and coffee making equipment. "Would you like a coffee?"

"Yes. Thank you. That would be nice."

"Tea with two sugars", Korpanski said shortly before settling on the farther sofa.

They waited until the mugs were in front of them before Joanna opened the questioning. "You've just come back from your holiday?"

"Yes. I've been walking – in Italy. I rang – just to make sure everything was going all right and they told me about poor Beattie." His eyes were watering as he spoke and he brushed them with the back of his hand. "I can't believe it, Inspector. I just can't. I would have thought her the last person in the world who would be murdered. She didn't seem…"

Korpanski butted in rudely. "So what sort of person *would* you expect to see murdered, Mr Grove?"

"Oh I don't know." Understandably Grove was rattled by the question. Joanna felt annoyed that Korpanski had confronted the librarian so soon in the interview. She shot him a warning look and he gave her one of his bland, innocent smiles back.

But she knew he'd got the message.

"Someone more glamorous," Grove came up with. "Someone who has an adventurous life."

Joanna knew then. She just knew that Grove read spy thrillers.

"Did you know anyone who might have disliked Mrs Pennington?"

"No." Grove stopped short and considered the question. "No. I can't say as I do. She wasn't the sort of person you'd take strong feeling against, if you see what I mean. She was easygoing. Pleasant, polite, private."

"Were you and she good friends?"

"Oh yes." Again the librarian stopped short. "Well – I mean – friends as colleagues of course."

No impropriety was what he was suggesting.

"I think I see." Korpanski was at it again, antagonising a potential witness.

"You mean you had no – special friendship?"

"Certainly not," Grove said indignantly.

"But you are divorced?"

"I am. Through no fault of my own."

A prig too. "But Mrs Pennington was a happily married woman."

"Was she?"

The rhetoric seemed to confuse Grove. His Adam's apple bobbed like a Halloween fruit as he swallowed. "I'm sure she was," he said. But there was a hint of doubt in his voice which both police picked up on.

"Good." Joanna treated him to one of her warmest smiles.

"How long had you worked together?"

"Around five years. We weren't close, you understand, but we were friends."

"Did you go out socially ever?"

"Only at the Christmas party."

"And were husbands and wives invited to that?"

"No – we never do. I'm on my own and I think out of respect for my situation we decided a few years ago not to invite partners."

Grove was reminding Joanna even more of Arthur Pennington. The same pedantic and wordy way of speaking.

"We usually go to Den Engels," he added irrelevently.

Den Engels, the Belgian Bar, good, plentiful food and wonderful beers. It was one of Matthew's favourite eating/drinking holes. Joanna had a sudden vivid vision of him with a brown beer bottle in his hand, grinning and waving at her, shouting over the noise. She savoured the snapshot. It had been the venue of such happy nights.

And again, she promised herself. Again. They will come again. A few more days and he would be home. But this silent promise was dangerous. It gave her a terrible impatience with this case. It should be simple. She should have arrested someone by now, charged them with the murder. This was not some complex case where an unknown psychopath had gone berserk. This was a simple domestic drama. Beatrice had known her killer, as he or she had known her. She had entered his or her car willingly, maybe smiled at her killer as she had faced him or her, possibly even continued to smile as the fingers had fastened around her throat and squeezed the life out of her before dumping her body under the hedge on the moors.

So why hadn't she found the killer?

Answer:

Because Beatrice had not been what she had seemed. She had led a very hidden life, concealed from everyone – even those who considered they knew her well and especially from her family. Beatrice had preserved her secrets to the grave and beyond. Only when they had exposed all the dark corners of her complex life would she know who had killed her.

Beatrice had not confided in anyone – merely dropped the tiniest of hints to her friends who had not been curious enough to follow them up. So she had preserved her secrecy.

Already, so early on in her interview of yet another of Beatrice's colleagues she was aware of the blind tunnel ahead with no glimmer of light. So she fumbled and stumbled.

"When did you last see Beatrice?"

"The Saturday morning just before I left to go on holiday. I bumped into her shopping in Leek. She was in one of the shops along the street."

"Which one?" Joanna asked idly, more to keep the conversation moving than with any real interest.

"That nice handbag shop halfway up Derby Street."

"I see. How did she seem?"

"Her usual self."

"Was she alone?"

"Well – yes – apart from Mrs Pirtek – the lady who..."

"Yes, I know she owns the shop and was a friend of Beatrice's."

Grove looked at her expectantly, waiting for the next question. The trouble was Joanna couldn't think of any other questions to ask Adrian Grove. He seemed pleasant, eager to please. Innocent was the word that sprang to mind. She couldn't sense any evil lying beneath his bland exterior. *Sense?* She could practically *hear* Korpanski scoffing at this most unscientific instinct. Maybe it was time she stopped depending on it so much.

They returned to the main library to speak to the two remaining librarians but even as they both looked up it all seemed too fantastic. Lisa Chorley was a young woman, attractive in her midriff-exposing jeans and t-shirt. She wore stud silver earrings, had long, silky dark hair. Joanna simply couldn't imagine her having some sort of lesbian affair with the deceased.

Maybe Kerry Beardmore was a more promising candidate.

Kerry was a few years younger than Beatrice. Plump too, with an innocent, motherly face, kind and doughy. In fact from certain angles she could have been mistaken for her dead colleague. They settled down again in the staff room and for once Joanna didn't quite know where to begin. She felt swamped with the idea that she was floundering blindly in a sticky bog. She looked helplessly at Mike. This was completely uncharacteristic but Korpanski, with surprising sensitivity, opened the interview.

"Married, are you, love?"

Joanna winced. Not quite her style of questioning. But it was better then nothing.

"Yeah." Kerry shared that same, eager-to-please expression with her friend.

"Got kids?"

You had to hand it to Korpanski – he had a certain blunt directness in the way he conducted his interviews.

"I've got two. A daughter and a son who – well – he isn't terribly well."

Joanna took over. "Sorry to hear that."

Kerry smiled. "Thanks. He's a bit of a tie. I mean – I adore him. Love him to bits but sometimes – well – let's just say, he's difficult."

"I expect Beatrice was quite understanding about your son?"

"She was." No mistaking the warmth here. "She was really lovely about him. You see – lots of people just don't understand. He comes out with things. But Beattie. Well – she took it all in his stride. She was a lovely person, you know. I mean – I've read in the papers just the bare bones of her life. The fact that she was married, worked here, had two children. It doesn't describe her at all. She was wonderful. Very kind and generous." Kerry's eyes began to fill up. She sniffed and tugged a tissue from the pocket of her cardigan. "And she was so dedicated to the Readers' Group. She was always looking for good books to introduce the readers to. Some classics, some bestsellers and other authors of whom no one had heard. That was such a special thing she did. And she never put anyone down. She'd always listen to their point of view."

Kerry's face changed. "The thing was – people weren't always so nice to her."

"Who do you mean?" Joanna asked curiously.

"Her son and daughter for one thing. Never bothered remembering her birthday. And Mothers' Day – well 'forget it, K,' she said to me. 'I'd faint if I got a card or a bunch of flowers or something. Crack me up it would."

"And her husband?" Joanna prompted.

Kerry Beardmore considered for a moment. "He wasn't bad," she said. "Just a bit long-winded. A bit boring. If you gave him half the chance he'd spout on for hours about law and order, politics, public toilets. Anything. And his voice never changed tone. He always spoke in the same way. No expression. Just flat. I found him very hard to listen to. No – I don't say there's anything *wrong* with Arthur. It's just there isn't very much right with him either." She forgot herself for a moment in a girlish giggle, which she quickly suppressed with a hand over her mouth and round eyes.

It was time for confidences. The librarian was wearing a low-cut, v-necked short-sleeved black woollen sweater. She leaned far enough forward for Joanna to have full view of a plump and extended cleavage. "I was glad when she found someone else."

"Even if it led to her death?"

Oddly enough Kerry Beardmore didn't answer this. She merely regarded both Joanna and then Mike with a perfectly expressionless face.

It was time to 'put the screws in'. "Come on, Kerry, you must have had some idea who this mystery lover was?"

Another giggle. "At first I thought it was Adrian," she said. "Then – just before Christmas she got very over-confident – very high-and-mighty. Almost flaunting herself. And then she changed. She got very secretive. Almost ashamed. I came in here one lunchtime and she was scribbling something. A letter I think. She covered it up really quickly with her hand and stuffed it into her handbag but I was very curious."

"So?" Mike asked bluntly.

"I didn't *read* it," Kerry said quickly. "I didn't. I just caught the odd word. I couldn't help it," she said defensively. "I couldn't. I didn't *deliberately* set out to read it but I couldn't help seeing that it was a love letter. There was no name at the top but it was full of romantic phrases. Things like '*When I think of you*' ...and stuff like that."

"Go on."

"I'd seen letters like that in her bag before. Quite often. She always used blue paper and envelopes, the long ones. And the envelopes were thick, as though there were sheets and sheets of writing."

"Who were they addressed to?"

Kerry took in a deep breath. "They weren't," she said. "There was no name on them. She must have filled it in later."

She must have realised that Joanna didn't believe her because she protested again. "Honestly – and in a way I was glad. I thought Beattie deserved to keep her secrets. If she'd wanted us to know who her lover was she would have said."

"So what *did* she say?"

The woman looked flustered. "Only that we were in for a shock one of these days."

"What did you think she meant?"

"I don't know. Beattie was a funny one. She half-lived in fantasyland. I suppose part of me wondered if any of it was true."

"Go on," Joanna prompted.

"When she left work that night I saw her walk past her bike."

Sometimes ordinary phrases can appear momentous.

"Why would she do that?"

"I asked her."

"And?" Joanna simply couldn't see where this was heading.

"She said 'I've got a letter to deliver.'"

Still Joanna couldn't see the significance.

"*Deliver*," Kerry said triumphantly.

Then the penny dropped and the slot machine started whirring. Cogs and spindles cranking around.

"So whoever this mystery person is lives or works near enough for her to walk rather than take her bike."

"Exactly."

They both stood up. "Thank you," Joanna said. "Thank you."

They left the Nicholson Institute a little more enlightened than when they had walked in.

So they returned to the little handbag shop on the High

Street. But this time Joanna had no intention of playing friendly with her. No more acting soft. She was beginning to feel angry and impatient with a casual and uninterested public.

She entered the shop in truculent mood and didn't make any attempt to return Jewel's smile. "I think you'd better put the *Closed for half an hour* sign up," Joanna said. "It's time you were a bit more honest with me."

Jewel said nothing but raised her eyebrows, marched to the door, turned the sign around, put the lock down and marched back to her post behind the counter, all the time keeping her eyes on Joanna with an air of frank defiance, waiting for the detective to speak.

"You knew that Guy Priestley had been 'making up' to Beatrice, didn't you?" Joanna accused.

She got the distinct feeling that Jewel's response was one of relief.

"It was nothing," she said quickly, studying her fingernails, which had been freshly rebuilt, squared off and painted white. French fingernails. "*Nothing*. Do you understand me? There was no harm in it. It was just a laugh. No one took it seriously."

"Except Beatrice."

"Well – that was the trouble. She hadn't much experience of that sort of thing. I mean it's obvious Guy's quite a hunk. Another woman would have been on her guard but Beattie. It just made us laugh. And she got quite *up herself.* Know what I mean?"

"Unfortunately I do," Joanna said. "I know exactly what you mean."

The picture was a cruel one, the three of them – her two best friends and Guy all laughing behind their hands at poor old Beatrice. Joanna sat down opposite the false friend and leaned across the counter. "Not much of a friend, are you?"

Jewel looked away, out of the window, at a couple of shoppers who were trying the door. No mention today of selling Joanna a handbag. Jewel Pirtek was a woman on the defensive. Joanna was curious to know how she would excuse her disloyalty.

"It was just a joke."

Joanna studied her face. There was a trace of shame there, giving her normal glamour a tinge of sadness that made her look suddenly vulnerable.

She continued looking

So did she really suspect one friend of murdering another?

No. It was no motive.

"Tell me about it," Joanna prompted, keeping one eye on Korpanski for his reaction.

"I think..."

"Never mind what you think. Your *friend* is dead. Understand? I believe that somewhere along the line this cruel practical joke contributed to her murder."

"No it didn't."

"Sure of that, are you?" Mike had stepped forward and even from ten paces Joanna could feel the heat of his anger.

But Jewel Pirtek was Korpanski's equal. She stood up. "Yes, I am bloody sure. It was just a bit of fun."

"Really?"

"Yes, Sergeant. Really."

It was up to Joanna to take the heat out of the situation. "Tell me about it."

"Well it was obvious that Beatrice was as jealous as hell of Marilyn's success with Guy. She was always making little comments about him like how lucky she was and what a nice body he had." Jewel gave a frank look over her half-moon bifocals. "At first it really surprised us. It was so out of character. It just wasn't her at all. We thought it was funny. And then we got sort of sick of it so Marilyn said if Guy came over all strong it would shut her up and she'd stop going on about him."

"Was she worried? Did she see Beatrice as a potential rival?"

"No. I kept telling her..."

Which meant she *had* been worried.

"So Guy did pounce on her. Did it have the desired effect?"

"No. It made her worse. She was convinced he fancied her rotten."

"At this point did Marilyn believe that Guy was attracted to Beatrice?"

The first sign of hesitation. "No."

Korpanski and Joanna simply waited.

"She told Guy it had to finish."

"Then?"

"She came across them together. It was a shock. I mean – she'd never really trusted Guy. She knew what he was like and that one day he'd move on to..." Jewel Pirtek made a wry face "fresh pastures. She just hadn't thought it would be with someone like Beatrice. It was that *bloody* adoration," she said, frowning. "He just fed on it. Like all men."

Korpanski's eyes opened wide.

"Is it possible," Joanna asked slowly, "that Marilyn was jealous enough to – ?"

"No. No. Surely not. I mean."

But Joanna could tell that the thought had crossed Jewel's mind.

Chapter Sixteen

Joanna had put this off for as long as she dared. Now she simply had to do it even though she already knew it could lose her two very good friends. But she knew from bitter experience that the minute she donned her policeman's helmet even friends could leak away like the sand in an egg timer. Not for the first time her career threatened to come between her and people she both liked and respected.

But it was her job and she owed it to the unfortunate Beatrice. She sighed so heavily Korpanski glanced across at her. "You all right, Jo?"

"Yes – and no," she said.

He bent back towards the computer screen, avoided looking at her and asked casually, "Anything I can help with?"

She reassured him quickly. "It's nothing to do with Matthew. I was just thinking I should talk to some of the other members of the cycling club. It's just possible..." She didn't need to say any more.

Korpanski stood up. All six feet plus of him. "I'll come with you."

She smiled at him, feeling a sudden rush of affection for the burly sergeant. Mike Korpanski would always do this, blunder into situations without realising it was the delicate touch which sometimes produced results. Delicate was not an adjective she would ever use to describe him. Yet he meant well. And sometimes his blunderbuss methods did produce results. But it is strange, she reflected, this relationship which builds up when two colleagues work closely together, even two such contrasting personalities. He knew her methods and she knew his.

She put a restraining hand on his arm. "I think it would make less waves if I went alone," she said. "He who hunts alone, and all that?"

"OK."

Lynn Oakamoor lived in a neat house on a modern development. Basically curving streets of individually designed brick-built houses, each with their own short drive and garage, neat front gardens sporting geraniums, miniature trees and some very imaginative stonework. It was typical Middle-England. Lynn and her husband had worked hard to afford this place and they kept it immaculately. A well-polished Fiat Uno sat on a drive you could have eaten your dinner from. As Joanna parked the police car close to the kerb she saw a movement at the window. Her friend was in. What she dreaded as she walked up the drive and squeezed passed the car was her friend's initial smile being replaced by a hostile glare when she told her the real reason for her visit.

Lynn answered the door quickly and with pure delight. "Joanna."

She quickly disillusioned her. "Hello, Lynn. Look – I'm sorry. This isn't a social call."

The surprise on her friend's face was almost as hurtful as the raised eyebrows. "Oh. Well come in anyway." She led her through the lounge, tossing back a comment. "So. I assume it's about Beatrice Pennington?"

"Yes." With relief Joanna took her seat in the UPVC conservatory furnished in Indian cane and cheese plants. "Lynn," she said frankly. "We're not getting on as well as we'd hoped. To put it bluntly, we're stuck."

"Poor Joanna," her friend said dryly. "Must be awful. So how do you think I can help?"

"Go over the conversations you had with her," Joanna pleaded. "At some point she *must* have said something of significance to you."

Lynn was quickly on the defensive. "Why me? She's just as likely to have said something to you." Already the distance between them was widening.

"I know what she's said to me," Joanna said. "I've gone over and over everything. I couldn't think of anything. That's why I came to you."

Her words mollified the situation a bit. Lynn leaned right back in the chair and let out a hearty sigh.

"You did *listen* to her, didn't you?"

"Oh yes. But it was nothing very interesting. She talked about men being insensitive. Said that women listened more, that they were gentler, less brash. I think she said something about touching." She screwed her face up. "It was just mumbo jumbo. Something about the power of touching. To be honest, Jo, I can't stand all this sort of rubbish. I must admit. I did switch off. She was full of beliefs and trust, a feeling that the world was really not such a bad place as we all thought. I can't remember *exactly* the words she used but you know the sort of thing."

"Anything else?"

"Oh, Jo. Not that I can remember."

"Did she say anything about her husband?"

"She *mentioned* him."

"In what vein?"

"Just that she found him boring, that there were no surprises left, that there was nothing hidden from her, that she'd got to the end of his character..." Lynn rolled her eyes. "Whatever *that's* supposed to mean. She wasn't exactly deep herself. She spoke a lot about losing weight, about the life she was going to lead when she got to her target weight, how fit she felt, clothes. Confidence. New life. She talked some twaddle about love."

"What sort of thing?"

"Complete tripe. Real romantic stuff. Almost Mills and Boon-y. You know the sort of thing, knees trembling, tingling feeling all over her body, heightened awareness."

"We think she was in love with another woman," Joanna said reluctantly.

Lynn opened her blue eyes wide. "Really? She didn't strike me as a lesbian. She seemed. I assumed she was hetero. You knew her as well or as little as we did. What did *you* think?"

Joanna thought back to a rainy Sunday morning in the

middle of June. Beatrice had arrived early. They had been the first ones there and she had sensed Beatrice was in the mood for a confidence. But she had arrived depressed. She had heard nothing from Matthew and the miscarriage had suddenly and inexplicably seemed terribly sad. Maybe it had been the hormones but listening to Beatrice's chatter had been beyond her so she had straddled her bike and stared in the direction from where she knew the others would come, hoping Beatrice would stay silent. Then she had turned around and read her eyes. Brown cow eyes, very appealing. Something very happy and excited in her face and she had felt guilty that she had been so wrapped up in her own problems. Joanna frowned away the unexpectedly vivid picture. Beatrice had seemed fulfilled – and dumb. Dumb in the American sense of bordering on stupid. No. That wasn't right. Dumb in the sense of being animal, manipulated and used, lacking control over her fate.

And now the memory provoked the same feeling of discomfort. Joanna stood up quickly. "Did she say *anything* that might give us a clue?"

"No," Lynn said. "If she had I would have been the first to get in touch with you."

She sounded hurt.

"Well – if you do recall anything else you will ring me, won't you? You know my number."

"Yes."

"And you're still coming on Sunday?"

"Yes. I'll be there." But her friend's voice had chilled into formality.

All sorts joined the cycling club. Sport is the great unifier. Pagan, in contrast to Lynn, lived in a tiny terraced house with her four children and even as Joanna lifted her hand to knock on the battered front door she could hear noise. Lots of it. Children shouting, pop music thumping, the sound of a washing machine whirring bronchitically.

She had to bang loudly to provoke any response. Pagan answered the door abruptly, a pair of eyes peering from behind her. "Joanna," she said with genuine amazement. "What on earth brings you here? Come in. Come in."

There was as much contrast between the two houses as there was in the two women. Pagan's was a tip. Washing strewn across the backs of chairs, books, fallen open on the floor, the TV blaring out. From upstairs thumped the thud of a bass guitar. There was not one spare inch of space. And two teenagers, disproportionately large compared to the size of the room, lolling across the chairs filled the airspace too. The house was filled with the scent of old fried food and Joanna spied a plate tucked underneath the settee.

"Come in the kitchen," Pagan said, vaguely searching around for a spare chair. "We can at least talk in there."

Joanna followed her into the tiny kitchen, messily painted green with pine units. Every cupboard door was wide open so you could see into fat-stained shelves. There were piles of dishes over every surface. Joanna parked herself on one of the kitchen chairs and as concisely as possible repeated the conversation she had just had with Lynn Oakmaoor. Pagan was less resentful at being questioned and her dark eyes opened wide in sympathy. It struck Joanna that she badly wanted to help.

And yet – this too can hamper police investigations. It was no use putting ideas into her head. She wanted the whole truth only. Pagan chewed her lip for a minute as Joanna stumbled through her lines.

"I liked Beattie," she said. "But she was the most frightful prude, you know?"

"No?"

Pagan puffed out a long sigh. "Ridiculous really. So screwed up about sex."

"Really?"

Pagan smothered her giggle with her hand. "Oh yes. She asked me all sorts of weird and wonderful things."

"Like what?"

"Sex toys, same-sex sex, how women managed it." She gave a throaty laugh. "Why the hell she was asking me I

really don't know. My life is devoid of anything *that* interesting. All *my* energy is taken up with managing this." She
waved her arms around her. She met Joanna's eyes with a
frank stare of her own and a hint of shame at her levity. "I'm
all right if I forget she's dead," she said. "I can cope then. If
I laugh I'm fine. It's when I think that some bastard. Oh
excuse me but that's what he is. When I think he's just
killed her I get really angry. I want to hit and punch."

"Who?"

"Him."

"Do you know who *him* is?"

"I just know he's young. And I also know that he made a
fool of her and that she knew it. She felt stupid."

Joanna was giving away nothing. Although she could
guess who this person was she said nothing, simply, "Do
you have a name?"

"No. I just have a picture of some arrogant bloke having
a laugh at her expense. Luckily for her she met someone
else."

Joanna was listening with every single fibre of her body.
"Someone else?" she said casually.

"A woman who healed her with her sympathy and kindness and the laying on of hands."

*The laying on of hands and the casting out of devils. The
question remained. Who killed her? Her jealous husband, this
young lover – or someone connected with him? The woman
who had finally shown her such kindness – or someone connected with her?*

The circle spun, expanding at the same time.

It was obvious that Pagan's way of thinking was nearer to
Beattie Pennington's than was Lynn's. "Do you know who
she is, this woman?"

"Just bits. It was obvious that Beattie didn't want people
to know. I know for a fact that she has warm brown eyes. I
know she is a professional woman whom Beattie met
through her work."

"Whose work? Beatrice's or the woman?"

"The woman's, I think." Pagan frowned. "That was the impression I got."

"I know that she was seeing her during the week that she last came out cycling with us, the week of the 13th of June."

"Do you know the day? The place? The time?"

"No. Only that it was sometime that week.. I think she said she had an appointment."

"Try and remember. Was it hair? A dentist?"

"Wait a minute. She was talking about her excitement, that she was going to buy herself something new."

"Something new," Joanna echoed. "Something new."

Something old, something new, something borrowed, something blue. Blue as in Beatrice Pennington's lips.

She needed to get hold of her diary.

A row was breaking out at Corinne Angiotti's house. Pete was standing, facing her, a letter in his hand. One of *the* letters. He'd found the drawer in her desk at home where she had put the overflow from her surgery.

"I've thought many things about you, Corinne," he jeered. "I know you're not over-keen on sex. I know some days you look at me as though you can't stand me. I know you despise me and dislike me for dragging you here when you were doing so well in your London clinic. I just didn't think you'd stoop to this."

"I haven't stooped to anything," Corinne defended herself. "The woman is a deranged patient. Obsessed and sick. Lonely and misguided."

"She's also dead."

Corinne said nothing but regarded her husband calmly.

He, on the other hand, was red and sweating, his emotions gaining control. "It strikes me, Corinne, that I don't know you, do I?"

"So what do you think you have just found out about me?"

"That you have been carrying on some sort of affair with another woman and on top of that she is a patient of yours. History repeats itself."

"Don't be ridiculous."

"It says here." Pete Angiotti was beside himself. His eyes were bulging with fury. *"When you touch me I am alive."*

He looked up. "I don't know how you can be so bare-faced as to deny it when it says it all here."

"I told you," she said coldly. "The woman was a deranged patient. That's all. A nutcase. A sad woman. Misguided and deluded. She believed herself in love with me and that I returned this love. It was pathetic. I simply felt sorry for her." She felt tired and defeated. "I kept trying to return her to reality. I kept pointing out that one day she would feel really stupid about it but all she did was to put various out-fits on and make appointments. I was frightened, Pete. I thought she might just convince someone from the General Medical Council that I'd made advances to her."

"That is just the sort of explanation I would expect you to make. And now she's dead and can neither confirm nor deny it so I'll never know."

It was this that finally defeated her. Pete would never believe her version. Therefore she would have this sitting on her shoulder – for ever. It struck her then how very tired she was. For months now her nightmare had been that Beatrice Pennington would make a complaint to the General Medical Council and they would spend years inves-tigating. All that time she might be suspended from prac-tice and the newspapers would have a field day – as they had for her husband. What a fine pair they were – the teacher husband who assaulted a pupil and the doctor wife who has an affair with a patient. Both abusing their positions of trust – except she hadn't. But the public have scant sympa-thy for professionals who mistreat the very people they are paid to protect. This small town would quickly turn hostile. Who would believe *her*? Husband and wife would be tarred with the same brush? She had watched doctors have their careers ruined by just such patients and wondered. Maligned? Guilty? Innocent? Who would ever know? And the pundits are right. Mud does stick. So hard that when it is removed it takes some of your skin away. You can never be the same again. How many times had she gone over and over each early consultation and wondered how she might have turned away the flood of emotion. What had *she* done to invite this devotion? Because if she did not know then it could happen again and again and again.

She never would be free of the shackles of a deluded patient's devotion.

Absorbed, obsessed, deluded. Beatrice had been only the first. A lonely woman who had clung to the one person who had dished out sympathy in great big dollops.

But it is part of the job, she might protest.

If she couldn't even convince her own husband who should know and trust her above all others what chance did she have with a wider audience? None.

"Why did you keep the letters?" he was saying.

Why had she? She didn't know. Only that they were beautiful. And dangerous. More poetic than anything that had ever been written to her or about her. In a subtle way they had given her more than she could have wanted, praised her above all others, elevated her. Canonised her even. Some devil in her had not wanted to to destroy them. Why not? Because they were beautiful? Because they were dangerous? Because they were *evidence*? The only tangible proof of the truth behind the fantasy.

Because they were all three. They had told her things she had *wanted* to be told.

"Did you ever write back to her?"

She had. Not love letters but curt notes explaining, as she thought, the principle of the doctor/patient relationship. Corinne looked at her husband. She would have loved him to have put his arms around her, hug her to him and tell her it would be all right. But this was as silly as wishing for the moon to be made of cream cheese and have a smiling man who lived in it. In his way Pete was another Arthur Pennington. Unaware.

Corinne looked at her husband and knew she could never begin to explain. He would never understand, never sympathise because he was at the centre of his universe and she was too far on the periphery to make impact.

Then she understood something else. This was not news to him. He had known before. This was a well-rehearsed scene, one he had played over a few times in his imagination. His shock was not new but second-hand. Thoughts began to tumble faster through her mind. He had been reading the letters long before she had brought them home from the tightly-jammed drawer in her surgery. He had seen them there and derived some sort of vicarious thrill from his secret knowledge. "How long have you been reading the letters for?"

"For a while."

Yes, now she thought of it Pete had seemed to find any excuse to call at the surgery and wait for her.

"Why didn't you say anything before?"

"I thought I'd watch you. After all – it's easy to fake things, deny the truth. I wasn't sure just what was going on."

"And what do you think now?"

Something in him seemed to crumple. "I don't know," he said. "I simply don't know."

Corinne was amazed. "You can't really believe I'd embarked on some sort of affair with one of my patients, can you?"

The mean side of her husband came to the fore then. "Well something was keeping that woman's fantasies going."

So he believed the worst. Pete's eyes narrowed and he looked at her with a tightness around his mouth.

That was when Corinne Angiotti felt the first stirrings of real fear. Pete was her husband. He knew her better than anyone. Or at least he should do. Beatrice Pennington was dead. The woman who could so easily have wrecked her career and ruined her life. Who would employ a woman doctor who had had an affair with her patient? Men were struck off for the like. It only remained for the first really high profile case of a woman to come to the fore. Equal opportunities? Equal trouble.

What a motive.

Beatrice was dead and looking at the suspicion in Pete's eyes she could see he believed she *could* have killed her. Simple really. She eyed him. No one but he knew about this. All right, stupidly she had kept the letters. Silly – but letters could be burnt. The real question was, could Pete be silenced?

"I didn't kill her," she said.

"Prove it."

Corinne fell quiet and thought. Nasty suspicious little worms were boring into her brain. Pete was a jealous, unstable man, prone to fits of petty jealousy and irrational behaviour. People knew that. And he had left his previous job under an ugly cloud. No one liked a teacher who was accused of suddenly losing his temper and assaulting a pupil. No one would believe *him* either. If push came to shove who would be believed? She – or him? It would be an interesting contest. What if…?

"Did *you* kill her, Pete?"

"Oh, I know what you're doing," he said nastily. "Trying to turn the tables on to me. It won't work."

"Give me the letters," she said.

"I've hidden them."

So – ultimately can marriage degenerate into this? Suspicion and hatred. The complete inability to communicate without pointing fingers. And finally – can it descend into fear?

Joanna was back in the station, reading through the statements. Arthur Pennington's, the colleagues. Her two friends. And into the picture swam someone else. Someone else. Someone who lived near the library, near enough for her to prefer to walk rather than cycle round there. She had worn a smart dress that day in honour of this person, this woman. She believed this woman loved her back. Maybe she had.

Why had the consequences been so great? Why had Beatrice died? Had it been similar to the Guy farce? A terrible showdown? There had been marks of violence on her body but no sign of sexual activity.

What a strange lover this secret person was.

Chapter Seventeen

At some point in July you become aware that the summer will not last forever. The nights are starting to lengthen; the swallows gather in increased numbers and chatter on telegraph wires. Late at night when the house is cooling you are reminded of the first breath of chilly autumn and think about gathering logs in preparation for the long winter's nights when a fire and the television beckon.

Apart from the odd few hot days the summer had been disappointing with so little sun Joanna had almost forgotten what a summer should be like: ice cubes and gay umbrellas, endless barbecues, the search for shade. However the plants and weeds were thriving. Many loved the luxury of so much rain although the flowers with large petals, petunias and roses in particular, suffered, rotting on their stems. Owners of country pubs and restaurants were unhappy too, thinking of lost business and doubtless the ice-cream manufacturers would have suffered a fall in their profits. The populace were staying in the towns, not tempted to lower the roofs on their convertibles, take in the country air, drink the country beer and eat the country food.

Joanna was conscious of autumn lurking around the corner as she climbed onto her bike that morning. There was a dull, unfriendly edge to the day. She freewheeled through the village of Waterfall and along the country lanes with their high banks of rosebay willow herb and scarlet corn poppies. Less than a week now and Matthew would be home. As usual when she thought of her partner, he provoked mixed feelings, a sense of intense pleasure, tinged with sick worry. They had unfinished business and they both knew it. Since he had left four months ago for Washington D.C. to study the effects of gunshot wounds he had said little in his emails, only the bare bones of his flight details. But she knew him well enough to know that

Matthew's style was to lock horns physically – not deal with the issue through letters, emails or telephone calls. He knew her well enough to know that she would move heaven and earth to be at the airport to meet him and that they would tackle their problems face to face. She also knew that their relationship had reached a watershed. Their ultimate test – so far. They never could go back now to those new and heady days of simply being together. Their relationship had entered the realms of being hugely complicated, with its imperfections exposed and raw. If they survived they might emerge stronger. If not – She didn't want to think about it. At heart Joanna was a fatalist. This was the reason she had embarked on the affair with Matthew while he had still been married to Jane. It was why too, she had fallen back into it when their work had brought them so close together. To her it had been inevitable. Fate. Kismet.

She sped down the hill, feeling the wind ruffle her hair. She would pay the price later; she would have trouble getting a comb through it. Matthew had bought her a helmet for safety after an accident when she was knocked off her bike but she frequently forgot to put it on and didn't bother putting her hair in an elastic band either so it blew, thick, unruly and tangling. Unbidden, she recalled Beatrice's hair, blowing in the wind too. Another woman who scorned the use of a helmet.

She reached the dip and glanced upwards before starting to stand up in the saddle, climbing the hill with the steady, rocking motion of a regular cyclist, pedalling steady and quick, panting a little as she reached the top, only to speed down the hill again and then start the slow climb back into Leek.

She arrived at the station breathless, warm – and still aware of the autumn sneakily hiding behind the summer mantle.

She showered quickly in the female changing room, bundling her trainers and cycling shorts in her locker, changing into a blue cotton summer skirt and a white t-shirt with sandals and spraying herself with eau de toilette before wandering into her office. She had scheduled a briefing for nine and wanted to talk to Mike first.

Oddly enough at the same time that Joanna was acknowledging the creeping presence of autumn so was Arthur Pennington. He had noticed that the daylight in the early morning was ebbing away like a late spring tide. Each day as he drew back the curtains he was aware of this dinginess which crept into the room. He turned back to look at the big double bed with its bright duvet cover and caught sight of his pale, strained face in the dressing table mirror. He dreaded being alone in the long winter nights. He had been used to Beattie being there, with him. Quiet they were but at least he hadn't been alone. He padded downstairs to make himself a cup of tea, hearing the ringing silence in the house and wincing when he saw the foil dishes of last night's takeaway still scattered all over the work surfaces. He hadn't realised how much Beattie had tidied up after him. She'd done it in such a quiet, unobtrusive way.

He felt a momentary panic which rose, sour and stale in his mouth.

He didn't want to be alone.

He couldn't depend on the children. Apart from a couple of very brief phone calls they'd given him a wide berth, almost as though they blamed *him* for their mother's murder. He stood, fighting the rising panic.

And then he heard the front gate open and close. He peered through the window to see Kerry, the next-door neighbour, in tight jeans and a cream sweater, which slipped off her shoulders so he could see pink bra straps. His mouth tightened in a prudish bunch as he opened the door.

"Morning, Arthur," she said jauntily. She already smelt of cigarettes and her hair was straw-dry with a dark inch of roots near the scalp. "I thought maybe we should go through Beattie's things," she said. "Time you moved on, Arthur."

He felt affronted. "It's early days yet," he said. *But how glad he was to see her.*

Korpanski looked fed up when he finally appeared at eight forty two.

He seemed grouchy and tired as he stumped into the corner and parked himself in front of his desk.

"Late night?" she asked sympathetically.

"Just tiresome," he said shortly and switched his computer on without adding anything more.

"We've a briefing in fifteen minutes, Mike," she said. "I'd really like to move forward in this one."

He swivelled round and she caught a flash of temper. "Forward? In our dreams, Joanna. We've been floundering now for days. I looked through the statements last night after you'd gone. There's nothing there. Not a flipping clue."

Korpanski had got out of bed on the wrong side.

"Then we need to look through the forensics again," Joanna said crisply. "And the diaries." She decided to ignore his mood. "I think I might have a lead, Mike."

Korpanski's face softened and his brown eyes rested on her. He swivelled his chair around quite slowly, his anger swiftly melting. "Get something last night, did you, Jo?"

She hadn't meant to do this – encourage over-optimism – but when she felt so sure they were breaking through it was hard not to share it. "Our mystery woman," she said. "Beatrice had an appointment with her in the week she died."

"How do you know?"

"Because she told Pagan, one of my cycling companions."

"Oh."

"We'd better look through her diaries again," she prompted.

Mike vanished through the door and returned five minutes later with Beatrice's diary.

It was a large, desk diary with two pages serving a week. They'd retrieved it from her study. Starting with Saturday and Sunday. Joanna turned to the week beginning Sunday the 13th of June.

She had obviously used the diary as an *aide memoir*. There was plenty in it, sometimes the entries spilling over the day-lines in her round, childish hand.

There was one entry for the Sunday: *Bike ride 9.30.*

Joanna recalled the day.

It had been one of the few really warm days in the entire summer with not a cloud in the sky. She'd overslept after a night out with Sarah and Jeremy the night before. She'd woken with a vague hangover, showered quickly and dressed in a sleeveless vest and cycling shorts and arrived at the rendezvous late. The others were already swigging from their water bottles and sweating profusely. But she knew once they had climbed from Thorncliffe to the top of the moors they would soon cool down. Because up there there was always a breeze. She had never known it too hot at that height.

They had greeted her arrival with relief and a few dark looks. It was one of the unwritten rules of the Femina Club that no one kept the others waiting but she was in no mood to care and didn't apologise to the already over-heated bunch of cyclists. But she remembered now that Beattie had looked more uncomfortable than the rest, already sweating profusely with half-moons of perspiration staining under the arms of her cycling top. She had thought then that maybe climbing to Thorncliffe wasn't such a good idea on such a hot day. But, she had argued, there were hills all around Leek. It was difficult to avoid climbing. Joanna had eyed Beatrice with reserve just as Beattie wiped her dripping face and their eyes had met, Joanna's with irritation, Beattie's with a dumb apology for needing special consideration.

So they had set out and halfway up the hill Joanna had turned around in the saddle to see Beattie doggedly pushing her bike up. Her resentment had melted then. The woman was trying fearfully hard and something in her admired her for it.

They'd waited for the straggler at the top, tipped some of their drinking water over her glowing face and t-shirt dampened with sweat then complimented her encouragingly on her grittiness and effort.

Beatrice had beamed around them all. "Oh, it'll be worth it," she'd said fervently and Joanna had stared at her dumbly for a long minute, thoughts pinging around her mind. *Nuns must look like this, she'd thought, when they enter the novitiate. New mothers, still tired with the effort of childbirth but exhilarated with their reward. There was something evangelical in the woman's face.*

Having managed the climb the rest of the cycle ride was much less strenuous and the climate cooler with a fresh breeze evaporating their sweat. They'd stopped at The Mermaid for a sandwich and a drink, Beatrice sitting quietly at the end of the table.

Joanna was downing an apple juice with tonic water and chewing on her sandwich when Beatrice had sidled up to her and fixed her with her short-sighted stare. "Do you know why they called this pub 'The Mermaid'?"

Joanna shook her head.

"Legend has it that a mermaid lives in Blakemore Pool," Beattie said, smiling. "And she drags unwary travellers to their deaths. Had you never heard the story? Leek and its surrounds are full of legend."

Legend is a consequence of remoteness, superstition and isolation.

Joanna had realised then that, like many quiet people, Beatrice Pennington was a fund of knowledge.

For herself she had never pondered the question of the pub name. She had merely accepted the fact that the pub, almost as far from the sea as is possible in England, had the name of a mythical sea creature. So she had looked at the quiet woman through new eyes and when they had all finished eating and drinking it had registered that Beattie had been the first to get back on her bike. Joanna had watched her cycle ahead and thought back ten minutes to that

almost beatific expression on the woman's face and wondered. *What had given it to her? What religion or love, what
desire or dream, had transformed the plain face into the face of
a saint?*

"Penny for them, Jo," Korpanski said in her ear. Abruptly
she stopped daydreaming.

"Oddly enough, Korpanski," she said dryly, "I was recalling a day out with the dead woman."

It shut him up.

She and Korpanski skimmed through the rest of the diary
entries. There was nothing penned in for Monday, June
14th. Tuesday, the 15th, was obviously the day for the
Readers' Group. Three p.m. She'd ringed the time and
underneath penned in some notes: *Discuss what was in the
writer's mind when he described the legal cocktail party! What
stopped Nic Gabriel from moving forward?* Joanna was
intrigued. Then she'd written:

*The dead woman smiled. How does the phrase work as an
attention grabber?*

*The rich man who burned in Paradise. The giant who
chopped himself in half. The boy who died of shock.*

The two police officers looked at one another. "Sounds
quite a story," Korpanski said.

"Yes." The point is, where is our clue to find our mystery
woman?

Joanna turned to Wednesday, June 16th. There was only
one entry for that day.

C 4 p.m.

"Could be anyone," Korpanski said grumpily, his bad
mood returning.

"Not anyone," Joanna said. "We don't have many suspects called, 'C'. It lets her two cronies off the hook. It isn't
Guy."

"I thought we were looking for a woman."

"I'm keeping an open mind," Joanna said.

"I think that's short cut for having no bloody idea,"

"Well, thanks, Mike. And now, with those encouraging
words, let's go to the briefing."

Arthur Pennington was composing a letter to a late-paying client when the phone rang.

"Someone for you," his secretary said. "A woman. She said it's personal." She put the phone down.

He pressed the Line 2 button. "Hello?" he said cautiously.

"Arthur? It's Kerry." There was panic in her voice. "I think you'd better come home. Right away."

"I can't just..."

"I mean it, Arthur."

His secretary was agog as he walked through. "I'm just going out for half an hour," he said uncomfortably. "I shan't be any longer."

He was conscious of his anger as he dropped down the stairs, two at a time. He couldn't have this, Kerry ringing him at work. What would people think? And his wife so recently dead.

Murdered.

It would make the police suspicious. He'd have to tell her.

He just couldn't have this.

Life was not quite so dull here recently, the secretary was musing, in fact it was hotting up very nicely.

Who would have thought that Arthur Pennington would have led such an exciting life.

Joanna surveyed the rim of expectant faces. It was difficult to tell them that, though they had no inkling that the net was closing around the small collection of suspects.

"The entry for 'C'," she started with.

She sensed that Hesketh-Brown was itching to make a contribution.

"I know we've been working on the assumption that it might have been a woman – this mystery person," he said tentatively, "but I thought I'd have another word with the pathologist, and see if he could tell anything from the hand-prints on Mrs Pennington's neck."

Joanna waited.

"He said he was ninety per cent sure it was a man's hand that had strangled her. He said it was too big for a woman's."

Bridget Anderton spoke up then. "That fits in with what her colleagues said. They just didn't believe she could possibly have been a lesbian. They said she'd never given any sign that she'd leaned in that direction."

WPC Kitty Sandworth stood up. "It's the impression I got too," she said.

Joanna walked in a daze back to her office without waiting for Mike. Ideas were buzzing around her head. She found the telephone number in the file and dialled.

Waited while they fetched Fiona Pennington then put the question to her.

"A lesbian? You must be joking. Far too avant-garde for mother," Fiona said, laughing. "I know you think I didn't really know mum but it wasn't that. We simply had nothing in common. Nothing to talk about but we did touch on that sort of thing once or twice. My mother had very normal leanings, I can tell you."

Joanna put down the phone and knew Fiona Pennington was right. This hadn't been a sexual relationship at all. They'd barked up the wrong tree. The play Beattie had made for Guy was proof enough.

But if not a sexual relationship then what?

Chapter Eighteen

Kerry did look upset; he had to hand it to her. Genuinely upset. She was waiting at the front door, holding something in her hand, her face as pale as milk.

It is a man's natural instinct to comfort a woman who is in distress, he told himself. Arthur put his arm around her. "What's up, love?"

Without saying anything she held out the letter.

PC Bridget Anderton had lived in the Staffordshire Moorlands all her life. She knew the people of the town of Leek, knew what was acceptable in their eyes and what was not. So as she sat in the car, opposite the Pennington house, and watched the little tableau being played out in front of her, she knew that this was quite definitely of interest – the bereaved man whose wife had died violently, being so easily comforted by his single, female neighbour.

Besides – Leek is a gossipy little town and Kerry Frost had a reputation for being a bit of a man-eater.

She smiled to herself. Against such a professional onslaught Arthur Pennington had no chance. But the real question which intrigued her was this: was Kerry simply being opportunistic with a newly unattached man or had this bond between Pennington and his neighbour existed for some time – maybe even pre-dating Beatrice's murder. Could it even be construed as a motive?

She watched the embrace with interest and strained to hear the words before they moved inside.

"What is it, love?"

Once inside Kerry handed him the letter. "It's Beattie," she said tearfully. "She'd been writing letters to someone." As she handed him the first page she added softly, "And you so nice, Arthur."

He read it through, looked up, looked down again. The passionate words leapt at him from the paper. Kerry's mouth was open, her eyes wide. She too had felt the scorch of intensity. And from Beatrice.

Arthur held it in his hand.

The unfinished epistle. He already knew every word contained in it. Right up to the half-finished sentence which began, *And when you touch me*... What she had intended to say no one would ever know. At the very point when she was writing he had walked into the room and seen her tuck the corner of this letter underneath a book she was pretending to read. When she had casually left the book lying closed on the sofa cushions and put the kettle on for a brew he had scanned through it.

The really hard bit had been to pretend to drink the tea without displaying any of the shock. The utter shock that he had felt as he had read through the treacherous words.

The sense of terrible, gut-wrenching betrayal. Beatrice. His loyal, faithful, quiet wife.

Except she wasn't.

Kerry was watching him so for show he read the letter through again, closing his eyes against surprisingly real pain which Kerry interpreted as a failure to understand the significance of the words. "She was having an affair, Arthur," she pointed out, suddenly shrewish. "Beattie had someone else."

Did he understand – or not?

Arthur Pennington couldn't find the right words so to soak up the time he read it through again. Once, twice, three times. It didn't matter how many times he read it through, did it? Its meaning was exactly the same. Clear as a pane of glass. A window, in fact, to the treachery of his wife's mind.

Betrayal.

Kerry opened her mouth to speak again but Arthur spoke first. "This is terrible," he said. "Terrible."

Her blue eyes rested on his face without comprehension for only a minute. Then she started to understand and in the same split second backed away. "Arthur?" she said uncertainly.

He smiled at her.

"Arthur?" she said again. She did not like that smile.

He was still smiling, that empty, frozen smile that failed to warm his face.

She suddenly felt very afraid. She backed out into the hall. "I've got to go now," she muttered, pulled the front door open and was gone.

While Bridget Anderton watched.

Now what had made flirty little Kerry Frost fancy her chances and then back off like a scalded cat, she wondered, before picking up the phone.

"I thought you'd be interested, Ma'am."

Corinne was tired of the rows, tired too of her husband's constant goading, of his threats and promises. There is only one way to deal with a would-be bully and it was an exhausting way. Confront him. Magic your weaknesses into strengths. Turn his perceived strengths into weaknesses. "I don't believe you'd do it," she said weakly. "I can't see you leaving me. Why would you? I believe you're too frightened of the scandal, of the loss of income, loss of status. You'd miss your bloody meal ticket," she ended savagely.

Pete made a feeble attempt to fight back. "Don't push me too far, Corinne," he warned. "You don't mean that much to me."

They were in the conservatory. The sun was trying to shine through thin wisps of cloud but the weather was cool. Corinne sank back on to the Lloyd loom chair. It creaked in protest. "I think I've learned," she said," that I don't actually mean anything to you. I'm just a means to an end. A convenience."

Hands on the armrests he leaned over and put his face close to hers. "How do you think I feel about you, knowing this?"

She shrank into the chair, aware of his fury. The fury of all men spurned as representative of their sex. "I am not a lesbian, Pete," she said. "I was the object of a lonely woman's affections. I helped her. That's it. Understand?"

The anger in her husband's eyes took her by surprise. She had seen him petulant before. Peevish and demanding but she had never before seen this furious, uncontrolled side of him. There was something quite wild in his face. She watched him, part fascinated, part frightened, part mesmerised.

The slap came out of nowhere. And yet she had seen it coming for years. She had always known her husband was capable of violence. When the assault accusation had been directed he had spent evenings trying to convince her that he had not moved to hit the girl. But she had known the truth. You cannot hide a violent nature. It surfaces. Afterwards, when she was pressing an ice cube to her face and worrying what she would say in surgery the next day to explain her injury, she tried to remember and knew. She had not seen his hand move. It was as though some disembodied thing had hit her – so hard her neck had jerked right back. She touched her face and saw blood on her hand. "Pete," she said. "Please. Don't."

I walked into a door.

How else do you explain away a black eye, a split lip, a bloodied, bruised nose?

Tell me. Because it is hard. And no one believes you. They all give a knowing look.

The battered wife syndrome.

You can always ring the police and they will press charges. Oh yes, expose yourself to the full force of publicity, a court case, pity – and behind that always the question, *what did she do to earn that?*

And this time there was an obvious answer glaring back.

Or you can do nothing but dab on extra foundation and tell a silly lie which nobody believes.

There comes a time when you stare facts in the face. You are unhappy. You are bored. You are frightened of your husband. You don't love him. You don't even like him.

Corinne Angiotti had reached this exact position.

He was still bending over her.

Staring at her with a look of triumph. He had done it, what he had wanted to do for months, wipe that confidence right off the sneering face and replace it with fright, uncertainty and apprehension. He would now dominate her for ever.

Corinne's eyes watched him warily. For a second – two seconds her fright persisted – that he would hit her again. And then she didn't care any more because the fright had been replaced with hot fury. She pushed him away with her feet. "Get out," she screamed.

"Pack your bags and get out of my life. I'll be with the solicitor first thing in the morning."

Startled he fell backwards and she moved. He followed her to the kitchen. "That's what you want, is it?" he jeered. "You want me to go to the law with the letters in my hand and tell them why I hit you? You don't think I'll get sympathy? You don't think the publicity might just cost you your job?"

She didn't respond. He jerked her shoulder back. "You don't think this evidence might just put you under the suspicion of the police?"

"You bastard," she spat out, running a towel under the cold tap.

"Where were you first thing on Wednesday morning?"

"Surgery."

"Oh no you weren't. I saw you, Corinne. You were late for work. I watched you sitting in your car outside the library. After I'd read the letters I was very curious. I saw you there on the morning she died."

"At what time?"

"You know what time."

"I was at surgery," she said again.

"Oh no you weren't. You were late. Liar."

She took the cold compress away from her face. "What's your point, you scum?"

"I can go with a noise or I can go like a little mouse, squeaking away behind the skirting board," he said. "The choice is yours."

Marilyn Saunders was speaking to her friend on her mobile. "I don't know," she said dubiously. "I don't know. Guy's such a liar. Who knows when he's telling the truth and when he's lying through his teeth? I know that I simply don't trust him any more."

"I'd give him a chance if I was you," Jewel advised. "Who knows what he knows?"

"What are you talking about?"

"Guy wasn't having an affair with Beattie," Jewel said again. "He was just mucking around. Playing."

"How do you know?"

"Oh come on." Her eyes screwed up. "I don't believe you ever thought those two had got it together."

"I did." A long pause. "Well...I...put it like this. I was never sure."

"Anyway." Jewel was anxious to move subjects. "If I was you I'd be worrying about something else."

"What?"

"I'd be worrying who killed Beattie. Because whoever it was just might think we know more about it than we do and strike again."

"Don't be so theatrical, Jewel."

"Well – the police haven't caught whoever it was, have they?"

There was silence from the other phone.

"Are you still there?"

"Yes."

Jewel made some more sympathetic noises down the line but her friend had stopped listening. She tried one more time to provoke a response then gave up.

Kerry had a friend too. Sonya. She'd bolted the front door after her and was still shaking as she found her name on her mobile phone directory. "Son," she started. "Are you all right to talk?"

Her friend picked up at once that something was wrong. "Yes. What is it?"

"Where are you?"

"Up the town. Shopping. What's the matter? You sound awful."

Kerry started to explain about the letter and the deduction she had made from it. "He already knew, Son. He said he didn't but I could see it in his eyes. He already knew."

"O-o-h." A pause while she struggled with something. "Do you mean *before* she died?"

"Yes. I think so."

Her friend was silenced. Then she added in a low voice. "You don't think…"

"That's the trouble. I don't know what to think. I just don't feel comfortable with him any more. I don't trust him. He had such an odd look in his eyes."

Sonya Darlington frowned, ignored the people hurrying past her and concentrated on the conversation. "You be careful, Kerry," she warned. I wouldn't go over there on your own if I was you. I'd just wait until the police have arrested someone."

"What if they don't arrest anyone? Ever?"

"Then I wouldn't go over at all."

"But he seems so nice."

"People aren't always what they seem," her friend said darkly. "I should give him a wide berth if I was you. Until somebody's arrested for the murder you don't know it wasn't him."

"Hmm." There was still some doubt in her friend's voice.

"Kerry," Sonya said warningly.

The moment she had stopped speaking to her friend Sonya Darlington rang Leek Police and was put through to Joanna.

Who listened intently.

Korpanski was watching out of the corner of his eye and from the stiffening of her shoulders he knew this was a significant phone call. He waited for her to put the receiver down.

"He knew," Joanna said slowly. "Pennington knew about

the letters."

"How can you be sure?"

The trouble was – she couldn't. Sonya had merely said her friend was convinced he already knew. Pennington had not admitted it but she had felt the sight of all that passion spilling out onto the blue notepaper had been no surprise.

"And if so," Mike, "it gives him a very clear motive."

"But no opportunity," he said.

Her shoulders drooped. Korpanski was right.

But it did mean that Pennington's protestations of ignorance of his wife's affair had been a deceit.

Well, he was a very good liar.

Joanna had reached the point in the case when she felt she knew all she needed to know. She simply didn't understand the significance of it all. So she had decided to have a brainstorm with every single officer who had been detailed to gather the information.

Dressed in tight black trousers and a red shirt with high-heeled black boots she was perched on the corner of a desk. "Chuck it at me," she said, fists clenched. "Start with the obvious. Move in, tell me specifics and any great ideas you have. I don't care if they're not logical or wise. I don't care if they're simply questions you don't think have been satisfactorily answered. Just – start – talking."

She'd ordered coffee and sandwiches for everyone. She wanted a nice, relaxed atmosphere, plenty of ideas and fact sharing.

Bridget Anderton kicked the ball off.

"The murder of Beatrice Pennington, aged fifty-two, married woman who had two grown-up children, who live away. Suspicions of having an affair with another woman."

PC Paul Ruthin took up the story. "Set off for work on the morning of Wednesday, June 23rd..."

"In an uncharacteristically smart dress," Kitty Sandworth put in.

"For work," Korpanski growled.

"Chained her bike to the railings and..."

"Disappeared."

"Reported missing on Thursday, 24th June by her husband. Body found almost a week later under a hedge on the Moorlands on a little-used road between Grindon and Butterton in a state of decomposition. Cause of death manual strangulation."

"The pathologist thought the hand was big." Bridget Anderton again. "He thought more likely a man's hand."

"And probably dumped under the hedge soon after she disappeared."

Joanna spoke. "Anomaly one. The affair was thought to be with a woman but the murder thought to be committed by a man." She searched around the room. "Inspiration anyone?"

"The husband of the woman she'd been having an affair with?"

"Or maybe her own husband," Joanna said thoughtfully. "Bridget? Would you like to tell the others what you saw"

"He came home from work hurriedly today," the WPC said. "His neighbour, Kerry, had spent the morning in his house. I was just keeping an eye," she replied to the sniggers around the room. "Anyway – she meets him on the doorstep holding out some pages of blue what looked like notepaper. They go inside. A couple of minutes later she bolts back out, runs across the road and back into her own house. A minute or two later Pennington's knocking on her door. She doesn't answer it and he drives back to work."

"Maybe he tried it on." Paul Ruthin suggested.

"No, it was obviously the letters,"

Joanna interrupted. "We know that Beatrice sent numerous letters on blue notepaper, sealed in blue envelopes to the object of her affections," she said, "because the librarians have told us. We know that she delivered them by hand, walking from the library so we assume it was somewhere near, in the town."

She paused. "And, according to a friend, who kindly rang us, Kerry Frost is convinced that Arthur Pennington had known about his wife's letters for some time. In other words *before* his wife was murdered. However, as Sergeant Korpanski has pointed out, he may have motive but he did not have the opportunity. Too many witnesses saw his wife after Pennington was safely in his office."

"The real question is – who were these letters addressed to?"

"C," Phil Scott said gloomily.

Joanna put her hands up to her face. "Surely it is not beyond our capabilities to find out who 'C' is? Surely if we find out who she is it will lead us to Beatrice's killer?"

At her side Korpanski let out a long, heaving sigh.

Time to move on. "Right – so. There are other problems. While plenty of witnesses saw Beattie cycling in to the town and even locking her bike to the railings it seems no one saw her get into a car or be abducted." Another thought struck her. "We *know* that the letters were sent to someone who either lived or worked very near the library. It's possible she went once too often to deliver one of these and that was where she met her death, her body being disposed of at some other time, maybe that night."

A few heads nodded. It seemed logical.

"Let's think about alibis. Her own husband?"

Korpanski shook his head. "It's not going to work," he said. "He's in an office with a secretary in the adjoining room. He has to go through her room to reach the outside.

"Even if he had slipped out he would have to work very quickly," Bridget Anderton objected. "Meet up with his wife, murder her, dispose of her body somewhere and get back to work – all in a pee-break. Unless," she said, "his wife's body lay in his boot all day."

Joanna stared at the back of the room. "No response to the boards, I don't suppose?"

"Plenty," PC Anderton said. "Everyone *saw* her in her best frock wobbling along the road. I mean – she was conspicuous but no one so far reports seeing her get into a car near the library or on the road at any time when the body was being dumped."

On this down beat the briefing seemed to pause.

There was a hard knocking at the door, the desk sergeant's face appearing in the round window.

"Oh no," Joanna said crossly. "Not now." She didn't want interruptions. She wanted to move on, consolidate their knowledge, pool their ideas. She wanted to find the killer, make an arrest.

But he opened it anyway. "I think you'll want to see this, Ma'am."

"What," she asked irritably. "We're in the middle of a very important briefing."

For answer the desk sergeant lifted his eyebrows and stared, the faintest hint of a smile touching his mouth. *Trust me*, it said.

"All right then. Korpanski," she said, "come with me."

"We'll continue later."

Chapter Nineteen

Joanna faced the determined, damaged face of Corinne
Angiotti. Her first instinct was one of shock. The last time
she had met the doctor she had been composed, in control,
confident to the point of arrogant. And now? Someone had
put a fist into the delicate features. Hard. And done a lot of
damage. The eyes that glared back at her were full of anger
and terror.

Joanna was curious; but first things first. "Do you need a
doctor?"

Corinne Angiotti shook her head.

"Some pain killers?" Joanna managed a smile. "We keep a
couple of aspirins around the place – for hangovers usually."

"I'm OK."

"Who did this to you?"

Corinne Angiotti stared back without speaking.

"Let's go in here." Joanna led her into one of the smaller
interview rooms. "Are you sure I can't get you anything?
Tea?"

She was struggling to conceal her shock and pity. She
hadn't expected this.

She closed the door behind them. "OK," she said. "Do
you want this on the record or off?"

"Off – for now," Corinne spoke with difficulty through
the split, swollen lip. "It'll all have to come out – eventually,
I expect."

"What?"

Corinne put a hand up – near her face. "This," she said,
"and other things."

*So this was "C", Joanna thought and could have kicked her-
self. The signs had all been there from the first. The numerous
calls to the doctor's surgery, the fact that it was round the corner from the library. And Corinne Angiotti had just the right
profile to fit. Beatrice Pennington would have adored the
woman who had given her so much attention. It was typical of*

her that she had misinterpreted the doctor's professional inter-est as being a return of her love. Oh what a tragedy – not only the woman's death but her life too.

She glanced across the room at Korpanski and knew he had worked it out in the same second that she had.

"So *you* were the one," she said. "The object of Beatrice Pennington's affections."

Corinne's eyes dropped instantly. "Can I have a glass of water?"

"Yes, of course."

Korpanski shot across the room to the sink, filled a plastic cup, handed it to her – all in the space of a second. Corinne Angiotti took it gratefully without looking at him once and drank.

"Beatrice Pennington," she said steadily, "was a sweet, kind woman who was cruelly mocked by her family, her friends and in particular Guy Priestley." Her eyes opened as wide as she could manage. "They were *all* laughing at her. People she'd loved and trusted, people she'd known all her life. They all let her down. Her husband hardly acknowl-edged her existence; her mother and father had little time for her, preferring her sister; her two friends used her and her children couldn't have cared less whether she was alive or dead. She had no one she could turn to. She was lonely and ignored so she came to consult me as her doctor because she felt so devastated by what had happened. I couldn't let her down."

"What was your understanding of what *did* happen?"

"I'm sure you've unearthed the full story. Urged on by Marilyn, Guy Priestley quite callously pretended to made a play for her. She fell for it. Beatrice was naïve beyond belief. She had low self-esteem. She felt a fool, completely unloved and unwanted. I just gave her some of my professional time."

"But her husband wanted her," Joanna pointed out.

"Her husband was *used* to her. That's all."

Corinne tried to smile but it started the lip bleeding.

"Ouch," she said, putting her hand to it.

Korpanski shot back to the sink and returned with some paper towels soaked in cold water. Corinne took it gratefully and dabbed the blood away. Joanna gave Mike a suspicious look. There was no need for him to compensate for the behaviour of the entire male race.

He caught her eye and gave her a bland, innocent smile but he knew that *she* knew what he was up to.

"Beatrice consulted me on a number of occasions," Corinne continued, "starting round about Christmas-time. Within a week, I think, of the Priestley incident. Her son and daughter had not let her know whether they would be home or not for the festive season. Her parents were going to her sister's. I felt really sorry for her." Corinne's fingers brushed over her face. "She seemed so low. I tried to prescribe some antidepressants but she refused them. She said it did her more good to talk to me. I tried to refer her to a counsellor but again she refused, again saying that she would prefer to talk to me, that she found it more helpful." She brought her hands up, palms outwards in a foreign gesture of appeal. "What was I to do? I'm a doctor. My work is to struggle against the forces of nature, do what I can to promote my patients' physical and mental health. I have taken the Hippocratic oath to that effect. In the circumstances the best option seemed to be to listen to her problems. At least she felt she could unburden herself of some of the humiliation and shame she'd experienced when Guy Priestley deliberately made such a fool of her. I knew how she felt. I have a – few problems myself." Her hands brushed over her face and even through the swollen eyelids Joanna could read the hurt held in her eyes.

In the circumstances the epithet, problems, seemed a bit of an understatement but Joanna reserved her comment. It would have been unkind to say anything.

"I felt a real empathy with her. Maybe that was my mistake," Corinne mused – more to herself than to the two detectives. "Maybe I shouldn't have empathised with her quite so much but it seemed natural at the time. We talked quite a lot about marriage, about relationships. That sort of thing. To be honest I too found it therapeutic. That was another mistake I made. I see it now so much more plainly."

"And then?" Joanna prompted.

"And then she started writing letters to me. Love letters. They were awful. Embarrassing, quite unbalanced. At first they professed a sort of romantic love. Adoration, almost. Then they got quite physical. Talking not about emotion but about touching, feeling, kissing. I felt terrible."

"When was this?" Joanna interrupted.

"Well after Christmas. March, sometime. I wrote back telling her this was a big mistake, that I had expressed a professional interest rather than personal, that I had treated her as a patient. The trouble was – I started to see myself as no better than Guy Priestley. I too had led her on and now was trying to let her down. It was just what she didn't need. You understand? I was letting her down more gently than he had. Without cruelty or malice. But the result was the same. It would make no difference to her. She'd perceived us both as potential lovers. At one point she threatened suicide."

"When was this?"

"May, June sometime. I…"

And suddenly Corinne's eyes became furtive and her manner evasive, face turning away, hands fidgeting, feet moving underneath the table. Joanna thought she understood. Although these consultations had taken place in the surgery, Doctor Corinne Angiotti had not kept accurate and detailed records which would make her story uncorroborated. And which left her, in turn, vulnerable.

"Did these exchanges take place in the surgery?"

"Yes."

"Entirely?"

"Up until then, yes."

"So they're all on record," she asked innocently.

Corinne covered her mouth with her hand. She scooped in a long breath. "Not fully, no."

The fidgeting stopped. It is interesting how truthful people are incapable of lying.

"And then things turned nasty and a bit frightening. She began waiting outside the house, bumping into me deliberately when I arrived at and left surgery. Often when I'd think I was alone in the house I'd look out of the window and see her just standing there. If I went shopping up the High Street I'd bump into her. It was terrible. I was always conscious that she was nearby. She became further detached from reality, imagining things I'd never said. Started to tell me she'd found a cottage where we could live, that we could build a new life together." Suddenly Corinne Angiotti covered her face with her hands and burst into tears. "It was horrible. I didn't want it. I didn't want to be with her. I simply thought of her as my patient, someone I treated. Not a bloody lover. I didn't know where it was all going to lead. I didn't know how to stop it and professionally I was frightened. She appeared so plausible, so lucid, so unimaginative and truthful. I was worried that if the story came out people would believe her and not me"

Joanna exchanged a swift glance with Korpanski. Did Angiotti know she was digging herself into a pit?

She gave her a chance. "Why didn't you come to the police?"

"Because in my more confident moments I still thought I could handle it. Because I didn't want to embarrass her. Because I was afraid that you would believe *her* – not me."

"We would have handled this with kid gloves," Joanna said. "We can be careful and considerate. Don't you understand?"

"You didn't know how convincing she was, nor the power of her conviction that she was right. She was deluded. She really was quite convinced that I did love her and had, at some time, promised that I would leave Pete to go away with her. She sensed that we weren't happily married and filled in the rest."

But Korpanski was staring, fascinated at the doctor. He

always stood in the same way, like the genie of the lamp, guarding the door, arms folded, legs apart. "There's more," he said.

Corinne Angiotti looked at Korpanski directly for the first time since entering the room. And she looked at him with fear.

"And then?" Joanna echoed.

"Then things turned even more threatening," Corinne admitted.

"She hid in the drive one evening. We have a long drive," she explained. "We live in one of the Victorian semis on the Buxton Road, on the fringes of the town. The drive is curved and lined with rhododendrons. Anyone could hide in there and she did. One evening when I'd been working for the Medical Deputising Service I was very late home. It was around 1 am. As I got out of my car I knew she was there, I could hear her breathing heavily. Did anyone tell you she had adenoids and very laboured breathing? Oh yes. As her doctor I knew that all right. I knew it every bloody time she phoned me at home. I could hear it. 'Your heavy breather again', Pete used to say."

"Go on." Joanna was wondering where all this was leading.

"She asked me where I'd been. I started off telling her it was none of her business. But she persisted, accusing me of having another lover. She was mad," Corinne said. "She said she had a knife. 'I mean it,' she said. 'I mean it. I will kill you if you don't stick by your word. I know you want to be my lover.'" Corinne's eyes were struggling to open against the bruising which was darkening by the minute. "How could she know that," she asked pitifully, "when it wasn't true?"

Joanna glanced across the room at Korpanski. He was watching the doctor with fascination.

It was he who broached the subject. "Tell us about the murder."

"I don't know about the murder," Corinne protested. "I

don't know. I only know that I didn't do it."

A gaze flickered between the two detectives. Joanna gave an almost imperceptible shake of her head and a swift glance downwards at the doctor's hands. Medium sized for a woman. Not the man's hands the pathologist had described.

"Then what?"

"She wanted us to go away together. You have to understand. I really liked her but there was no way I was going to ride off into the sunset with her. I'd hoped..." Her voice softened. "I suppose I'd always hoped that my husband and I would somehow work things out."

They waited for her to draw the inevitable conclusion.

"It seems that was a bit of a vain hope."

Joanna exhaled noisily, blowing out in relief.

"I knew I really had to confront her," Corinne said, "somewhere on neutral ground and somewhere where I would be safe. I was feeling increasingly threatened. She was unbalanced, you know. There was no appealing for her to understand that it was all in her mind. She simply wasn't listening." She drew in a deep breath. "I was late for work on the Wednesday she disappeared and as I passed the library I saw her bending over, locking her bike to the railings. She was wearing a fifties-style cotton thing with a full skirt." She smiled. "It looked odd with a cycling helmet. I honked my horn and tried to do a U-turn in the road but when I arrived back she'd vanished. There was just the bike locked against the railings. I don't know whether she'd seen me or not. She didn't wave but I thought she'd started to look round." Her hand covered her mouth again as though she was distressed by her memory. "I lost the chance to talk to her – for ever, it seems."

Now it was Joanna's turn to look wide-eyed at Korpanski. Corinne Angiotti must have been so close to the killer.

"Did you see anyone else approach her?"

The doctor shook her head. "No."

"Did you notice anything that might give us a clue?"

"I've thought and thought about it, gone over that little street scene so often in my mind but the only thing I keep coming up with is that for some reason she didn't want to see me that morning." Corinne's face was puzzled. "I don't know why but I'm convinced it's true."

Joanna eyed the tape-recorder with frustration. If it had been switched on they could have recorded this interview.

The case had never seemed more ridiculous. For Beatrice Pennington to shrink away from the woman she had professed to love? It didn't make sense.

Corinne Angiotti must have read her mind.

"I know," she said. "It doesn't make any sense at all."

"How were you when you arrived at the surgery?"

"Agitated," Corinne said. "Very."

"Did anyone witness these events? See you turning in the road?"

The doctor shook her head. "Well – loads of people must have *seen* me turning around on such a busy road. No cars hit me but I don't suppose anyone would remember. It's an insignificant thing. I really wasn't conscious of other people. I simply felt an overwhelming sense that I must have it out with her for once and for all." She paused. "My husband saw me."

"He was in Leek that morning?"

"Yes." She and Mike exchanged glances. This was like a horse race. And right now Pete Angiotti was way out in the lead. He had motive, opportunity and the right twisted character too.

Joanna leaned across the table. "Can I point out, doctor," she said. "We have a murder investigation on our hands and you have come in of your own free will and told us a completely unbelievable story."

"It's true."

"What strikes me is why have you come in to make confession today?"

Corinne touched her face. "Because my husband found

the letters," she said. "And even *he* did not give me the benefit of the doubt. I knew I had to tell my story first – before you found out from another source. The whole thing was bound to come out." She bent down, reached something from her bag and put sheets of blue notepaper on the desk. Joanna leaned back in her chair, eyed the sheets of paper, glanced at Korpanski triumphantly and resisted the temptation to punch a hole in the air.

"We'd like to keep these," she said.

Corinne Angiotti simply nodded.

"Where are you going now? You can't go home."

Corinne shrugged. "I don't know. I must speak to people at work and take some time off. I'd like to go away from Leek for now."

"I don't think that's going to be possible for a while."

"Well then?"

"We do have accommodation. A safe house."

Corinne stood up. "I should go home," she said.

"I take it it was your husband?"

Corinne nodded. Then she touched her face. "This is what husbands do to women they believe have betrayed them." She swallowed. "I don't think Pete will try anything again. He's probably gone."

"We can arrest him. But that isn't the problem," Joanna said.

Corinne's face moved. Had it not been so swollen it is possible she would have looked questioning.

"Beatrice's killer is still out there," Joanna said.

Corinne managed the faintest of smiles. "Well – at least you don't think it was me."

"We know it wasn't you," Joanna said. "The hand that strangled her was a man's."

Corinne flinched. "So it isn't a matter of your believing me or not," she said. "It's down to the facts."

"I'm a policewoman," Joanna said. "We're not known for our blind trust in the human race."

Corinne bowed her head.

"So you really do intend to go home?"

"Where else?" Corinne said steadily.

"We'd be only too happy for you to go home," Joanna said, "on one condition, that you have a WPC with you 24 hours a day. We can't risk this happening to you again. And the killer may have some animosity against you or even believe that you saw him on that morning."

"If Pete sees a policewoman in our house he'll think she's there to arrest him."

"I don't care what your husband thinks," Joanna said. "We can't risk anything further happening to you. Understand?"

Corinne nodded.

"And you accept the terms – just until we've made an arrest?"

Again Corinne Angiotti nodded.

"Why did you keep the letters?" Joanna asked curiously. "They were so incriminating. Why didn't you destroy them?"

"Because." Corinne Angiotti looked helpless. "Because they were such beautiful letters. Because they were such lovely words, because she had a vision of me that was intensely flattering. Because no one had ever said such beautiful things to me before and probably never will again."

"When did your husband find them?"

"I don't know."

"Could it have been before June the 23rd?"

Corinne licked her cracked lips. "It's possible. I think it might have been."

"Where is he now?"

"I don't know. I just left."

"Does he have a mobile phone?"

Corinne nodded.

Joanna pushed a pad and biro across the table at her and Corinne wrote the number down, copying from her own mobile phone menu.

She pushed the pad back at Joanna.

"Thank you."

The action must have released some tension in the doctor. She gave Korpanski a flirtatious look as she spoke to Joanna. "I don't suppose the first watch could be your detective sergeant, could it? I think I'd feel safe with him."

Korpanski shifted his weight onto the other foot.

"OK by me," Joanna said, laughing at him. "But if I were you," she added soberly, "I think I'd make very sure your husband is out of the way. Detective Sergeant Korpanski is a chivalrous soul. I can't imagine him being very merciful to the person who messed up your face."

Korpanski's stared back woodenly at the two women. Only the hint of a smile warmed his dark eyes to indicate that he had heard her. "I'll follow you in my car, doctor," he said.

Chapter Twenty

So Joanna was left alone again. Immediately she returned to her office she dialled Pete Angiotti's mobile number and wasn't a bit surprised to find it switched off.

She left her message, *"Mr Angiotti, this is Detective Inspector Joanna Piercy here of the Leek police. We would like to talk to you about two matters. These are quite important. I suggest you return my call on Leek 01538...and ask to speak to me as soon as possible. It is now 3 p.m. on Tuesday July 14th."* She ended the message with an ultimatum. *"If I have heard nothing by tomorrow morning I shall put out a stop and search."*

So – that was that. She rang Korpanski's phone. "Where are you?"

"Just turning into the drive."

"Any sign of him?"

"Not so far."

"We need his car details," she said. "I want him in here for questioning."

"OK, Jo. Umm – how long do you want me to stay here for?"

"Enough time to make her comfortable. A couple of hours. Until a replacement arrives. I shall go and talk to Arthur, I think."

"See you later then."

It was five o'clock, an awkward time. Would she catch Pennington still at the office or would he already have set out for home? Leek would be gridlocked at this time of evening and she didn't particularly want to sit in traffic for the next half hour. Neither could she justify putting the siren on which would have reduced her journey time to less than ten minutes to the Pennington home. Equally it was out of the question to use her bike. Even she had to acknowledge that arriving on a bike like Inspector Plod hardly gave out the message of the police force for the new millennium!

She picked up the phone and got straight through to the increasingly inquisitive secretary.

"Is Mr Pennington still there?"

"Yes. Have you got the person?"

"We're getting there slowly. May I talk to him?"

"I'll put you through right away." Said breathily.

"What is it, Inspector?" Spoken wearily. It was obvious that grieving husband or not Pennington was getting tired of this case and of her constant attention. How quickly we adjust to new situations. A couple of weeks ago he had been distraught.

"I need to talk to you again, Mr Pennington," she said.

"What about? Can't it be done over the phone?"

No – because I would not be able to read your face – and all that it can tell me.

"Is there any chance that you could call in on the way home from work?"

"I – suppose so."

"Good." The exchange was finished.

But Pennington did not put the phone down. He cleared his throat. "I don't suppose you could give me a clue what this is about? Are you likely to be making an arrest before long?"

"Better we talk face to face."

Joanna wanted to rattle him, enough to make him nervous and talkative. Nervous people make mistakes. They babble out secrets.

And that was just what she wanted.

She sat back and waited.

She leaned back in her chair, rolling a biro between her two hands and thought. Two men were under suspicion. Pennington and Pete Angiotti. Motives? As Corinne had observed, they were both wronged husbands.

Pennington was easy to understand. He was an unimaginative man who would be easily shocked by his wife's profession of love for another woman. But would it drive him to murder?

Who knows what will drive a man to murder?

But Arthur Pennington couldn't have done it.

Angiotti, on the other hand, was a different kettle of fish. Instinctively she mistrusted him. There was something inherently weak about him. *And* he was a bully.

On instinct she searched his name on the PNC. Nothing. So why had they left London? Why had they come here? If he already knew about the letters his wife had been receiving why erupt now? Why had he hit her? Lastly was he capable of murder?

She continued rolling the biro between her hands and answered her own question. Yes. She thought so. Yes.

She heard the commotion outside and had a feeling she knew it who it would be.

Her phone rang in the same moment, as there was a knock on the door.

Hesketh-Brown peered round, excitement flushing his face. "We've got Doctor Angiotti's husband here," he said. "And he's kicking up a right old fuss."

That was when she missed Korpanski. Stolidly taking up position at the door, standing with his arms akimbo, feet planted wide apart, minding the proceedings. But this would not do. He could not always be there. "Are you free?" she asked the constable.

"Yep."

"Well then, you and I are going to interview him."

Hesketh-Brown grinned. "Great."

She smiled to herself and watched Hesketh-Brown out of the corner of her eye, reflecting how long ago it was that she had expressed such enthusiasm for a mere interview. Maybe the young PC fancied his chances as a detective?

In a few years.

The desk sergeant had already put Pete Angiotti in Interview Room 2 and as she peered through the spy window she could see him pacing around, obviously agitated. He must have sensed her presence because he whipped around and glared at her. She felt her pulse quicken as she pushed the door open. By any yardstick this promised to be a significant exchange.

She sat herself down opposite Angiotti and took a good long look at his face. He looked pale and wild, his eyes staring back at her with real fear. He was a typical bully. Cruel to those he felt he had the advantage of and cowering in the presence of one he feared.

But it did not suit her questioning to have him fearful. She wanted him relaxed so she began by smiling and thanking him for responding so swiftly to her appeal.

"Good afternoon, Mr Angiotti," she said politely. "I think you know me already. Detective Inspector Piercy."

He nodded. "I know who you are all right."

"And this is PC Hesketh-Brown."

Angiotti nodded at the young PC briefly and then turned his attention back to Joanna.

"Do you want a solicitor present?"

He shook his head.

Joanna guessed he was somewhere in his early forties. It is always difficult to decide someone's age when they are under duress. He looked tired and haggard, his forehead resting on his hand as he spoke. But there was something belligerent too.

"Am I under arrest?"

"No. Not at the moment. We are simply interviewing you about two matters which are almost certainly connected, aren't they, Mr Angiotti?"

Again he nodded that world-weary gesture before attempting to justify his action, directing his comment at Hesketh-Brown – not at Joanna. "I think most blokes would have flipped if they'd learned what I just did about my wife."

Joanna played the innocent. "What did you learn?"

Angiotti flushed. "That she..."

She knew he was about to lie.

"That she was having an affair."

Joanna raised her eyebrows. He was not convincing her. "With a woman."

She waited for him to flash his third trump card.

"One of her patients."

Hesketh-Brown looked down at Angiotti's right hand spread on the table. It was puffy and swollen. The knuckles were reddened and grazed. A spot of blood had congealed on the middle finger. It had been quite a blow.

"It was the woman who was murdered," he finished then sneaked a direct look at both police officers.

"How long had the affair been going on?"

"Months – I think. They were planning to go away together."

"When did you find out?"

For the first time Pete Angiotti looked distinctly uneasy. Because he was about to lie.

"Today. I found the letters in my wife's bag." He gave a swift glance at Hesketh-Brown for sympathy. "They gave me quite a shock."

"You didn't know before that?"

"I was suspicious."

"Why?"

"Because she didn't..." His voice trailed away. No man likes to confess that his wife is reluctant to have sex with him. They all consider it a failing on their part. If they were a better lover their wife would be panting for them.

Joanna watched Angiotti closely.

He met her eyes, flushed and looked away.

"She wasn't keen on sex," he said reluctantly.

"Right. Let's move to the assault earlier on today."

Angiotti looked ashamed. "I just lost my rag," he said.

"Well – in cases of alleged domestic violence," Joanna said, "we almost always press charges. And we will in this case – whatever your wife says. Now where are you going to be?"

Angiotti looked surprised. "Home," he said.

"I don't think that's a good idea," Joanna said. "My

detective sergeant is with your wife at the moment, in your home. I suggest you go elsewhere."

She paused, trying to mentally suppress any response from Hesketh-Brown. He didn't know her methods as well as Korpanski. "Can I just clarify a few points?"

"Yes."

"You allege that your wife and Beatrice Pennington were having an affair?"

"Ye-es."

"Are you suggesting that your wife killed her?"

She felt Hesketh-Brown's surprised gaze. He knew as well as she did that Beatrice Pennington had been killed by a man.

But Angiotti didn't. "I didn't say that."

"I know you didn't *say* it. What I'm asking is did you *think* it?"

Angiotti looked even more uncomfortable. "I don't know. Possibly."

"But why? If they were planning to go away together I can't understand what would be her motive."

Angiotti gaped. He hadn't worked this one out. "Perhaps they'd fallen out," he said. "Maybe Mrs Pennington was threatening to expose my wife. The General Medical Council take a very dim view of professional misconduct with patients. If Mrs Pennington had claimed that my wife took advantage of her position my wife would have been struck off." A nasty smirk crossed his face. "Just think of the publicity. The first ever woman doctor to be struck off for having an affair with another woman. It would really hit the headlines, wouldn't it?"

"It would," Joanna agreed. "Can I ask you something else?"

"Sure – anything."

This was how she liked her suspects. Over confident. Cocky. Off their guard.

"Why did you leave London?"

For a moment the wariness was back. Angiotti looked at

her for a minute. She knew he was wondering which lie to feed her.

"We'd had enough of living in a big city," he said.

This was not the truth.

"Corinne wanted to live up here. We'd been to Buxton for a holiday – years ago."

Neither was this.

"I'd had a few problems in the school where I taught."

"What sort of problems?"

"Allegations. No truth in them at all."

She simply raised her eyebrows and waited for the whole truth.

"A thirteen-year-old. She said I'd assaulted her. Got hold of her too roughly. She claimed I'd lost my temper."

"Did you?"

"No."

"So what happened in the end?"

"Nothing. The girl dropped charges and I left the area. The whole thing fizzled away. But if I'd stayed I would never have been free of it so we left. Scandal sticks, Inspector. Can I go now?"

"Just one more thing. I take it you admit you did hit your wife?"

Angiotti nodded.

"And lastly," She wanted to rattle him further. She wanted him to know that he was in the picture for being a murder suspect. "Did you kill Beatrice Pennington?"

"No. No."

"OK then." She stood up. "We will want to speak to you again and probably caution you but for now you may go."

Angiotti nodded, bowed his head and eyed the door.

"Keep your mobile on," Joanna said.

She watched him file along the corridor, looking some-how smaller than when he had come in. As he passed her he met her eyes. She knew what he was dumbly asking her. *Am I a suspect?*

She gave an imperceptible nod.

So – she was again alone in her office and found it strange. She and Korpanski always worked together. They were almost like Siamese twins. Joined at the hip. Except for annual leave it was rare for her to be alone in the office they shared, an overcrowded small room with a view over a brick wall, two desks, two computers, a notice board.

On impulse she rang the desk sergeant. "Put me in touch with Bridget Anderton," she said. But WPC Anderton had already left to play nursemaid to Corinne Angiotti.

Chapter Twenty-One

The two men passed in the corridor, these two rather ordinary men who had a strange, thin thread connecting them, a thread which was knotted with twisted emotions and misunderstandings, their feelings stretched as taut as the "E" string on a violin.

They did not acknowledge each other but Joanna noticed that both shrank back against the wall to leave feet of space between them even though the corridor was only narrow.

She wondered.

A briefing had been arranged for the afternoon. Korpanski arrived back at one, cheerful – with good reason. Apparently after telephoning the surgery to explain that she would not be at work for a few days Corinne Angiotti had cooked him lunch – meat and two veg. and they had sat together, chatting.

He'd obviously enjoyed the morning.

The first thing that caught Joanna's eye as she entered the briefing room were the blown-up photographs of Beatrice's body, lying under the hedge, neatly arranged, just as she had been when they had first found her. Joanna crossed the room and stood in front of the board to take a good, long look. Periodically, during a murder investigation, you have to remind yourself what it is that you are investigating. Immersing yourself in the life of your victim can sometimes be too much of a distraction so you lose sight of your goal – to make an arrest and avenge a death.

Joanna paid close attention to every single detail: the aspect of Beatrice's body, the staring, bulging eyes, the dress pulled up over her torso, her face, knickers tidily arranged, shoes off. One missing, one found near the body. The handbag and missing shoe had been discovered tossed into the verge on the road between Grindon and Leek, probably out of a car window.

She moved on.

The second photograph had been taken after the body had been moved and showed the vegetation flattened where the body had lain.

Joanna sensed a shuffling behind her and turned to see the assembled officers waiting impatiently.

"OK. Let's continue," she said, "right where we left off. I think we should consider timing a bit more carefully.

"At 8.50 Arthur Pennington leaves for work."

"At 9.30 Corinne Angiotti saw Beatrice Pennington locking her bike to the railings outside the library. She tried to speak to her but either Beatrice didn't see her or if she did she didn't want to speak. By the time Corinne Angiotti arrived at the bike Beatrice Pennington was nowhere to be seen."

"And Mr Angiotti?" Mike muttered in her ear.

She half-turned. "We don't know his movements," she said, "except that he was in Leek that morning and at school later." But something struck her as cold and heavy as granite. "Speaking of Angiotti," she said, "who's with Corinne now?"

"Bridget Anderton."

She didn't like it. She had sensed around Pete Angiotti something devious and cruel. That had been quite a blow to his wife's face. "I think we should detail a male officer," she said. "There's something about Angiotti that I don't trust."

Korpanski looked sour. "Like giving black eyes to women?"

"Like what's the true story behind his leaving that school in Wandsworth?" She answered her own question. "Temper. That sudden, flashing temper that we've seen in killers before plus conceit. He won't accept humiliation."

Call it instinct. Call it years of working with criminals. Call it what you like but Joanna was very uneasy. Perhaps it was the vision of that neglected old house, hidden from view, up a long curving drive, overgrown with rhododendrons.

Rich, with plenty of places to hide. Perhaps it was the sight of Corinne Angiotti's face, evidence of latent fury.

"Danny," she said urgently to Hesketh-Brown. "Ring Pete Angiotti on his mobile number. Find out where he is and go straight round to his wife. Bridget can take over your duties for the afternoon." She frowned. "I want you there."

A house in the middle of a summer's day appears so much safer than the same house on a winter's night but in reality this is not so. People are so much more careless in the day and neighbours take less notice of the unusual. Doors are left unlocked, windows too, handbags and purses clearly visible on chairs. Neighbours are less vigilant. They ignore odd noises, which in the middle of the night would mean a 999 call. Friends can wander in and out of the house and garden, from room to room, in the day. No one keeps guard as they do at night. So if someone wants to enter the house in daylight it is much easier as the same building would be a virtual fortress after dusk. Houses are vulnerable in daylight. People too. And felons know this. He watched. The house was perfect for his intent.

He knew how he could approach it without being seen. He had done it before. It was not just Beatrice who could do this, take two, three steps, hiding from behind from a low slung branch, concealed by large leaves and dark shadows before waiting for a safe moment and advancing. Like the SAS or the Special Services. Watching. Stalking. Waiting for the right moment.

He drew nearer, seeing them through the window. From the outside looking in.

They were sitting at the table, drinking coffee. Feeling safe.

His lip curled. How women loved to do this, waste time, gossiping, exchanging pleasantries and confidences, sharing flatteries which drew them nearer.

He saw the WPC, neat in her dark uniform skirt, cross her legs, caught a glimpse of pale thigh above dark stocking and wondered. Did *she* love women too? The two of them certainly seemed to be hitting it off very nicely.

He saw Corinne hold a tea-towel under the tap and dab her face with it. It must be throbbing. Good. He had no sympathy to waste for her.

But time was marching forward and he had work to do. He must separate them. Even *he* could not deal with them both together.

Joanna would punish herself afterwards, thinking that she had failed to protect both women.

Until they are caught you have a killer on the loose, a person who has tasted blood. And like a man-eating lion, this memory has imprinted dangerously deep inside their brain.

What has been done once can be done again. Second time around is easier.

Inside The Firs WPC Bridget Anderton was refusing a fourth coffee with a laugh. "No thanks. No more coffee." She giggled. "I'll never get off the loo. Besides, I think coffee's supposed to be bad for you, isn't it?"

Corinne gave the WPC a rueful laugh. "Everything's bad for you in excess," she said. "Sometimes I think doctors are absolute killjoys."

In the hallway outside the telephone rang.

They looked at one another. Corinne stood up. "I'd better get it."

So she was gone. Only the WPC sat alone at the table, relaxed and off her guard. He took two steps forward and ducked behind a branch, still dripping with the recent rain. He was less than ten yards away from her and she couldn't see him.

"Who was it?"

Corinne frowned. "No one was there," she said. "I picked it up but no one spoke. I thought I heard someone breathing. Even some background noise but no one answered."

She had caught Bridget Anderton's full attention." What background noise?"

Corinne considered. "Traffic," she said, "I think."

"Did you dial 1471?"

"Caller withheld their number." Corinne looked only mildly concerned and sat down to consider. She had never really thought about Beatrice's murder. Not the actual murder. There was no hint that another person could be in danger. In between the lines the papers had conveyed the opinion that it was a domestic crime. But now, in this very moment, alone with a WPC, in a large and rambling house, Corinne could sense that a killer was out there. And what had struck once could strike again.

It suddenly seemed terribly important to learn. Who had killed Beatrice Pennington? Why had she died?

She turned her attention back to the WPC. "Why are you here?"

"To protect you."

"From whom?"

But this, WPC Anderton could not answer.

Back at the station the briefing was almost over. Paul Ruthin had stood up to go when Joanna called him back. "I want you to do something for me," she said. "Dig the dirt up on Pete Angiotti. It's no use your going into the PNC. I don't believe there was a charge – not one that stuck anyway. Try here." She gave him the name of the school. "Speak to whoever you can. I want to know how much of a danger this guy is."

Ruthin looked surprised but he took the paper and smiled. "Leave it with me," he said.

Joanna felt nothing but relief.

Bridget Anderton picked up on the woman's unease but she was an active, confident, fit policewoman. "Lock your door," she advised. "You stay inside. I'm going to take a look around the garden."

She was making the mistake of believing she was not in

danger, that no one could possibly wish her harm.

She took her truncheon from her belt. Ready. Just in case.

He grasped the knife in his hands and watched the police-woman step through the French windows, down onto the terrace, looking around her. He could feel her thoughts, searching him out. But *he* would find *her*. Not *she* him. He did not care what happened to him afterwards – as long as he got her.

From the other side of the door Corinne turned the key, peering through the glass anxiously.

He could almost swear they could both sense his near-ness *and* his intent. It pleased him that they felt so threatened. In fact he was so pleased it was hard for him to resist rubbing his hands together. This stalking of prey brought the adrenaline to his system like no other action. He smiled.

Policewomen are trained in self-defence. They are also trained to be observant. So when Bridget, from the corner of her eye, saw the changing light in the dark shadows of the trees she forced herself not to turn her head but tightened her grip on her truncheon, touched her pepper spray and moved forward, affecting a nonchalance which would have earned her a place in RADA.

He stalked her quietly, moving two small steps to her one, keeping in the shade all the time.

It was Corinne, peering through the window, who saw him and screamed.

Outside Danny Hesketh-Brown's car skidded to a halt.

Threats quickly turn to farce.

Hesketh-Brown charged through the trees.

I have a knife. I am not afraid.

Pete Angiotti turned to face him. Hesketh-Brown pulled him into an arm-lock. "Well," he said. "What have we here?"

"Any reason why I shouldn't be in my own garden?"

"We told you to keep away."

Angiotti took in the scene very quickly. Two police officers. He was outnumbered.

"Prove it," he challenged. "Prove any of it."

Bridget Anderton held out her hand. "Give me that," she said. Angiotti lunged at her and Bridget fell, gasping.

It is always the worst decision. Whether to apprehend your felon or help a colleague.

Corinne Angiotti was at Bridget's side, mobile in hand, dialling 999 and holding her hand over the wound in Bridget's chest. The policewoman's eyes rolled. Hesketh-Brown snapped the Quikuffs on and knelt on Pete Angiotti, the caution snarling from his lips and sounding a threat.

Within minutes the garden was swarming with blue lights and men in uniform. An ambulance man snapped an oxygen mask on the WPC's face.

"Her lung is pierced," Corinne said calmly. "She'll need surgery."

Her husband gave her a look of pure venom and said nothing.

Chapter Twenty-Two

Joanna took the questioning, she and Mike working together as they had now over the years.

As they approached the interview room, she warned Korpanski. "No outbursts, Mike," she said. "Make no assumptions."

His eyes blackened. "What on earth do you mean?"

"Just that," she said quietly. "We're not there yet."

Korpanski almost exploded. "What more does he have to do, Jo? He virtually killed Bridget. If Hesketh-Brown hadn't arrived in the nick of time you would have had a double murder on your hands."

"It still doesn't prove that he killed Beatrice Pennington."

Angiotti looked calm. Hands on table, eyes giving her a hard stare. "I was only in the garden," he said. "It's my garden. I can't understand why your police officer grabbed me the way he did."

"You had a knife," Joanna said.

Angiotti gave her a hard stare.

She didn't understand. "You *knew* we were watching her. You *knew* you wouldn't get away with it. We were waiting for you."

Angiotti continued to stare at her and suddenly she understood how deep his hatred was. Yes – he had known he wouldn't get away with it. In fact he had had no intention of escaping because he would have turned the knife on himself. Oddly enough this earned him some respect from her.

"Bitch," Angiotti snarled.

She was still struggling to comprehend. "Why? When she'd done nothing?"

Angiotti's face was a mask. "Because," he said and folded his arms.

Korpanski's face was like thunder. Joanna knew he was dying to punch Pete Angiotti right on the nose. She shot him a warning glance.

She put her arms flat on the table. "You do understand we're investigating a murder," don't you?"

It was meant to ruffle the doctor's husband. "You can't pin anything on me," he said.

Joanna merely lifted her eyebrows. "A serious assault on a police officer? You call that nothing?"

The knock at the door was a welcome diversion. Even better that it was Paul Ruthin.

"I think you'll be interested, Ma'am."

Joanna moved outside, closed the door behind her and kept a watchful eye on Korpanski.

"Go on," she prompted.

"Pete Angiotti left under a cloud," the PC said. "He was accused of assaulting a thirteen-year-old girl."

"Accused? Give me the circumstances."

"She'd been kept behind for bad behaviour. Her mother had signed a detention slip and the girl was there until five o'clock. It was November and very dark. When her mother picked her up the girl said Angiotti had 'roughed her up'."

Joanna gave a deep sigh. "The girl could easily have made the allegation through spite – or just wanting to get her own back. I take it the allegations were later dropped?"

"There were full investigations."

"And?"

"There are two schools of thought," Ruthin said, looking troubled. "Some thought Angiotti was a bit of a slime-ball. Others believed there was something behind the allegations. The investigations unearthed nothing concrete and Angiotti was reinstated. Not before there was a hoohah right through the school. It divided everyone."

"Anything more?"

"Nothing concrete."

"Any rumours?" She glanced anxiously through the porthole window.

Again Ruthin shook his head.

"It's just that I can't see the connection."

"Except one thing. The girl claimed that at one point Angiotti put his hands around her neck."

"Really?"

"She said he lost his temper with her when she cheeked him."

"Now that is interesting."

She re-entered the room. Korpanski was studiously watching Angiotti, dislike making his eyes shine.

Angiotti was staring away from the Detective Sergeant, into the corner. His eyes flickered over her.

"Well then, Pete," she said. "We've heard a little story about you."

"I hope it was entertaining," he responded sulkily.

"An allegation that you tried to strangle a thirteen-year-old girl in your old school?"

"It wasn't true."

"So let's get the real truth, Pete. You assaulted your wife and you knifed Bridget Anderton. It was attempted murder."

"No it wasn't."

Joanna was close to losing her temper. "I don't care what *you* bloody well call it. I call it attempted murder and that will be the charge we bring before the Crown Prosecution Service."

"It won't stick," he said.

Joanna gave a deep sigh. "We'll see," she said. "And now the murder charge. Where *were* you on the morning of Wednesday June the 23rd?"

"At school," he said, "teaching."

"Your wife tells us that around the time that Beatrice Pennington went missing you were in the town, near the library."

Angiotti stared straight ahead and something inside Joanna went cold. She would not like to be Corinne at this moment.

"You understand we'll be searching your house, your car, for forensic evidence?"

"You can search where you like, Inspector," Angiotti said truculently. "You won't find anything. I didn't do it."

Joanna's head was feeling muzzy. She felt confused because too many thoughts were flying through her head. She excused herself and left Korpanski to conduct the interview. She wanted to be alone. She wanted to think.

She found Dawn Critchlow working in the main office and asked to see the statements again.

Once inside her office she closed the door behind her and read through each statement very carefully then sat, alone, thinking. She sat down at her desk, trying out her new theory to see if it fitted all the facts.

Fact one: Beatrice had appeared to bolt when Corinne Angiotti had tried to speak to her when she should have welcomed contact with the object of her love.

Fact two: Pennington's words, "What have *they* done to you?"

Fact three: Beatrice's flashy dress, guaranteed to be noticed, almost drawing attention to herself.

Fact four: she had worn a cycling helmet for that last, fateful journey which was also out of character.

Fact five: the fact that both husbands had been aware of the existence of the letters and therefore the relationship between the two women.

And gradually a picture began to emerge.

She felt herself smile. So that had been it.

It fitted.

Chapter Twenty-Three

She called Korpanski from the interview room. He looked irritated.

"I was just getting somewhere," he said. "What is it?"

"Just listen to me for a minute, Mike. Not here. Let's go somewhere more private."

She could feel his resentment heating her back as he followed her along the corridor towards their office. "OK." She closed the door behind them and sat down opposite him.

He waited, irritation all over his face.

"I'll ask you the same questions I've been asking myself. Then I'll give you the answers."

"OK."

"Why was Beatrice wearing such a flashy dress that morning when she usually cycled in more practical clothes?"

He regarded her steadily. "Possibly because she had an assignation."

"Why was she wearing a cycling helmet when she didn't normally?"

"Safety?"

"And in the statements they say she was wearing sunglasses?"

"What are you getting at?"

"Why did she bolt when Corinne Angiotti tried to approach her?"

"I don't know," he said. "Maybe because...OK."

"Why did Pennington say what have *they* done to you?"

He shook his head.

Again he shrugged, confused.

"I'll tell you why. Because the woman who cycled in the flowered dress into the library that morning wasn't Beatrice. She was already dead."

"So who was it?"

"Arthur Pennington."

"That's not possible. One he was at work at the time when we *know* she was on her bike and two nobody could possibly mistake him for his wife. For a start she was plumper."

"He could have worn something bulky underneath the dress."

"But?"

"Who looks at a cyclist? Particularly one in a helmet and sunglasses. People simply saw a woman on Beatrice's bike wearing a flowery dress."

Korpanski smothered a smile. "I don't think Arthur Pennington could have thought up such an idea."

"Not even fuelled by the fury with his wife?"

Korpanski's eyes were fixed on hers.

"He knew about the letters and like the pedantic, unimaginative, unforgiving man he is he couldn't hack it. He strangled her over breakfast that morning and left her body at home. He went to work to create his alibi then drove back. He dressed himself in his wife's dress to make sure people remembered him when we started asking questions. He isn't stupid. He would have known the way our minds work and that he would be prime suspect. He cycled in, assuming the other librarians would already be at work. He was just locking up the bike when horror of horrors Corinne Angiotti drives passed and tries to attract his attention by sounding her horn and manoeuvring in the road. By the time she's pulled up he's already bolted; my guess is to the area behind the iron staircase which is dark and unvisited. There he pulls off the dress, rolls his trouser legs down, takes off the helmet and glasses, probably bundling it into a carrier bag. Then he goes back to work."

Korpanski leaned right back in his chair. "It won't wash, Jo. How did he get out of his office without the secretary seeing him? She's like a guard dog."

"The fire door, Mike. He slipped out of the fire door,

probably told his secretary not to disturb him – a tricky bit of work or something."

Korpanski sat up. "And evidence?"

"We've got the bike," she said. "Let's look for DNA, a hair from his leg, prints on the handlebars. We get the cycling helmet – well – I bet you we find some of his hair. And then we already have Beatrice's fashion statement. Unless he's a cross-dresser his skin cells or hair shouldn't be inside."

He stroked his chin. "And the murder scene?"

"We've probably already got evidence. We're just waiting for the results on his car to be matched."

Korpanski shook his head. "It could work," he said. Then he smiled. "But the thought of Pennington wobbling along on his bike, dressed in his wife's clothes. Well," he said, "it doesn't bear thinking about."

"I told you from the first it was a ridiculous case. A domestic. Our instincts told us correctly. Pennington murdered his own wife then started acting the part of innocent, bemused husband. The burden of proof might not be heavy. I think once we face him with our story he'll confess. My guess is he'll plead guilty."

"Why did he ask the question? Why use the plural? What have *they* done?"

"I've thought of two possible explanations," she said. "It *could* have been simply to put us off. He'd blamed his wife's two cronies for her changed behaviour or else it was the maggots," she said, "and remember the nibbling of the animals on her legs? Maybe *that* was the *they*. I don't know everything, Mike."

Korpanski looked at the door. "And Angiotti?" He had not given up on the teacher.

"Pete Angiotti still tried to kill one of our officers," she said. "We'll get him on an attempted murder charge, I hope. That's if the CPS don't water it down to a GBH." A mischievous thought suggested itself to her. Everyone in the station knew that Bridget Anderton had a soft spot for the burly sergeant. "I suggest you pop over the hospital at some point and take WPC Anderton a nice big bunch of flowers."

It would cheer her up.

They cornered Pennington at his office and arrested him for the murder of his wife, Korpanski reciting the caution with undisguised relish. It is always satisfying to wind up a murder case.

Pennington looked astonished and for a while tried to bluster. "And how do you think I did it when I was busy working here at the very time when my wife, still alive, was riding her bicycle into work?"

"We can discuss that in the police station," Joanna said, "where we can record all your explanations."

On the way out she stopped by the secretary's desk. She was watching, round-eyed, open-mouthed. "Can you remember back to the morning of June the 23rd? The morning that Mrs Pennington disappeared?"

The girl nodded. "What was Mr Pennington working on that he couldn't be disturbed for half an hour?"

"It was the solicitor's account," the girl said. "He said to put no calls through as it was a really tricky one and would take some time."

"How long?"

"An hour."

"Thanks," Joanna said. "I wondered what it was."

They left the girl frowning after them. Joanna could read her mind. *And what has that got to do with it?*

They set up the interview room and waited for Pennington's solicitor. This case had to be watertight. Arthur Pennington sat opposite them, arms folded, looking comfortable – at first.

Joanna opened the questioning. "I want you to think back to the last morning your wife was seen alive," she started.

And then she remembered the post-mortem findings.

The story was there, written in tissue and blood.

"I believe that you lost your temper that morning, at breakfast time," she said, "and thumped your wife twice, once on her back, between her shoulder blades and again on her head."

Pennington gaped at her.

"She must have tried to explain to you why she had fallen in love with her doctor and written her so many romantic letters," she continued. "So you throttled her."

It was the turning point. Pennington looked shaken. She had done this before, studied the post-mortem findings and used them when questioning a suspect. It was the spookiness of it – that they believed she must have been there to describe the attack in such detail. But it was never that. It was the simple rule of forensics – that encounters, particularly violent ones, invariably leave traces which can, in turn, be picked up by careful laboratory work.

Pennington had one last try. "And how do you explain," he challenged, "that my wife was seen riding her bike half an hour after I'd arrived at work?"

"That," Joanna said, "is the really clever bit. Your wife was already dead when you arrived at work. It was you, wearing a dress, cycling and pretending to be Beatrice."

The solicitor looked startled. "This is preposterous."

"Well," Joanna said softly. "Preposterous or not it is what I believe happened and we shall search for forensic evidence to support my theory. In the meantime we shall hold your client here."

Pennington began to laugh. "I think you're mad, Inspector. Excuse me laughing but it's so funny."

"You think murdering the woman you've been married to for more than twenty years, leaving her body at home while you impersonate her before dumping her underneath a hedge for flies to lay their eggs in her eyes and rats to nibble her feet is funny?"

It was as though she had struck the man. Pennington visibly crumpled.

"I don't..."
His voice ebbed away.

Joanna couldn't resist turning round to give Korpanski a swift look. He raised his eyebrows and returned the ghost of a grin.

They had him.

The solicitor sat silently at Pennington's side. He knew that they were in trouble. She knew he was already bringing up the word, *provocation*.

"Perhaps," he said, "I should advise my client."

Joanna nodded. "Yes," she said. "Perhaps you should."

Pennington was as good as in the bag.

In the end Corinne Angiotti had given her the solution on a plate. This is what men do to women they feel have betrayed them.

It was the cruel cost of misdirected adoration.

Chapter Twenty-Four

Friday, July 16th, 7 a.m.

She had hardly slept, worrying she would not wake and she would miss Matthew at the airport. It had been easy to check with the airline a direct flight from Washington DC to Manchester. There was only one a day. It was due in at 10. She had put her alarm on for eight.

At some time in the middle of the night she had sat bolt upright, finding the answer to yet another of the little mysteries which had dogged her.

Another domestic.

And the answer was so blindingly obvious she could only blame the murder case for preventing her from reading the signs.

What had lain behind Eloise Levin's newfound friendliness?

Her father, of course. He had promised to leave Joanna alone, to allow her to make her own mind up about him and the baby, undertaking not to influence her in any way, not knowing that nature would take one of the decisions from her. He had charged his daughter to keep some sort of watch over his mistress. The flowers had been from Matthew – not Eloise.

She gave a silent laugh. How could she possibly have thought that Eloise would ring *her* with such concern?

She padded downstairs and made herself a cup of tea to return to bed and ponder this new knowledge. As she passed by the photograph of Matthew holding his baby daughter it hit her. He had asked a lot of his daughter and she had complied.

How much a father and daughter love each other.

She went back to bed, nursing the mug of tea.

Would it have been so very terrible to have given Matthew what he wanted more than anything else in the world – another child? Women the world over combined careers and a family. What was so different about her?

She sat up in bed, drained the mug and knew that when Matthew returned he would expect some changes in her. He was right. She had given up nothing for him. He had done all the sacrificing, his wife, his daughter.

As for her, she had refused to marry him, evaded the issue of further children, always always put her career before any other considerations.

She put the mug down on the bedside table and glanced at her radio alarm. Three a.m.

She switched her lamp off and tried to go back to sleep.

But all she could see were adoring faces. Beatrice's as she must have looked at her doctor, Matthew's face in the photograph, looking down at his baby daughter, Matthew's face when he had looked at her, across the desk in his office, and first asked her to have dinner with him. Her own father, proud of her achievements. Even her sister, holding baby Daniel, her godson.

She went back to sleep, still seeing those green eyes fixed on hers with an optimistic expression. It had been that which had persuaded her to accept the dinner invitation even though she had suspected the pathologist must be married. That bright optimism.

The other questions which punched into her dreams at some time in the night was, had Matthew met someone who could return his love while he was in Washington?

She must wait for his answer.

She woke again to the alarm and half an hour later, fortified with plenty of coffee she felt wide-awake and alert.

She dressed carefully, in tight black trousers, a pink blouse and high-heeled black leather boots, arrived at the airport early, with plenty of time to park the car and browse the early morning papers. Time seemed to move all too slowly, the minute hand creeping around the clock reluctantly. Sometimes it seemed it slipped back a minute or two when she wasn't looking.

At nine thirty-five she made her way to the arrivals barrier and waited.

Passport Control, Baggage Reclamation, Customs. It all takes so long.

Finally the moment came. A swell of people spilled out looking tired after their transatlantic flight.

What is it that we notice first about someone we love? With Matthew it was always his hair. The colour of darkened corn, invariably tousled. Shorter than it had been when he had left. That and his tall, slim figure, jacket slung carelessly over his shoulders, beige jeans, holding a black flight bag and pulling behind him a large suitcase on wheels. His walk. Loose limbed, long-legged. Quick. He was overtaking people walking slowly. No two people walk the same. It is the reason police line-ups often include a walk. She stood transfixed and inexplicably oddly nervous. Would he sense a grass roots change in her?

He looked up and saw her.

She held back, feeling her welcome smile stretch from ear to ear in a *Risus sardonicus*.

And then he was there, wrapping his arms around her, holding her so tightly they might have been glued together and never separated. He held her for long minutes before moving back, cradling her face in his hands and kissing her mouth. Then, at last, they could speak.

"Matthew, I'm so sorry," she said.

He kissed her again. "Don't speak," he said. "I'm knackered. It was a vile flight. I was wedged between a thirty stone man and an infant. Let's get home, Jo." He passed. "Then we can talk."

For the time being there were to be no more questions.

Love is a many splendoured thing...

Author's Note

For those of you who are wondering what the book was which the Readers' Group were enjoying, it was *Take My Breath Away* by Martin Edwards. Enjoy...